KU-201-787

LOVE & GELATO

JENNA EVANS WELCH

WALKER
BOOKS

First published in Great Britain 2017 by Walker Books Ltd
87 Vauxhall Walk, London SE11 5HJ

2 4 6 8 10 9 7 5 3

Text © 2017 Jenna Evans Welch
Illustration © 2017 Sam Brewster

This book has been typeset in Adobe Caslon Pro

Printed and bound in Great Britain by Clays Ltd, St Ives plc

British Library Cataloguing in Publication Data:
a catalogue record for this book is available from the British Library

ISBN 978-1-4063-7232-8

www.walker.co.uk

To David,

for being my love story

Prologue

YOU'VE HAD BAD DAYS BEFORE, RIGHT? YOU KNOW, the ones where your alarm doesn't go off, your toast practically catches on fire, and you remember way too late that every article of clothing you own is soaking wet in the bottom of the washer? So then you go hurtling into school fifteen minutes late, *praying* no one will notice that your hair looks like the Bride of Frankenstein's, but just as you slide into your desk your teacher booms, "Running late today, Ms Emerson?" and everyone looks at you and notices?

I'm sure you've had those days. We all have. But what about really bad days? The kind that are so pumped up and awful that they chew up the things you care about just for the fun of spitting them back in your face?

The day my mom told me about Howard fell firmly in the *really bad* category. But at the time, he was the least of my worries.

It was two weeks into my sophomore year of high school and my mom and I were driving home from her appointment. The car was silent except for a radio commercial narrated by two Arnold Schwarzenegger impersonators, and even though it was a hot day, I had goose bumps up and down my legs. Just that morning I'd placed second at my first-ever cross country meet and I couldn't believe how much that didn't matter anymore.

My mom switched off the radio. "Lina, what are you feeling?" Her voice was calm, and when I looked at her I teared up all over again. She was so pale and tiny. How had I not noticed how *tiny* she'd gotten?

"I don't know," I said, trying to keep my voice even. "I feel like I'm in shock."

She nodded, coming to a stop at a traffic light. The sun was doing its best to blind us, and I stared into it, my eyes scalding. *This is the day that changes everything*, I thought. *From here on out there will only be* before *and* after *today*.

My mom cleared her throat, and when I glanced at her, she straightened up like she had something important to tell me. "Lina, did I ever tell you about the time I was dared to swim in a fountain?"

I whipped around. "What?"

"Remember how I told you I spent a year studying in Florence? I was out photographing with my classmates, and it was such a hot day I thought I was going to melt. I had this friend – Howard – and he dared me to jump into a fountain."

Now, keep in mind, we'd just gotten the worst news of our lives. The *worst*.

"… I scared a group of German tourists. They were posing for a photo, and when I popped out of the water, one of them lost her balance and almost fell back into the fountain with me. They were furious, so Howard yelled that I was drowning and jumped in after me."

I stared at her, and she turned and gave me a little smile.

"Uh … Mom? That's funny and everything, but why are you telling me this now?"

"I just wanted to tell you about Howard. He was really a lot of fun." The light changed and she hit the gas.

What? I thought. *What, what, what?*

At first I thought the fountain story was a coping mechanism, like maybe she thought a story about an old friend could distract us from the two blocks of granite hanging over our heads. *Inoperable. Incurable.* But then she told me another story. And another. It got to the point where she'd start talking and three words in I'd know she was going to bring up Howard. And then when she finally told me the reason for all the Howard stories, well … let's just say that ignorance is bliss.

"Lina, I want you to go to Italy."

It was mid-November and I was sitting next to her hospital bed with a stack of ancient *Cosmo* magazines I'd swiped from the waiting room. I'd spent the last ten minutes taking a quiz called "On a Scale of One to Sizzle: How Hot Are You?" (7/10).

"Italy?" I was kind of distracted. The person who'd taken the quiz before me had scored a 10/10 and I was trying to figure out how.

"I mean, I want you to go live in Italy. After."

That got my attention. For one thing, I didn't believe in *after*. Yes, her cancer was progressing just the way her doctors said it would, but doctors didn't know everything.

Just that morning I'd bookmarked a story on the Internet about a woman who'd beaten cancer and gone on to climb Mt Kilimanjaro. And for another, *Italy*?

"Why would I do that?" I asked lightly. It was important to humor her. Avoiding stress is a big part of recovery.

"I want you to stay with Howard. The year I spent in Italy meant so much to me, and I want you to have that same experience."

I shot my eyes at the nurse's call button. *Stay with Howard in Italy?* Did they give her too much morphine?

"Lina, look at me," she said, in her bossiest I Am the Mother voice.

"Howard? You mean that guy you keep talking about?"

"Yes. He's the best man I've ever known. He'll keep you safe."

"Safe from *what*?" I looked into her eyes, and suddenly my breath started coming in short and fast. She was serious. Did hospital rooms stock paper bags?

She shook her head, her eyes shiny. "Things will be … hard. We don't have to talk about it now, but I wanted to make sure you heard my decision from me. You'll need someone. After. And I think he's the best person."

"Mom, that doesn't even make sense. Why would I go live with a stranger?" I jumped up and started rifling through the drawers in her end table. There had to be a paper bag *somewhere*.

"Lina, sit."

"But, Mom—"

"Sit. You're going to be fine. You're going to make it. Your life will go on, and it's going to be *great*."

"No," I said. "*You're* going to make it. Sometimes people recover."

"Lina, Howard's a wonderful friend. You'll really love him."

"I doubt it. And if he's that good of a friend, then why haven't I ever met him before?" I gave up on finding a bag, collapsing back into my chair and putting my head between my knees.

She struggled to sit up, then reached out, resting her hand on my back. "Things were a little bit complicated between us, but he wants to get to know you. And he said he'd love to have you stay with him. Promise me you'll give it a try. A few months at least."

There was a knock on the door, and we both looked up to see a nurse dressed in baby blue scrubs. "Just checking in," she sang, either ignoring or not noticing the expression on my face. On a Scale of One to Tense, the room was at about 100/10.

"Morning. I was just telling my daughter she needs to go to Italy."

"Italy," the nurse said, clasping both hands to her chest. "I went there on my honeymoon. Gelato, the Leaning Tower of Pisa, gondolas in Venice… You'll love it."

My mom smiled at me triumphantly.

"Mom, *no*. There's no way I'm going to Italy."

"Oh, but, honey, you have to go," the nurse said. "It will be a once-in-a-lifetime experience."

The nurse ended up being right about one thing: I did have to go. But no one gave me even the tiniest hint about what I'd find once I got there.

Chapter 1

THE HOUSE LOOMED BRIGHTLY IN THE DISTANCE, like a lighthouse in a sea of headstones. But it couldn't be *his* house, right? We were probably just following some kind of Italian custom. *Always drive newcomers through a cemetery. That way they get a feel for the local culture.* Yeah, that must be it.

I knit my fingers in my lap, my stomach dropping as the house got closer and closer. It was like watching Jaws emerge from the depths of the ocean. *Duuun dun.* Only it wasn't a movie. It was real. And there was only one turn left. *Don't panic. This can't be it. Mom wouldn't have sent you to live in a cemetery. She would have warned you. She would have—*

He flipped on the turn signal, and all the air came rushing out of my lungs. *She just didn't tell me.*

"Are you OK?"

Howard – my dad, I guess I should call him – was looking at me with a concerned expression. Probably because I'd just made a wheezing noise.

"Is that your…?" Words failed me, so I had to point.

"Well, yes." He hesitated for a moment and then gestured out the window. "Lina, didn't you know? About all this?"

"All this" didn't even come close to describing the massive moonlit cemetery. "My grandma told me I'd be staying on American-owned land. She said you're the caretaker of a World War II memorial. I didn't think…" Panic was pouring over me like hot syrup. Also, I couldn't seem to finish a single sentence. *Breathe, Lina. You've already survived the worst. You can survive this, too.*

He pointed to the far end of the property. "The memorial is that building right up there. But the rest of the grounds are for the graves of American soldiers who were killed in Italy during the war."

"But this isn't your *house* house, right? It's just where you work?"

He didn't answer. Instead we pulled into the driveway, and I felt the last of my hope fade along with the car's headlights. This wasn't just a house. It was a *home*. Red geraniums lined the walkway, and there was a porch swing creaking back and forth, like someone had just gotten up. Subtract the crosses lining the surrounding lawns and it was any normal house in any normal neighborhood. But it wasn't a normal neighborhood. And those crosses didn't look like they were going anywhere. Ever.

"They like to have a caretaker on-site at all times, so they built this house back in the sixties." Howard took the keys out of the ignition, then drummed his fingers nervously on the steering wheel. "I'm really sorry, Lina. I thought you knew. I can't imagine what you're thinking right now."

"It's a cemetery." My voice was like weak tea.

He turned and looked at me, not quite making eye contact. "I know. And the last thing you need is a reminder of everything you've been through this year. But I think you'll find that this place grows on you. It's really peaceful and it has a lot of interesting history. Your mother loved it. And after being here almost seventeen years, I can't imagine living anywhere else."

His voice was hopeful, but I slumped back in my seat, a swarm of questions taking flight in my mind. *If she loved it so much, then why didn't she ever tell me about it? Why didn't she ever talk about you until she got sick? And for the love of all that's holy, what made her leave out the teeny-tiny detail that you're my father?*

Howard absorbed my silence for a moment, then opened his car door. "Let's head inside. I'll get your suitcase."

All six foot five of him walked around to the back of the car, and I leaned over to watch him in the side mirror. My grandma had been the one to fill in the blanks. *He's your father; that's why she wanted you to live with him.* I probably should have seen it coming. It's just that good old buddy Howard's true identity seemed like the sort of thing my mother would have at least *mentioned*.

Howard closed the trunk, and I straightened up and started rifling through my backpack, buying myself another few seconds. *Lina, think. You're alone in a foreign country, a certifiable giant has just stepped forward as your father, and your new home could be the setting for a zombie apocalypse movie. Do something.*

But what? Short of wrestling the car keys from Howard, I couldn't think of a single way to get out of going into that house. Finally I unbuckled my seat belt and followed him to the front door.

* * *

Inside, the house was aggressively normal – like maybe it thought it could make up for its location if it just tried hard enough. Howard set my suitcase down in the front entryway, and then we walked into a living room with two overstuffed chairs and a leather sofa. There were a bunch of vintage travel posters on the walls, and the whole place smelled like it had been soaking in garlic and onions. But in a good way. Obviously.

"Welcome home," Howard said, switching on the main light. Fresh panic smacked me in the face, and he winced when he saw my expression. "I mean, welcome to Italy. I'm so glad you're here."

"Howard?"

"Hi, Sonia."

A tall, gazelle-like woman stepped into the room. She was maybe a few years older than Howard, with coffee-colored skin and rows of gold bracelets on each arm. Gorgeous. And also a surprise.

"Lina," she said, enunciating my name carefully. "You made it. How were your flights?"

I shifted from one foot to the other. Was someone going to introduce us? "They were OK. The last one was really long."

"We're so glad you're here." She beamed at me, and there was a thick moment of silence.

Finally I stepped forward. "So … you're Howard's wife?"

Howard and Sonia looked at each other and then practically started howling with laughter.

Lina Emerson. Comic genius.

Finally Howard got himself under control. "Lina, this is

Sonia. She's the assistant superintendent of the cemetery. She's been working here even longer than I have."

"Just by a few months," Sonia said, wiping her eyes. "Howard always makes me sound like a dinosaur. My house is on the property too, a little closer to the memorial."

"How many people live here?"

"Just us two. Now three," Howard said.

"And about four thousand soldiers," Sonia added, grinning. She squinted at Howard, and I glanced back just in time to see him frantically running one finger across his throat. Nonverbal communication. Great.

Sonia's smile vanished. "Lina, are you hungry? I made a lasagna."

That's what that smell was. "I'm pretty hungry," I admitted. Understatement.

"Good. I made my specialty. Lasagna with extra-garlicky garlic bread."

"Yes!" Howard said, pumping his arm like a contestant on *The Price Is Right*. "You decided to spoil us."

"It's a special night, so I thought I'd go all out. Lina, you probably want to wash your hands. I'll dish up and you can meet us in the dining room."

Howard pointed across the living room. "Bathroom's over there."

I nodded, then set my backpack on the nearest chair before practically fleeing the room. The bathroom was miniature, barely big enough for a toilet and a sink, and I ran the water as hot as I could stand it, scrubbing the airport off my hands with a chip of soap from the edge of the sink.

While I scrubbed, I caught a glimpse of myself in the mirror and groaned. I looked like I'd been dragged through three different time zones. Which, to be fair, I had. My normally tan skin was pale and yellowish-looking, and I had dark circles under my eyes. And my *hair*. It had finally figured out a way to defy the laws of physics. I wet both my hands and tried to smash down my curls, but it seemed to only encourage them. Finally I gave up. So what if I looked like a hedgehog who'd discovered Red Bull? Fathers are supposed to accept you as you are, right?

Music started up outside the bathroom and my nervousness kindled from a flame to a bonfire. Did I really need to eat dinner? Maybe I could go hide out in a room somewhere while I processed this whole cemetery thing. Or didn't process it. But then my stomach roared in protest and *ugh*. I did have to eat.

"There she is," Howard said, getting to his feet as I walked into the dining room. The table was set with a red-checkered cloth, and an old rock song I sort of recognized was playing from an iPod next to the entryway. I slid into the chair opposite them, and Howard sat down too.

"I hope you're hungry. Sonia's such a great cook, I think she missed her calling in life." Now that it wasn't just the two of us, he sounded way more relaxed.

Sonia beamed. "No way. I was destined for life at the memorial."

"It does look good." And by "good," I meant *amazing*. A steaming pan of lasagna sat next to a basket of thickly sliced garlic bread, and there was a salad bowl piled high with tomatoes and crisp-looking lettuce. It took every ounce of willpower I had not to dive right onto the table.

Sonia cut into the lasagna, placing a big gooey square right in the center of my plate. "Help yourself to bread and salad. *Buon appetito*."

"*Buon appetito*," Howard echoed.

"*Buon appe* ... something," I mumbled.

The second everyone was served, I picked up my fork and attacked my lasagna. I knew I probably looked like a wild mastodon, but after a full day of nothing but airline food, I couldn't help myself. Those portions were *miniature*. When I finally came up for air, Sonia and Howard were both staring at me, Howard looking mildly horrified.

"So, Lina, what kinds of things do you like to do?" Sonia asked.

I grabbed my napkin. "Besides scare people with my table manners?"

Howard chuckled. "Your grandmother told me you love running. She said you average about forty miles a week, and you're hoping to run in college."

"Well, that explains the appetite." Sonia scooped up another piece, and I gratefully held out my plate. "Do you run at school?"

"I used to. I was on the varsity cross-country team, but I forfeited my spot after we found out."

They both just looked at me.

"... When we found out about the cancer? Practice took up a lot of time, and I didn't want to leave town for all the meets and stuff."

Howard nodded. "I think the cemetery is a great place for a runner. Lots of space, and nice smooth roads. I used to run here all the time. Before I got fat and lazy."

Sonia rolled her eyes. "Oh, please. You couldn't get fat if you tried." She nudged the basket of garlic bread toward me. "Did you know that your mother and I were friends? She was lovely. So talented and lively."

Nope, didn't tell me that, either. Was it possible I was falling prey to some elaborate kidnapping scheme? Would kidnappers feed you two pieces of the best lasagna you'd ever had? And if pressed, would they give you the recipe?

Howard cleared his throat, snapping me back to the conversation. "Sorry. Um, no. She never mentioned you."

Sonia nodded, her face expressionless, and Howard glanced at her, then back at me. "You're probably feeling pretty tired. Is there anyone you want to get in touch with? I messaged your grandmother when your plane arrived, but you're welcome to give her a call. I have an international plan on my cell phone."

"Can I call Addie?"

"Is that the friend you were living with?"

"Yeah. But I have my laptop. I could just use FaceTime instead."

"That might not work tonight. Italy isn't exactly on the cutting edge of technology, and our Internet connection has been pretty slow all day. Someone's coming by to take a look at it tomorrow, but in the meantime you can just use my phone."

"Thanks."

He pushed back from the table. "Would anyone like some wine?"

"Yes, please," Sonia said.

"Lina?"

"Uh … I'm kind of underage."

He smiled. "Italy doesn't have a drinking age, so I guess it's a little different around here. But no pressure either way."

"I'll pass."

"Be right back." He headed for the kitchen.

The room was quiet for about ten seconds, and then Sonia set her fork down. "I'm so happy you're here, Lina. And I want you to know that if you need anything, I'm just a stone's throw away. Literally."

"Thanks." I trained my eyes on a spot just over her left shoulder. Adults were always trying too hard around me. They thought that if they were nice enough they could make up for the fact that I'd lost my mom. It was kind of sweet and horrible at the same time.

Sonia glanced toward the kitchen and then lowered her voice. "I wanted to ask you, would you mind stopping by my place sometime tomorrow? I have something I want to give you."

"What?"

"We can talk about it then. Tonight you just focus on settling in."

I just shook my head. I was going to do as little settling in as possible. I wasn't even going to unpack my bag.

After dinner Howard insisted on carrying my suitcase upstairs. "I hope you like your room. I repainted and redecorated it a couple of weeks ago, and I think it turned out really nice. I keep most of the windows open in summer – it's a lot cooler that way – but feel free to close yours if you'd prefer." He spoke quickly, like he'd spent all afternoon rehearsing his welcome speech. He set my bag down in front of the first door.

"Bathroom is right across the hall, and I put some new soap and shampoo in there. Let me know what else you need and I'll pick it up tomorrow, OK?"

"OK."

"And like I said, the Internet's been pretty spotty, but if you decide you want to try it out, our network is called 'American Cemetery.'"

Of course it was. "What's the Wi-Fi password?"

"Wall of the Missing. One word."

"'Wall of the Missing,'" I repeated. "What does that mean?"

"It's a part of the memorial. There are a bunch of stone tablets listing the names of soldiers whose bodies were never recovered. I can show you tomorrow if you'd like."

Nooo, thank you. "Well, I'm pretty tired, so…" I edged toward the door.

He took the hint, handing me a cell phone along with a slip of paper. "I wrote down instructions for dialing the States. You have to put in a country code as well as an area code. Let me know if you have any trouble."

"Thanks." I put the paper in my pocket.

"Good night, Lina."

"Good night."

He turned and walked down the hall, and I opened the door and dragged my suitcase into the room, feeling my shoulders sag with the relief of finally being alone. *Well, you're really here,* I thought, *just you and your four thousand new friends*. There was a lock on the door and I turned it with a satisfying *click*. Then I slowly turned around, steeling myself for whatever Howard had meant by "really nice." But then my heart practically stopped, because *wow*.

The room was perfect. Soft light glowed from this adorable gold lamp on the nightstand, and the bed was antique-looking, with about a thousand decorative pillows. A painted desk and dresser sat on opposite sides of the room, and a large oval mirror hung on the wall next to the door. There were even some picture frames standing empty on the nightstand and dresser, like they were waiting for me to fill them up.

I stood there staring for a minute. It was just so *me*. How was it possible that someone who hadn't even met me had managed to put together my perfect bedroom? Maybe things *weren't* going to be so bad –

And then a gust of wind blew into the room, drawing my attention to the large open window. I'd ignored my own rule: *If it seems too good to be true, it probably is.* I walked over and stuck my head out. The headstones gleamed in the moonlight like rows of teeth, and everything was dark and eerily silent. No amount of pretty could make up for a view like that.

I pulled my head back in, then took the slip of paper out of my pocket. Time to start plotting my escape.

Chapter 2

SADIE DANES MAY BE ONE OF THE WORST PEOPLE ON the planet, but she'll always have a special place in my heart. After all, I owe her my best friend.

It was the beginning of seventh grade. Addie had just moved to Seattle from Los Angeles, and one day after gym class she'd overheard Sadie make a comment about how some of our classmates didn't actually need bras. Which, be real – we were in seventh grade; only about one percent of us actually needed bras. It's just that I was *particularly* less in need of one, and everyone knew she'd meant me. While I'd just ignored her (i.e., stuck my twelve-year-old head in my locker and blinked back tears), Addie had taken it upon herself to clothesline Sadie on her way out of the locker room. She'd stuck up for me that day and then never stopped.

"Go away. It might be Lina." Addie's voice sounded distant, like she was holding the phone away from her face. "Hello?" she said into the speaker.

"Addie, it's me."

"Lina! IAN, GET AWAY FROM ME." There was some muffled yelling and then what sounded like a Mexican knife fight going on between her and her brother. Addie had three older brothers, and rather than baby her, it seemed they'd unanimously agreed to treat her as one of the guys. It explained a lot about her personality.

"Sorry," she said when she was finally back on the phone. "Ian's an idiot. Someone ran over his phone, and now my parents say I have to share mine. I don't care what happened. I am not giving his caveman friends my phone number."

"Oh, come on, they're not *that* bad."

"Stop it. You know they are. This morning I walked in on one of them eating our cereal. He'd poured an entire box into a mixing bowl and was eating it with a *soup* ladle. I don't think Ian was even home."

I smiled and shut my eyes for a moment. If Addie were a superhero, her power would be Ability to Make Your Best Friend Feel Normal. Those first dark weeks after the funeral, she'd been the one to get me out of the house on runs and insist I do things like eat and shower. She was the kind of friend you knew you couldn't possibly deserve.

"Hold up. Why are we wasting time talking about Ian's friends? I'm assuming you've met Howard."

I opened my eyes. "You mean my father?"

"I refuse to call him that. We didn't even know he was your father until like two months ago."

"Less," I said.

"Lina, you're killing me. What's he *like*?"

I glanced at my bedroom door. Music was still playing downstairs, but I lowered my voice anyway. "Let's just say I need to get out of here. Right away."

"What do you mean? Is he a creep?"

"No. He's actually kind of OK. And he's like basketball tall, which is surprising. But that's not the bad part." I took in a deep breath. She needed the full dramatic effect. "He's the caretaker of a cemetery. Which means I have to live in a cemetery."

"WHAT?"

I was ready for her outburst, holding the phone a good three inches from my ear.

"You have to live in a *cemetery*? Is he like a *gravedigger or something*?" She whispered the last part.

"I don't think they do burials here anymore. All the graves are from World War II."

"Like that's any better! Lina, we have to get you out of there. It isn't fair. First you lose your mom, and then you have to move halfway across the world to live with some guy who suddenly claims to be your father? And he lives in a *cemetery*? Come on, that's too much."

I sat down at the desk, scooting the chair around until my back was to the window. "Believe me, if I'd had any idea of what I was getting into, I would have pushed back even harder. This place is *weird*. There are headstones all over the place, and it feels like we're really far from civilization. I saw some houses on the road coming in, but besides that it looks like there's just forest surrounding the cemetery."

"Shut up. I'm coming to get you. How much does a plane ticket cost? More than three hundred dollars? Because that's all I have after our little run-in with the fire hydrant."

"You didn't even hit it that hard!"

"Tell that to the mechanic. Apparently the whole bumper had to be replaced. And I blame it on you entirely. If you hadn't been jamming out, I probably wouldn't have had to join in."

I grinned, pulling up my feet to sit cross-legged. "It is *so* not my fault that you can't control yourself when old-school Britney Spears comes on the radio. But do you need help paying for it? My grandparents are in charge of my finances, but I get a monthly allowance."

"No, of course not. You're going to need your money to get home from Italy. And I really do think my parents will be on board with you living here again. My mom thinks you're a good influence. It took her like a month to get over the fact that you put your dishes in the dishwasher."

"Well, I *am* pretty remarkable."

"Tell me about it. OK, I'll talk to them soon. I just have to wait until my mom chills out. She's in charge of this big football fundraiser for Ian, and you'd think she was throwing a debutante ball. Seriously, she is stressing out *way* too much. She totally lost it last night when none of us ate her noodle casserole."

"I like her noodle casserole. The one with tuna, right?"

"Ew, you do not like it. You were probably just starving because you'd gone on a nine-hundred-mile run. Also, you eat everything."

"True," I admitted. "But, Addie, remember, it's my grandma we need to worry about convincing. She's super on board with me living here."

"Which makes absolutely no sense. Why would she send you halfway across the world to be with a stranger? She doesn't even know him."

"I don't think she knew what else to do. On the drive to the airport she told me she's thinking about moving with my grandpa into an assisted care center. Taking care of him is getting to be too much."

"Which is why you should live with *us*." She exhaled. "Don't worry. You just leave Grandma Rachelle to me. I'll take her out to buy some of those butterscotch candies all old people love, and we'll talk about why the Bennett house is your best option."

"Thanks, Addie." We both stopped talking, and the sound of insects and Howard's music filled the brief silence between us. I wanted to crawl right through the phone back to Seattle. How was I going to survive without Addie?

"Why are you being so quiet? Is Gravedigger there?"

"I'm in my bedroom, but I get the feeling that sound travels in this house. I don't know if he can hear me or not."

"Great. So you can't even speak freely. We'd better come up with a code word so I know if you're OK. Say 'bluebird' if you're being held hostage."

"'Bluebird'? Isn't it supposed to be a word that doesn't sound out of the ordinary?"

"Crap. Now I'm confused. You said the word, but I don't know if you meant it. Are you or are you not being held hostage?"

"No, Addie. I'm not being held hostage." I sighed. "Except maybe to the promise I made to my mom."

"Yeah, but do promises really count if you make them under false pretenses? No offense, but your mom wasn't exactly forthcoming about why she wanted you to go to Italy."

"I know." I breathed out. "I'm hoping there was some reason for that."

"Maybe."

I looked over my shoulder at the window. The moon was skimming the dark tree line, and if I hadn't known any better I would have thought the view was crazy pretty. "I'd better go. I'm using his cell phone, and this is probably costing a fortune."

"OK. Call me again as soon as you can. And seriously, don't worry. We'll have you out of there in no time."

"Thanks, Addie. Hopefully we can FaceTime tomorrow."

"I'll be waiting by my computer. How do they say good-bye in Italy? 'Choo'? 'Chow'?"

"I have no idea."

"Liar. You're the one who's always talked about traveling the world."

"Hello and good-bye is '*ciao*.'"

"I knew it. *Ciao*, Lina."

"*Ciao*."

Our call disconnected and I set the phone on the desk, my throat tight. I missed her already.

"Lina?"

Howard! I practically tipped over in my chair. Had he been eavesdropping?

I scrambled to my feet, then opened the door a couple of inches. Howard was standing in the hallway holding a bunch of folded white towels that had been stacked up like a wedding cake.

"I hope I didn't interrupt you," he said quickly. "I just remembered I meant to give you these."

I studied his face, but it was as bland as whipped cream. Apparently being related meant nothing. I had no idea if he'd overheard my conversation with Addie.

I hesitated for a second, then opened the door wider and took the towels from him. "Thank you. And here's your phone." I grabbed it from the desk, then handed it to him.

"So … what do you think?"

I flushed. "About… ?"

"About your room."

"Oh. It's great. Really pretty."

A big, relieved grin spread across his face. It was definitely the first genuine one of the night, and he looked about a hundred pounds lighter. Also, his smile was kind of lopsided.

"Good." He leaned against the door frame. "I know I don't have the best taste, but I wanted it to be nice. A friend helped me paint the desk and dresser, and Sonia and I found the mirror at a flea market."

Ugh. Now I had the image of him traipsing around Italy looking for stuff he thought I'd like. Why the sudden interest? As far as I knew, he'd never even sent me a birthday card.

"You didn't have to go to all that trouble," I said.

"It wasn't any trouble. Really."

He smiled again, and there was a long uncomfortable pause. The whole night had felt like being on a blind date with someone I had nothing in common with. No, it was worse. Because we *did* have something in common. We just weren't talking about it. *When are we going to talk about it?*

Hopefully never.

Howard bobbed his head. "Well, good night, Lina."

"Good night."

His footsteps faded down the hall and I shut and locked the door again. My nineteen hours of travel had worked its way to the center of my forehead, and I had an insane headache. Time for this day to be over.

I put the towels on my dresser, then kicked off my shoes and took a flying leap onto the bed, sending sprays of decorative pillows in every direction. *Finally.* The bed was as soft as it looked and the sheets smelled awesome, like when my mom had sometimes hung ours on the line to dry. I wriggled under the covers and switched off the lamp.

Loud laughter erupted from downstairs. The music was still at full blast, and either they were doing the dishes or playing a loud round of indoor croquet, but who cared? After the day I'd had, I could fall asleep anywhere.

I had just drifted into that murky half-sleep phase when Howard's voice brought me back to consciousness.

"She's really quiet."

My eyes snapped open.

"I don't think that's surprising, considering the scenario," Sonia answered.

I didn't move a muscle. Apparently Howard didn't think sound traveled through open windows.

He lowered his voice. "Of course. It was just kind of a surprise. Hadley was so…"

"Lively? She really was. But Lina might surprise you. I wouldn't be a bit surprised if she turned out to have some of her mother's oomph."

He laughed quietly. "'Oomph.' That's one way to put it."

"Give her a little time."

"Of course. Thanks again for dinner – it was delicious."

"My pleasure. I'm planning on posting up at the visitors' center tomorrow morning. Will you be in the office?"

"In and out. I'd like to be off early so I can take Lina into town."

"Sounds good. Night, boss." Sonia's footsteps crunched down the gravel driveway and a moment later the front door opened and then closed again.

I forced my eyes shut, but it was like I had soda pop running through my veins. What had Howard expected? That I'd be overjoyed about moving in with someone I'd never met? That I'd be superexcited about living in a cemetery? It's not like it was a big secret that I hadn't wanted to come here. I'd agreed only when my grandma had pulled out the big guns: *You promised your mom.*

And why did he have to call me "quiet"? I *hated* being called quiet. People always said it like it was some kind of deficiency – like just because I didn't put everything out there right away, I was unfriendly or arrogant. My mom had understood. *You may be slow to warm up, but once you do, you light up the whole room.*

Tears flooded my eyes and I rolled over, pressing my face into my pillow. Now that it had been more than six months, I could sometimes go whole hours pretending to be OK without her. But it never lasted long. Turns out reality is as hard and unforgiving as that fire hydrant Addie and I had run into.

And I had to live the whole rest of my life without her. I really did.

Chapter 3

"LOOK, THAT WINDOW'S OPEN. SOMEONE MUST BE HERE."

The voice was practically in my ear and I sat bolt upright. Where was I? Oh. Right. In a cemetery. Only now it was saturated with sunlight, and my bedroom was 890 degrees. Give or take a hundred.

"Wouldn't you think they'd have signs telling you where to go?" It was a woman's voice, her accent as tangy as barbeque sauce.

A man answered. "Gloria, this looks like a private residence. I don't think we should be poking around—"

"Yoo-hoo! Hello? Anyone home?"

I pushed off my covers and got out of bed, tripping over a smattering of decorative pillows. I was still fully dressed. I'd been so tired that pajamas hadn't even crossed my mind.

"Hell-ooo," the woman trilled again. "Anyone there?"

I gathered my hair into a bun so I wouldn't scare anyone, then went over to the window to see two people who matched their voices *exactly*. The woman had fire-engine-red hair and wore high-waisted shorts, and the man wore a fishing hat and had a massive camera around his neck. They were even wearing bum bags. I stifled a giggle. Addie and I had once won a costume contest dressed as Tacky Tourists. These two could have been our inspiration.

"Hell-o," Real-Life Tacky Tourist said slowly. She pointed at me. "Do you speak-a the English?"

"I'm American too."

"Thank the heavens! We were just looking for Howard Mercer, the superintendent? Where can we find him?"

"I don't know. I'm ... new here." The view caught my eye and I looked up. The trees outside my window were a rich, velvety green and the sky was maybe bluer than I'd ever seen. But I was still in a cemetery. I repeat: Still. In. A. Cemetery.

Tacky Tourist looked at the man, then back up at me, settling her weight into one hip like *You can't get rid of me that easily*.

"I'll check to see if he's in the house."

"Now you're talking," she said. "We'll be around front."

I unzipped my suitcase and changed into a tank top and running shorts, then found my shoes and headed downstairs. The main floor was pretty small and, besides Howard's bedroom, the only room I hadn't seen yet was the study. I knocked just in case, then pushed my way inside. The walls were lined with framed Beatles albums and photographs, and I stopped to look at a picture of Howard and a few other people throwing buckets of water on a huge, gorgeous elephant. Howard was wearing cargo pants and a safari hat and looked like the star of some kind of adventure nature show. *Howard Bathes Wild Animals*. He obviously hadn't spent the past sixteen years sitting around missing my mom and me.

"Sorry, Tacky Tourists. No sign of Howard." I headed for the front, all ready to tell The Tackys I couldn't help them, but when I walked into the living room I jumped like I'd stepped on a live wire. The woman was not only waiting for me out front, but she'd pressed her face up against the window and was peering in at me like an enormous bug.

Over here. Over here! she mouthed, pointing to the front door.

"You've got to be joking me." I put my hand to my chest. My heart was going like a million beats per minute. You'd think life in a cemetery would be a lot more ... dead. *Ba dum tss!* My first official cemetery joke. And first official eye rolling at own cemetery joke.

I pushed the door open and the woman trundled back a couple of inches.

"Sorry, darling. Did I startle you? You looked like your eyes were going to bug out of your head." She was wearing one of those stick-on name tags. HELLO, MY NAME IS GLORIA.

"I didn't expect you to be ... looking in." I shook my head. "I'm sorry, but Howard's not here. He said something about having an office; maybe you could go look for him there?"

Gloria nodded. "Uh-huh. Uh-huh. Well, here's the problem, doll. We only have three hours before the tour bus comes back for us, and we want to be sure we see everything. I just don't think we have the time to be traipsing all over looking for. Mercer."

"Did you see the visitors' center? There's a woman who works there who might know where he is."

"I told you we should try that," the man said. "This is a *home*."

"Which one's the visitors' center?" Gloria asked. "Was it that building near the entrance?"

"I'm sorry, I really don't know." Probably because the night before I'd been way too panicked to notice anything but the army of headstones staring me down.

She raised an eyebrow. "Well, I hate to inconvenience you, *darlin'*, but I'm sure you know this place better than a couple of tourists from Alabama."

"Actually, I don't."

"What?"

I sighed, casting one more hopeful glance back into the house, but it was as quiet as a tomb. (*Ack!* Second cemetery joke.) Guess I was going to have to jump headfirst into this whole living-in-a-memorial thing. I stepped out onto the porch and pulled the door shut behind me. "I don't really know my way around, but I'll try to help."

Gloria smiled beatifically. "Grah-zee-aye."

I walked down the stairs, the two of them following after me.

"They sure do keep this place up nice," Gloria observed. "Real nice."

She was right. The lawns were so green they looked spray-painted, and practically every corner had a grouping of Italian and American flags surrounded by patches of *Wizard of Oz*–worthy flowers. The headstones were white and sparkly and didn't look nearly as creepy in the daylight. But don't get me wrong. They were still creepy.

"Let's go this way." I marched toward the road Howard and I had driven in on.

Gloria nudged me with her elbow. "My husband and I met on a cruise."

Oh, no. Was she going to tell me their life story? I slid a quick glance at Gloria and she smiled engagingly. Of course she was.

"He'd just lost his wife, Anna Maria. She was a nice lady, but real particular about how she kept house – one of those who puts plastic on all the furniture? Anyway, my husband, Clint, had passed a few years earlier, so that's why we were both there on the singles cruise. They had great food – just mountains of shrimp and all the ice cream you could eat. You remember that shrimp, Hank?"

Hank didn't appear to be listening. I sped up and Gloria did too.

"There were a bunch of horny old dogs on that boat, just nasty things, but lucky for me, Hank and I were assigned the same table for dinner. He proposed before the ship had even docked – that's how sure he was. We got married just two months later. Of course, I'd already moved in, but we really rushed things because we didn't want to be, you know…" She paused, looking at me meaningfully.

"What?" I asked hesitantly.

Her voice fell an octave. "Living in sin."

I looked desperately around the cemetery. I either needed to find Howard or someplace to vomit. Maybe both.

"First order of business was ripping all the plastic off that furniture. A person's got to live without their buttocks sticking to the darn sofa. Right, Hank?"

He made a guttural noise.

"This is sort of like a second honeymoon for us. I've wanted to visit Italy my whole life, and now here I am. You sure are a lucky duck, living here."

Quack, quack, I thought.

The road curved and a small building appeared just ahead of us. It was right next to the main entrance and had a giant sign that said, VISITORS CHECK IN HERE. Easy to confuse with VISITORS, FIND THE NEAREST HOUSE AND THEN YELL THROUGH THE WINDOWS.

"I think this is it," I said.

"Told you," Hank said to Gloria, breaking his silence.

"You didn't tell me anything." Gloria sniffed. "You just followed me around like a lost puppy dog."

I practically ran for the building's entrance, but before I could reach for the handle, the door swung open and Howard stepped out. He was wearing shorts and flip-flops, like he planned to catch a flight to Tahiti later.

"Lina. I didn't think you'd be awake yet."

"These two came looking for you at the house."

Gloria stepped forward. "Mr Mercer? We're the Jorgansens from Mobile, Alabama. You probably remember my e-mail? We're the ones who wanted a private, *special* tour of the cemetery? You see, my husband, Hank, has a real love for World War II history. Tell them, Hank."

"A real love," Hank said.

Howard nodded thoughtfully, but the corners of his mouth twitched. "Well, there's just the one tour, but I'm sure Sonia would be happy to take you. Why don't you two head inside and she'll get you started."

Gloria clapped her hands. "Mr Mercer, I can hear you're a Southerner yourself. Where are you from? Tennessee?"

"South Carolina."

"That's what I meant. South Carolina. And who is this lovely young woman who came to our aid? Your daughter?"

He paused for a nanosecond. Just long enough for me to notice. "Yes. This is Lina."

And we just met last night.

Gloria shook her head. "Glory be. I don't think I've ever seen a daddy and his daughter look quite so different. But sometimes it's like that. I got this red hair from my great-aunt on my mother's side. Sometimes the genes just skip a few generations."

We both looked at her skeptically. There was absolutely no way Gloria's red hair had come from anywhere but a box, but you had to admire her commitment.

She squinted at me, then turned to Howard. "Is your wife Italian?" She pronounced it "Eye-Talian."

"Lina's mother is American. She looks a lot like her."

I shot him a grateful look. Present tense keeps things a lot less complicated. But then I remembered his and Sonia's conversation on the porch, and I turned away, sucking my grateful look right back into my eyeballs.

Gloria put her hands on her hips. "Well, Lina, you just fit right in here, don't you? Look at those dark eyes and all that gorgeous hair. I'll bet everyone thinks you're a local."

"I'm not a local. I'm just visiting."

Hank finally found his voice. "Gloria, let's shake a leg. If we keep chatting like this, we're going to miss the whole dang-blasted cemetery."

"All right, all *right*. No need for strong language. Come on, Hank." She gave us a conspiratorial look, like her husband was a little brother we were all being forced to hang out with, and then she opened the door. "You two have a good day now. A-river-dur-chee!"

"Wow," Howard said when the door had closed behind them.

"Yeah." I folded my arms.

"Sorry about that. People don't usually go to the house. And they're usually a little less…" He paused, like he thought he could come up with a polite word to describe the Jorgansens. Finally he just shook his head. "Looks like you're headed out for a run."

I looked down at what I was wearing. It was such a habit to get dressed this way I hadn't even thought about it. "I usually go first thing."

"Like I said, you're welcome to run through the cemetery, but if you want to get out and explore, just head out those front gates. There's only one road, so you shouldn't get lost."

The visitors' center door opened again and Gloria poked her head out. "Mr Mercer? This *woman* in here says the tour only lasts thirty minutes. I specifically requested two hours or longer."

"I'll be right in." He glanced at me. "Enjoy your run."

As he walked away I impulsively stepped forward so I could see both our reflections in the glass door. Gloria may be ridiculous, but she hadn't been afraid to point out the obvious. Howard was well over six feet tall with strawberry blond hair and blue eyes. I had dark features and had to buy all my clothes in the petites section. But sometimes genes just skip a few generations.

Right?

I jogged out the front gates of the cemetery and crossed through the visitors' parking lot. Right or left? I guess it didn't matter. I just needed to get away from the cemetery for a while. *Left. No, right.*

The road that ran past the memorial was only two lanes, and I stuck to the strip of grass along the side, picking up my pace until I was almost at a sprint. I could usually outrun disturbing thoughts, but this one was pretty hard to shake. *Why don't I look anything like Howard?*

It was probably just one of those things – I mean, lots of people look nothing like their parents. Addie was the token blonde of her family, and there was this guy I'd grown up with who was taller than both his parents by the sixth grade. But still. Shouldn't Howard and I look at least a *little* bit alike?

I kept my eyes glued to the ground. *You'll adjust in no time. He's really a nice man.* That from my grandmother, who as far as I knew had never even met Howard. At least not in person.

An enormous blue bus went whooshing past, sending a

blast of hot air into my face, and when I looked up, I gasped. *What the…* ? Was I running through a scene from an Olive Garden menu? It was so *idyllic*. The road was lined with trees and curved gently past rustic-looking houses and buildings painted in soft, buttery colors. Patchwork hills stretched out into the distance and there were honest-to-goodness vineyards behind half the houses. So *this* was the Italy people were always talking about. No wonder people were always losing their minds over it.

Another vehicle came roaring up behind me, honking loudly and jolting me from my Italian moment. I sprang away from the road and turned to look back. It was a small red car that looked like it was really, really trying to come across as more expensive than it was and as it neared me it slowed down. The driver and his passenger both had dark hair and were in their early twenties. When we made eye contact, the driver grinned and started honking again.

"Calm *down*. It's not like I'm in your way," I said under my breath. The driver slammed on his brakes, like he'd somehow managed to hear me, then came to a stop right in the middle of the road. Another guy, maybe a year or two older, rolled down the window of the backseat, a big grin on his face.

"Ciao, bella! Cosa fai stasera?"

I shook my head and started running again, but the driver just pulled ahead a few yards, coming to a stop on my side of the road.

Great. After four years of running I knew all about this breed of guy. I don't know who told them that "out running alone" was code for "please pick me up," but I'd learned that telling them you weren't interested wasn't enough. They just thought you were playing hard to get.

I crossed to the other side of the road and turned toward the cemetery, taking a second to tighten my shoelaces. Then I inhaled deeply, hearing an imaginary starting pistol in my mind. *Go!*

There was a shout of surprise from the car. *"Dove vai?"*

I didn't even look back. If properly motivated I could pretty much outrun anyone – even Italian men in cheap red cars. I'd scale a fence if I had to.

By the time I got back to the cemetery the guys had passed me twice more and then given up, and I'm pretty sure even my eyelids were sweating. Howard and Sonia were standing with their backs to the gate, but they both turned quickly when they heard me. Probably because I sounded like an asthmatic werewolf.

"You weren't gone long. Are you OK?" Howard asked.

"I … got … chased."

"By who?"

"A car … full of guys."

"They were probably just smitten," Sonia said.

"Wait a minute. A car full of guys *chased* you? What did they look like?" His jaw tightened and he looked toward the road like he was considering charging out there with a base-ball bat or something.

It kind of made up for the *She's so quiet* comment.

I shook my head, finally catching my breath. "It wasn't really a big deal. I'll just stay inside the cemetery next time."

"Or you could run behind the cemetery," Sonia said. "There's a gate that leads out behind the grounds. Those hills would probably give you a great workout, and it's beautiful back there. And there'd be no cars to chase you."

Howard still had steam curling out of his nostrils, so I changed the subject. "Where are the Jorgansens?"

Sonia grinned. "There was a bit of a ... conflict. They opted for the self-guided tour." She pointed across the cemetery to where Gloria was marching Hank past a row of headstones. "Your dad was just telling me he wants to take you into Florence for dinner tonight."

Howard nodded, his face finally decompressing. "I was thinking we could walk around the Duomo and then get some pizza."

Was I supposed to know what that was? I shifted from one foot to the other. If I said yes, I'd be agreeing to what was sure to be an awkward dinner alone with Howard. But if I said no, I'd probably be stuck here in the exact same scenario. At least this way I'd get to see the city. And the Duomo. Whatever that was. "All right."

"Great." His voice was enthusiastic, like I'd just told him I really, *really* wanted to go. "It will give us a chance to talk. About things."

I stiffened. Shouldn't I be allowed some sort of grace period before I had to deal with whatever big explanation Howard had in store for me? Just being here was already putting me into overload.

I turned to wipe the sweat off my forehead, hoping they wouldn't see how upset I was. "I'm going back to the house."

I started to walk away, but Sonia hurried after me. "Would you mind stopping by my place on your way? I have something that belonged to your mother, and I'd love to give it to you."

I stepped sideways, putting an extra six inches between us. "Sorry, but I really need to take a shower. Maybe some other time?"

"Oh." The space between her eyebrows creased. "Sure. Just let me know when you have a minute. Actually, I could just—"

"Thanks a lot. See you around."

I broke into a jog, Sonia's gaze heavy on my back. I didn't want to be rude, but I also *really* didn't want whatever it was she had for me. People were always giving me things that belonged to my mother – especially photographs – and I never knew what to do with them. They were like souvenirs of my previous life.

I looked out over the cemetery and sighed. It's not like I needed any more reminders that things had changed.

Chapter 4

AS SOON AS I GOT INSIDE I HEADED STRAIGHT FOR the kitchen. I had a feeling that if asked, Howard would give the standard *mi casa, su casa* speech – probably with Italian pronunciation – so I skipped the asking and went straight to raiding the fridge.

The top two shelves of the refrigerator were packed with things like olives and gourmet mustards – stuff that makes food taste good, but isn't actually food – so I rifled through the drawers, finally coming up with a carton of what looked like coconut yogurt and a thick loaf of bread. I was pretty much devastated not to find any lasagna leftovers.

After devouring half the bread and practically licking the bottom of the yogurt carton (hands down the best yogurt I've ever had), I looked through the cupboards until I found a box of granola that said CIOCCOLATO. Jackpot. Chocolate spoke to me in any language.

I ate a huge bowl of the granola, then cleaned the kitchen like a crime scene. *Now what?* Well, if I were still in Seattle I would probably be getting ready to go to the pool with Addie or maybe pulling my bike out of the garage and demanding we go get one of those triple chocolate shakes I pretty much lived on. But here? I didn't even have the Internet.

"Shower," I said aloud. Something to do. And besides, I really needed one.

I went upstairs and grabbed the stack of towels from my bedroom, then went into the bathroom. It was incredibly clean, like maybe Howard scrubbed it every week with bleach. Maybe that was the reason he and my mom hadn't worked out. She'd been unbelievably messy. Like once I'd found a Tupperware of pasta on her desk that had been sitting so long it had turned blue. *Blue.*

I pulled back the shower curtain but had no idea what to do next. The showerhead was tiny and flimsy-looking and underneath it were two nozzles that read *C* and *F*.

"Cold and frigid? Chilly and frosty?"

I turned on the *F* and let it run for a few seconds, but when I put my hand under the stream it was still ice-cold. *OK. So maybe C?*

Exact same results, maybe half a degree warmer. I groaned. Were freezing showers part of what Howard had meant when he'd said Italy wasn't on the cutting edge of technology? And what choice did I have? I'd traveled for a full day and then done one of the hardest speed workouts of my life. I *had* to shower.

"When in Rome." I gritted my teeth and jumped in. "Cold! Cold! Ahh!"

I grabbed a bottle of something off the edge of the tub and rubbed it over my hair and body, rinsing and jumping out of there as fast as I could. Then I grabbed the entire stack of towels and started wrapping myself up like a mummy.

There was a knock on the door and I froze. Again. "Who is it?"

"It's me, Sonia. Are you … all right in there?"

I grimaced. "Um, yeah. Just having some water issues. Does this place not have hot water?"

"We do, it just takes a while. At my house I sometimes have to let the water run for a good ten minutes before its ready. *C* stands for '*caldo.*' It means 'hot.'"

I shook my head. "Good to know."

"Listen, I'm sorry to bother you again, but I just wanted to tell you that I left the journal on your bed."

I froze. The *journal*? Wait, I'd probably just misheard her. Maybe she'd said "the gerbil." A gerbil would be a totally thoughtful gift. And if I were giving someone a gerbil I would definitely put it—

"Lina … did you hear me? I brought you a journal that—"

"Just a minute," I said loudly. OK, she'd definitely said "journal." But that didn't mean it was any journal in particular. People gave each other journals all the time. I quickly dried off and got dressed. When I opened the door Sonia was standing in the hallway holding a potted plant.

"You got me a *new* journal?" I asked hopefully.

"Well, an old one. It's a notebook that belonged to your mother."

I slumped against the doorway. "You mean like a big leather one with lots of writing and photographs?"

"Yes. That's exactly what it's like." Her forehead scrunched up. "Is it something you've already looked at?"

I ignored her question. "I thought you were just going to give me one of her photographs or something."

"I actually do have a photograph of hers, but it's hanging on the wall in my guest bedroom and I don't have any plans to part with it. It's a close-up of the Wall of the Missing. Quite a beautiful shot. You should come see it sometime."

Apparently the Wall of the Missing was a big deal around here. "Why do you have one of her journals?"

My voice came out kind of bad-cop-sounding, but she just bobbed her head. "She sent it to the cemetery back in September. There wasn't a note, and the package wasn't addressed to anyone, but when I opened it I recognized it right away. When she was living at the cemetery she carried that journal around everywhere."

Living at the cemetery?

"Anyway, I thought about giving it to your dad, but your mom had always been kind of a taboo subject. Whenever I brought her up, he got…"

"What?"

She sighed. "It was hard on him when she moved out. Really hard. And even after all these years, I was nervous about bringing her up. Anyway, I stalled for a couple of days, and then your dad told me about the plan for you to come stay here. That's when I realized why she'd sent the journal."

She gave me a funny look and suddenly I realized that I'd been slowly gravitating toward her. We were only like five inches apart. Oops. I sprang back, and questions started flying out of my mouth.

"My mom lived at the cemetery? For how long?"

"Not very long. Maybe a month or so? It was right after your dad got the job. He'd just barely moved into this house."

"So they were like, *together* together? It wasn't like a one-night stand between friends or something?" That was Addie's theory.

Sonia cringed. "Uh ... no. I don't think it was ... that. They seemed very in love. Your dad adored her."

"So then why did she leave? Was it because she was pregnant? Howard wasn't ready to be a dad?"

"No. Howard would have been a great dad – I thought..." She put her hands up. "Wait a minute. Haven't they talked to you about what happened? Your mom didn't explain things?"

I dropped my head. "I don't know anything. I didn't even know Howard was my dad until after my mom died." Great. Now I was going to cry. Losing my mom had turned me into a human faucet. The regular hot/cold kind.

"Oh, Lina. I didn't know. I'm so sorry. I assumed they'd talked to you about what happened. To be honest, *I* don't even know what went wrong. It seemed like their relationship ended pretty suddenly, and then your dad never wanted to discuss it."

"Did he ever talk about me? Before now?"

She shook her head, her long dangly earrings swinging back and forth. "No. I was pretty surprised when I heard about you coming to live here. But you really need to talk to Howard. I'm sure he'll answer all of your questions. And maybe the journal will too." She held the flower pot out to me. "I went into town early this morning and your dad asked me to pick these up for you. He said your room was missing flowers and that violets were your mother's favorite."

I took them from her and studied them suspiciously. The flowers were deep purple and had a subtle scent. I was ninety-nine percent sure my mom hadn't had any special feelings for violets.

"Would you rather I keep the journal for a while? It sounds like it's a lot to process. Maybe you should spend some time talking to your dad first."

I shook my head. Slowly at first, and then more forcefully. "No, I want it."

Technically a lie. I'd packed up the rest of her journals several months earlier when I'd finally given up on the idea that I'd ever be able to read them without falling apart. But I had to read this one. She'd sent it to me.

I blinked a couple of times, then put on my best *I'm in control now* smile for Sonia, who was looking at me with the expression of a hapless bystander trapped in a hallway by an emotionally unstable teenager. Which she was.

I cleared my throat. "It'll be nice. I can read about what she did while she was in Italy."

Her expression softened. "Yes, exactly. I'm sure that's why she sent it. You'll be experiencing Florence just like she did, and maybe it will be a nice connection."

"Yeah, maybe."

If I could make it past the first page without falling apart.

"Lina, it really is great having you here. And stop by anytime to see that photograph of your mother's." She walked to the top of the stairs and then looked back. "I meant to tell you, it's best to water violets from the bottom. Just fill up a saucer and set the whole pot in there. That way you won't overwater. They could probably use a drink right away."

"Thanks, Sonia. And I'm, uh … sorry for all those questions."

"I understand. And I really liked your mother. She was pretty special."

"Yeah. She was." I hesitated. "Would you mind not mentioning this conversation to Howard? I don't want him to think I'm … uh … mad at him or something." *Or instigate any awkward conversations that aren't strictly necessary.*

She nodded. "My lips are sealed. Just promise me you'll talk to him. He's a great guy, and I'm sure he'll answer any questions you have."

"OK." I looked away and there were a long few seconds of silence.

"Have a nice day, Lina."

She went down the stairs and out the front door, but I just stood there staring into my bedroom. It was practically glowing with urgency. Cue panic.

It's just one of her journals. You can do this. You can do this. I finally started making my way down the hall, but at the last minute veered toward the stairs, the violets teetering dangerously.

I had some seriously thirsty violets on my hands. Sonia had said so. I'd just take care of that first. I plummeted down the stairs, then looked through the cupboards twice before finding a shallow dish big enough for the flower pot.

"Here you go, buddy." I filled the dish with an inch of tap water *(F)* and set the pot inside. My violets didn't seem particularly interested in having company, but I sat down at the kitchen table and watched them anyway.

I wasn't stalling. Really.

Chapter 5

JOURNALING WAS KIND OF MY MOM'S THING. WELL,
a lot of things were kind of her thing. She also liked hot yoga
and food trucks and really terrible reality TV shows, and once
she'd gotten really into the idea of homemade beauty prod-
ucts and we'd basically spent a month with coconut oil and
mashed avocado all over our faces.

But journaling ... that was a constant. A couple of times
a year she'd splurge on one of these thick artists' notebooks
from our favorite bookstore in downtown Seattle, and then
she'd spend months filling it with her life: photographs, diary
entries, grocery lists, ideas for photo shoots, old ketchup
packets ... anything you could think of.

And here was the strange part: She let other people read
them. And even stranger? People loved to. Maybe because
they were creative and hilarious and after you read one you felt
like you'd just taken a trip through Wonderland or something.

I walked into my bedroom and stood at the foot of my
bed. Sonia had left the journal right in the center of my pillow,
like maybe she was worried I wouldn't notice it otherwise,
and it was weighing down the bed like a pile of bricks.

"Ready?" I said aloud. I was definitely not ready, but I walked over and picked it up anyway. The cover was made of soft leather and had a big gold fleur-de-lis in its center. It didn't look anything like her journals back home.

I took a deep breath, then cracked open the cover, half expecting confetti to come shooting out at me, but all that happened was a bunch of brochures and ticket stubs fell out onto the floor and I got a whiff of something musty. I picked up all the papers, then started flipping through the pages, ignoring the writing and focusing on the photographs.

There was my mother standing in front of an old church with her camera slung over her shoulder. And there she was grinning over a gigantic bowl of pasta. And then … *Howard*. I practically dropped the book. OK, of *course* he was in her journal. It's not like I'd appeared out of thin air, but still. My mind totally resisted the idea of the two of them together.

I studied the picture. Yep, it was definitely him. Younger, longer-haired (and was that a *tattoo* on his upper arm?), but definitely Howard. He and my mom were sitting on stone steps and she had short hair and Old Hollywood lipstick and this *I've been swept off my feet* kind of look.

I sat down on my bed with a *thud*. Why hadn't she just told me her and Howard's story herself? Did she think that her journal would do a better job? Was she worried I wasn't ready to hear their story?

I hesitated for a moment, then shoved the journal in the drawer of my nightstand and shut it with a loud *slam*. Well, I wasn't ready.

Not yet.

* * *

A car alarm burst into full vibrato somewhere in the cemetery and the sound rained down on my head like a thousand tiny Glorias. *This headache brought to you by Jet Lag & Stress.* Thanks, Italy.

I rolled over and looked at the clock on the wall. Three p.m. Which left me with so much time to kill, it was ridiculous.

I slowly got out of bed, then went over to my suitcase and made a halfhearted attempt at organizing my things – shirts in the right-hand corner, pants in the left, pajamas over there... I'd done a horrible job packing, and it was all basically a jumble. Finally I settled on putting a couple of pictures of my mom and me into my room's empty frames, then laced up my shoes and headed for the front porch.

I didn't have a plan of where to go, so I just sat on the porch swing and rocked for a while. I had a good view of the memorial. It was a long, low building with a stretch of engravings that I would bet money went by the name of Wall of the Missing. Out in front of it was a tall post with a statue of an angel holding an armful of olive branches. Two men stood taking pictures in front of it, and one of them noticed me and waved.

I waved back but jumped up and headed for the back fence. I really didn't have it in me to handle another Jorgansen situation.

The back gate was easy to find, and as I headed out I realized that Sonia hadn't been kidding – the hill behind the cemetery was *steep*. For the second time that day, sweat dripped down my back, but I forced myself to keep running.

I will *conquer you, hill.* Finally I reached the top, my legs and lungs on fire. I was just about to keel over when a *thud-thud* noise made my neck snap up. I wasn't alone.

There was a boy playing with a soccer ball. He was my age, maybe a little older, and he was at least three months overdue for a haircut. He wore shorts and a soccer jersey and was juggling the soccer ball back and forth from knee to knee, singing quietly in Italian to whatever was playing on his headphones. I hesitated. Could I sneak away without him noticing me? Maybe a tuck-and-roll-type escape?

He looked up at me and we made eye contact. *Great.* Now I had to keep going or look like a weirdo. I nodded at him and walked quickly along the path, like I was late to a meeting or something. Totally natural. People were probably always hurrying off to important meetings on the top of Italian hills.

He pulled off his headphones, his music blaring. "Hey, are you lost? The Bella Vita hostel is just down the road."

I stopped. "You speak English."

"Just a little bit-a," he said with an exaggerated Italian accent.

"Are you American?"

"Sort of."

I studied him. He sounded American, but he looked about as Italian as a plate of meatballs. Medium height, olive skin, and a distinct nose. What was he doing here? But then again, what was *I* doing here? For all I knew, the Tuscan countryside was crawling with displaced American teenagers.

He crossed his arms and scowled. He was imitating me. Rude.

I dropped my stance. "What do you mean by 'sort of American'?"

"My mom's American, but I've lived here most of my life. Where are you from?"

"Seattle. But I'm living here for the summer."

"Really? Where?"

I pointed in the direction I'd come from.

"The cemetery?"

"Yeah. Howard – my dad – is the caretaker. I just got here."

He raised an eyebrow. "Spooky."

"Not really. It's more of a memorial. All the graves are from World War II, so it's not like there are burials going on." Why was I defending the cemetery? It *was* spooky.

He nodded, then put his headphones back on.

Guess that was my cue.

"Great to meet you, mysterious Italian–American. Guess I'll see you around."

"I'm Lorenzo."

I blushed. Apparently Lorenzo had sonic hearing. "Nice to meet you, Lo-ren—" I tried to repeat his name but got stuck on the second syllable. He'd made this rolling sound with the *R* that my tongue refused to do.

"Sorry, I can't say it right."

"That's OK. I go by 'Ren' anyway." He grinned. "Or 'mysterious Italian–American,' that works too."

Argh. "Sorry about that."

"What about you? Do you go by 'Carolina,' or do you have a nickname too?"

For a second I felt like I was in a dream. A weird one. No

one but my mother or teachers on the first day of school ever called me by my full name. "How do you know my name?" I said slowly. Who *was* this guy?

"I go to AISF. Your dad came in to ask about enrollment. Word spread."

"What's AISF?"

"The American International School of Florence."

I exhaled. "Oh, right. The high school." The school I'd theoretically attend if I decided to stay longer than just the summer. *So* theoretical. Like not even in the realm of possibility.

"It's actually kindergarten through high school, and our classes are really small. There were only eighteen of us last year, so new students are a big deal. We've been talking about you since January. You're kind of a legend. One guy, Marco, even claimed you as his biology partner. He totally bombed his final project and he kept trying to blame it on you."

"That's really weird."

"You don't look anything like I thought you would."

"Why?"

"You're really short. And you look Italian."

"Then how'd you know to speak to me in English?"

"Your clothes."

I looked down. Leggings and a yellow T-shirt. It's not like I was dressed as the Statue of Liberty or something. "What's so American about my outfit?"

"Bright colors. Running shoes…" He waved his hand dismissively. "Give it a month or two; you'll totally get it. A lot of people here won't go anywhere unless they're wearing something Gucci."

"But you're not wearing Gucci or whatever, right? You're in soccer clothes."

He shook his head. "Soccer clothes are exempt. They're about as Italian as they get. Plus, I *am* Italian. So everything naturally looks stylish on me."

I couldn't tell if he was joking or not.

"Weren't you supposed to transfer to AISF in February?" he asked.

"I decided to finish out the school year in Seattle."

He took his phone out of his back pocket. "Can I take a picture of you?"

"Why?"

"Proof that you exist."

I said "no" at the exact moment he took the picture.

"Sorry about that, Carolina," he said, sounding very unsorry. "You should really speak up."

"You're saying my name wrong. It looks like 'Carolina,' but it sounds like 'Caro*leen*a.' And I go by 'Lina.'"

"Carolina Caroleena. I like it. Very Italian-sounding."

He put his headphones back on, then tossed his ball in the air and started playing again. Ren definitely needed some etiquette classes or something. I turned to walk away, but he stopped me again.

"Hey, do you want to come meet my mom? She's basically starving for American company."

"No thanks. I have to get back soon to meet up with Howard. He's taking me into Florence for dinner."

"What time?"

"I don't know."

"Most restaurants don't even open until seven. I promise we won't be gone that long."

I turned back toward the cemetery, but the thought of facing Howard or the journal again made me shudder. "Is it far?"

"No, just right over there." He pointed vaguely at a grouping of trees. "It will be fine. And I promise I'm not a serial killer or anything."

I grimaced. "I didn't think you were. Until now."

"I'm way too scrawny to be a serial killer. Also, I hate blood."

"Ew." I looked back at the cemetery again, mentally weighing my options. Emotionally challenging journal? Or visit with a socially inept potential serial killer's mother? Either option was pretty grim.

"OK, I'll come with you," I relented.

"Nice." He tucked his soccer ball under his arm and we headed for the other side of the hill. He was only about a head taller than me and we both walked quickly.

"So when did you get here again?"

"Last night."

"So you're pretty much jet-lagged within an inch of your life right now, right?"

"I actually slept OK last night. But yeah. I kind of feel like I'm underwater. And I have maybe the worst headache of my life."

"Wait until tonight. The second night is always the worst. Around three a.m. you're going to be wide-awake and you'll have to think of weird stuff to keep yourself occupied. Once I climbed a tree."

"Why?"

"My laptop was out of commission and the only other thing I could come up with was playing Solitaire and I suck at that."

"I'm really good at Solitaire."

"And I'm really good at climbing trees. But I don't believe you. No one is good at Solitaire unless they cheat."

"No, I really am. People stopped playing games with me when I was in like second grade, so I taught myself how to play Solitaire. On a good day I can finish a game in like six minutes."

"Why did people stop playing games with you when you were in second grade?"

"Because I always win."

He stopped walking, a big grin on his face. "You mean because you're really competitive?"

"I didn't say that. I just said I always win."

"Uh-huh. So you haven't played a game since you were like seven?"

"Just Solitaire."

"No Go Fish? Uno? Poker?"

"Nothing."

"Interesting. Look, that's my house. Race you to the gate." He broke into a run.

"Hey!" I took off after him, lengthening my stride until I caught up and then passed him, and I didn't slow down until I hit the gate. I whirled around triumphantly. "Beat you!"

He was standing a few yards back, that stupid grin still on his face. "You're right. You're totally not competitive."

I scowled. "Shut up."

"We should play Go Fish later."

"No."

"Mah-jongg? Bridge?"

"What are you, an old lady?"

He laughed. "Whatever you say, Carolina. And by the way, that isn't really my house. It's that one over there." He pointed to a driveway in the distance. "But I'm not racing you there. Because you're right – you'd win."

"Told you."

We kept walking. Only now I just felt stupid.

"So what's the deal with your dad?" Ren asked. "Hasn't he been the caretaker at the cemetery for like forever?"

"Yeah, he said it's been seventeen years. My mom died, so that's why I came to live with him." *Ah!* I mentally clamped my hand over my mouth. *Lina, stop talking.* Bringing up my mom was a surefire way to create awkwardness around people my age. Adults got sympathetic. Teenagers got uncomfortable.

He looked at me, his hair falling into his eyes. "How'd she die?"

"Pancreatic cancer."

"Did she have it for a long time?"

"No. She died four months after we found out."

"Wow. Sorry."

"Thanks."

We were quiet for a moment before Ren spoke again. "It's weird how we talk about that. I say 'I'm sorry' and you say 'thanks.'"

I'd had that exact thought maybe a hundred times. "I

think it's weird too. But it's what people expect you to say."

"So what's it like?"

"What?"

"Losing your mom."

I stopped walking. Not only was this the first time anyone had ever asked me that, but he was looking at me like he actually wanted to know. For a second I thought about telling him that it was like being an island – that I could be in a room full of people and still feel alone, an ocean of hurt trying to crash in on me from every direction. But I swallowed the words back as quickly as I could. Even when they ask, people don't want to hear your weird grief metaphors. Finally I shrugged my shoulders. "It really sucks."

"I bet it does. Sorry."

"Thanks." I smiled. "Hey, we just did it again."

"Sorry."

"Thanks."

He stopped in front of a set of curlicue gates and I help him push them open with a loud *creak*.

"You weren't kidding. Your house is close to the cemetery," I said.

"I know. I always thought it was weird that I live so close to a cemetery. And then I meet someone who lives *in* a cemetery."

"I couldn't let you beat me. It's my competitive nature."

He laughed. "Come on."

We walked up the narrow, tree-lined driveway, and when we got to the top he held both arms out in front of him. "Ta-da. *Casa mia*."

I stopped walking. "This is where you *live?*"

He shook his head grimly. "Unfortunately. You can laugh if you want. I won't be offended."

"I'm not going to laugh. I think it's kind of ... interesting." But then a tiny snort slipped through and the look Ren shot me pretty much blew my composure to pieces.

"Go ahead. Get it all out. But people who live in cemeteries really shouldn't be throwing stones, or whatever that saying is."

Finally I stopped laughing long enough to catch my breath. "I'm sorry. I shouldn't be laughing. It's just really unexpected."

We both looked back up at the house, and Ren sighed wearily while I did my best not to insult him again. Just this morning I'd thought I lived in the weirdest place possible, but now I'd met someone who lived in a *gingerbread house*. And I don't mean a house sort of loosely inspired by a gingerbread house – I mean a house that looked like you could possibly break off a couple of its shingles and dip them in a glass of milk. It was two stories high with a stone exterior and thatched roof lined with intricate gingerbread trim. Candy-colored flowers blanketed the yard, and small lemon trees were planted in cobalt-blue pots around the perimeter of the house. Most of the main-floor windows were stained glass with swirling peppermint patterns, and there was a giant candy cane carved into the front door. In other words, picture the most ridiculous house you can imagine and then add a bunch of lollipops.

"What's the story?"

Ren shook his head again. "There has to be one, right? This eccentric guy from upstate New York built it after making a fortune on his grandmother's fudge recipe. He called himself the Candy Baron."

"So he built himself a real-life gingerbread house?"

"Exactly. It was a present for his new wife. I guess she was like thirty years younger than him, and she ended up falling for a guy she met at a truffle festival in Piedmont. After she left him, he sold the house. My parents just happened to be looking, and of course a gingerbread house was just the right kind of weird for them."

"Did you guys have to kick out a cannibalistic witch?"

He gave me a funny look.

"You know … like the witch in Hansel and Gretel?"

"Oh." He laughed. "No, she still comes to visit on major holidays. You meant my grandmother, right?"

"I'm so telling her you said that."

"Good luck. She doesn't understand a single word of English. And whenever she's around, my mom conveniently forgets how to speak Italian."

"Where's your mom from?"

"Texas. We usually spend summers in the States with her family, but my dad had too much work for us to go this year."

"So that's why you sound so American?"

"Yep. I pretend to be one every summer."

"Does it work?"

He grinned. "Usually. You thought I was American, didn't you?"

"Not until you talked."

"That's what counts, though, right?"

"I guess so."

He led me to the front door and we walked inside. "Welcome to Villa Caramella. *'Caramella'* means 'candy.'"

"Holy ... books."

It was like a librarian's worst nightmare. The entire room was lined with floor to ceiling bookcases, and hundreds – maybe thousands – of books were mashed haphazardly into the shelves.

"My parents are big readers," Ren said. "Also, we want to be prepared if there's ever a robot uprising and we need to hide out. Lots of books equals lots of kindling."

"Smart."

"Come on, she's probably in her studio." We made our way through the piles of books to a set of double doors that opened to a sunroom. The floor was shrouded in drop cloths and there was an ancient-looking table holding tubes of paint and a bunch of different ceramic tiles.

"Mom?"

A female version of Ren lay curled up on a daybed, yellow paint streaked through her hair. She looked about twenty years old. Maybe thirty.

"Mom." Ren reached down and shook her shoulder. "*Mamma*. She's kind of a deep sleeper, but watch this." Bending close to her face, he whispered, "I just saw Bono in Tavarnuzze."

Her eyes snapped open and in about half a second she'd scrambled to a standing position. Ren cracked up.

"Lorenzo Ferrara! Don't *do* that."

"Carolina, this is my mom, Odette. She was a U2 groupie. Followed them around for a while in the early nineties while they were on tour in Europe. Clearly she still has strong feelings for them."

"I'll show you strong feelings." She reached for a pair of glasses and slipped them onto her nose, giving me a once-over. "Oh, Lorenzo, where did you find her?"

"We just met on the hill behind the cemetery. She's living here with her dad for the summer."

"You're one of us!"

"American?" I asked.

"Expatriate."

"Hostage" was more like it. But that wasn't the sort of thing you told someone you'd just met.

"Wait a minute." She leaned forward. "I heard you were coming. Are you Howard Mercer's daughter?"

"Yes. I'm Lina."

"Her full name is 'Carolina,'" Ren added.

"Just call me Lina."

"Well, thank the heavens, Lina – we need more Americans here. Preferably *live* ones," she said, waving her hand dismissively in the direction of the cemetery. "I'm so glad to meet you. Have you learned any Italian?"

"I memorized like five phrases on the flight over."

"What are they?" Ren asked.

"I'm not saying them in front of you. I'll probably sound like an idiot."

He shrugged. *"Che peccato."*

Odette grimaced. "Promise me you'll never use even one of those phrases in this house. I'm spending the summer pretending to be somewhere other than Italy."

Ren grinned. "How's that working out for you? You know, with your Italian husband and children?"

She ignored him. "I'm going to get us some drinks. You two make yourselves comfortable." She squeezed my shoulder, then walked out of the room.

Ren looked at me. "Told you she'd be happy to meet you."

"Does she really hate Italy?"

"No way. She's mad that we can't go to Texas this summer, but every year it's the same thing. We get there and she spends three months complaining about the terrible food and all the people she sees wearing their pajamas in public."

"Who wears their pajamas in public?"

"Lots of people. Trust me. It's like an epidemic."

I pointed to the table. "Is she an artist?"

"Yeah. She paints ceramics, mostly scenes of Tuscany. There's a guy in Florence who sells them in his shop, and tourists pay like a gazillion dollars for them. They'd probably have a conniption if they found out they're done by an American." He picked up a tile and handed it to me. She'd painted a yellow cottage nestled between two hills.

"This is really pretty."

"You should see upstairs. We have a whole wall of tile that she's replacing one by one with the ones she's worked on."

I set the tile down. "Are you artistic?"

"Me? No. Not really."

"I'm not either. But my mom was an artist too. She was a photographer."

"Cool. Like family portraits and stuff?"

"No. Mostly fine-art kinds of stuff. Her work was

displayed in galleries and at art shows, places like that. She taught in colleges, too."

"Nice. What was her name?"

"Hadley Emerson."

Odette reappeared, carrying two cans of orange Fanta and an opened sleeve of cookies. "Here you go. Ren goes through about a pack of these a day. You'll love them."

I took one. It was a sandwich cookie with vanilla on one side and chocolate on the other. An Italian Oreo. I bit into it and a choir of angels started singing. Did Italian food have some kind of fairy dust that made it way better than its American counterparts?

"Give her more," Ren said. "She looks like she's going to eat her arm."

"Hey—" I started, but then Odette handed me the rest of the cookies and I was too busy eating to properly defend myself.

Odette smiled. "I love a girl who can eat. Now, where were we? Oh – I didn't really introduce myself, did I? I swear, this place is turning me into a savage. I'm Odette Ferrara. It's like 'Ferrari,' but with an *a*. Pleased to meet you." She extended her hand, and I wiped crumbs off mine so we could shake. "Can we talk about air-conditioning? And drive-thru restaurants? Those are the two things I've been missing most this summer."

"You never even let us eat fast food when we're in the States," Ren said.

"That doesn't mean *I* don't eat it. And whose side are you on anyway? Mine or the Signore's?"

"No comment."

"Who's the Signore?" I asked.

"My dad. I have no idea how they ended up together. You know those weird animal friendship videos, where a bear and a duck become best friends? They're kind of like that."

Odette cackled. "Oh, come on. We're not *that* different. But now I'm curious. In that scenario, would you consider me the bear or the duck?"

"I'm not going there."

Odette turned to me. "So what do you think of my Ren?"

I swallowed and handed the rest of the cookies to Ren, who was eyeing them like they were *his precious*. "He's ... very friendly."

"And handsome, too, isn't he?"

"*Mom*."

I felt myself blush a little. Ren *was* cute, but in that kind of way that you don't really notice at first. He had deep brown eyes fringed with ridiculously long lashes, and when he smiled he had a little gap between his front teeth. But again, that wasn't the sort of the thing you told someone you just met.

Odette waved her hand at me. "Well, we're so glad to have you in town. I'm pretty sure Ren has been having the most boring summer of his life. I told him just this morning that he needs to get out more."

"Come on, Mom. It's not like I just sit home all day."

"All I know is that once a certain *ragazza* went out of town, you suddenly had no interest in going out."

"I go out when I feel like it. Mimi has nothing to do with it."

"Who's Mimi?" I asked.

"His crush," Odette said in a stage whisper.

"Mooom," Ren growled. "I'm not nine."

A phone started ringing, and Odette began pulling papers and art supplies off the table. "Where in the...? *Pronto?*"

A little girl appeared in the doorway wearing a pair of ruffled underpants and black dress shoes. "I pooped!"

Odette gave her a double thumbs-up and then walked into the house, speaking on the phone in rapid Italian.

Ren groaned. "Gabriella, that is so embarrassing. Get back in the bathroom. We have company here."

She ignored him, turning to me instead. "*Tu chi sei?*"

"She doesn't speak Italian," Ren said. "She's American."

"*Anch'io!* Are you Lorenzo's girlfriend?" she asked.

"No. I just met him when I was out for a walk. My name's Lina."

She studied me for a minute. "You're kind of like a *principessa*. Maybe like Rapunzel because of your crazy hairs."

"It's *hair*, not hairs, Gabriella," Ren said. "And it's not nice to tell someone their hair is crazy."

"My hairs *are* crazy," I confirmed.

"Do you want to see my *criceto*?" Gabriella ran over and grabbed my hand. "Come now, *principessa*. You will really like him. His furs are so soft."

"Sure."

Ren put his hand on her shoulder. "Carolina, no. And, Gabriella, she doesn't want to. She has to leave soon."

"I don't mind. I like kids."

"No, seriously, trust me. Going into her room is like

stepping into a time warp. Before you know it, you'll have been playing Barbies for like five hours and you'll be answering to Princess Sparkle."

"*Non è vero*, Lorenzo. You're so mean!"

Ren answered in Italian, and Gabriella gave me a betrayed look and then ran out of the room, slamming the door behind her.

"What's a *criceto*?"

"In English … a hamster, I think? Little annoying animal, runs on a wheel?"

"Yep. Hamster. She's cute."

"Sometimes she's cute. Do you have any brothers or sisters?"

"No. But I used to babysit a lot for a family in my apartment building. They had triplet boys who were five."

"Whoa."

"Whenever their mom left, she'd say, *Just keep them alive. Don't worry about anything else.*"

"So you tied them up or something?"

"No. The first time I babysat I wrestled them, and after that they loved me. Also, I always came over with my pockets full of fruit snacks." At my mom's funeral, one of the boys asked where I'd been and his brother said, *Her mom is sleeping for a really long time. That's why she can't play with us anymore.*

My throat tightened at the memory. "I'd better get going. Howard might wonder where I am."

"Yeah, sure." We walked back through the living room and Ren stopped at the front door.

"Hey, do you want to go to a party with me tomorrow?"

"Um…" I looked away, then quickly bent to tie my shoe-lace. *It's just a party. You know, the things normal teenagers go to?* Losing my mom had somehow made social events feel like a quick jaunt up Mt Everest. Also, I was doing an alarming amount of self-talk these days.

"I'll have to ask Howard," I finally said, straightening back up.

"OK. I can pick you up on my scooter. Around eight?"

"Maybe. I'll call you if I can go." I reached for the doorknob.

"Wait. You need my number." He grabbed a pen from a nearby table, then cupped my hand in his, writing his number quickly. His breath was warm, and when he finished, he held my hand for just a second longer.

Oh.

He looked up at me and smiled. "*Ciao*, Carolina. I'll see you tomorrow."

"Maybe." I stepped out of the house and left without looking back. I was afraid he'd see the sparkly smile plastered across my face.

Chapter 6

THE WHOLE REN-HAND-HOLDING THING HAD LAUNCHED
a teeny butterfly in my stomach, but all it took was two minutes in the car with Howard for the butterfly to fall flat. It was
just so *awkward*.

Howard had these big comb marks in his freshly
showered hair, and he'd changed into a pair of slacks and a
nicer shirt. I'd missed the memo on dressing up and was still
wearing my T-shirt and sneakers.

"Ready?" he asked.

"Ready."

"Well, then off to Florence. You're going to love the
city." He popped a disc in his CD player (who was still using
CDs?) and AC/DC's "You Shook Me All Night Long" filled
the car. You know, the official soundtrack of Ignore How
Uncomfortable Your First Father-Daughter Outing Is.

According to Howard the city was only about seven
miles away, but it took us like thirty minutes to get there.
The road into town was packed with scooters and miniature
cars and every building we passed looked old. Even with the
weird atmosphere in the car, excitement started building up

in me like steam in a pressure cooker. Maybe the circumstances weren't ideal, but I was in *Florence*. How cool was that?

When we got to the city Howard pulled down a narrow, one-way street, then pulled off the most impressive feat of parallel parking I'd ever witnessed. Like he would have made a great driver's ed teacher, if he weren't so into the whole cemetery thing.

"Sorry about the long drive," he said. "Traffic was bad tonight."

"Not your fault." I practically had my nose pressed against the window. The street was made of gray crisscrossing square stones and there was a narrow sidewalk on either side. Tall pastel-colored buildings were smashed close together and all the windows had these adorable green shutters. A bike flew past on the sidewalk, practically clipping my side mirror.

Howard looked at me. "Want to take the scenic route? See a little bit of the city?"

"Yes!" I unclicked my seat belt and then jumped out onto the street. It was still hot out, and the city smelled slightly of warm garbage, but everything was so interesting-looking that it was completely OK. Howard started up the sidewalk and I trailed after him.

It was like walking through a scene from an Italian movie. The street was lined with clothing stores and little coffee shops and restaurants, and people kept calling to one another from windows and cars. Halfway down the street a horn beeped politely and everyone cleared out of the street to make way for an entire family crowded onto a scooter. There was even a string of laundry hanging between two buildings, a billowy red housedress flapping right in the middle of it. Any second now a director was going to jump out and yell, *Cut!*

"There it is." We turned a corner and Howard pointed to a sliver of a tall building visible at the end of the street.

"There's what?"

"That's the Duomo. Florence's cathedral."

Duomo. It was like the mother ship. Everyone was funneling into it and we had to slow down even more the closer we got. Finally we were in the middle of a large open space, and I was looking up at a gargantuan building half-lit by the setting sun.

"Wow. That's really…" Big? Beautiful? Impressive? It was all that and more. The cathedral was easily the size of several city blocks and the walls were patterned in detailed carvings of pink, green, and white marble. It was a hundred times prettier and more impressive and *grander* than any building I'd seen before. Also, I'd never used the word "grander" in my life. Nothing had ever required it before.

"It's actually called the Cathedral of Santa Maria del Fiore, but everyone just calls it the Duomo."

"Because of the domed roof?" One side of the building was capped with an enormous orange-red circular roof.

"No, but nice catch. '*Duomo*' means 'cathedral,' and the word just happens to sound like 'dome' in English, so a lot of people make that mistake. The cathedral took almost a hundred and fifty years to build, and that was the largest dome in the world until modern technology came around. As soon as I get a free afternoon, we'll climb to the top."

"What's that?" I pointed to a much smaller octagonal building across from the Duomo. It had tall gold doors with carvings on them, and a bunch of tourists were taking pictures in front of them.

"The baptistery. Those doors are called the Gates of Paradise, and they're one of the most famous works of art in the whole city. The artist's name was Ghiberti, and they took him twenty-seven years to make. I'll take you on a tour of that, too." He pointed to a street just past the baptistery. "The restaurant is right over there."

I followed Howard across the big open space (*piazza*, he told me) and he held the restaurant's door open for me. A man wearing a necktie tucked into his apron looked up from behind his stand and stood a little straighter. Howard was like two feet taller than him.

"And tonight, how many?" he asked in a nasally voice.

"Possiamo avere una tavolo per due?"

The man nodded, then called to a passing server.

"Buona sera," the server said to us.

"Buona sera. Possiamo stare seduti vicino alla cucina?"

"Certo."

So … apparently my father spoke Italian. Fluently. He even rolled his *R*s like Ren. I tried not to stare at him as we followed our server to our table. I literally knew nothing about him. It was so weird.

"Can you guess why I like it here?" Howard asked as we settled into our seats.

I looked around. The tables were covered in cheap paper cloths and there was an open kitchen with a wood-fire pizza oven blazing away. "She's Got a Ticket to Ride" was playing in the background.

He pointed up at the ceiling. "They play the Beatles all day every day, which means I get two of my favorite things together. Pizza and Paul McCartney."

"Oh, yeah. I noticed the framed Beatles records in your office." I gulped. Now he was going to think I'd been snooping. Which technically I guess I had been.

He just smiled. "My sister sent those as a gift a few years ago. She has two boys, ten and twelve. They live in Denver and they usually come out every other summer or so."

Did *they* know about me?

Howard must have had a similar thought, because there was a moment of silence, and then we both suddenly got superinterested in our menus.

"What do you want to order? I always get a prosciutto pizza, but everything here is good. We could get a few appetizers or—"

"How about just a plain pizza. Cheese." Simple and quick. I wanted to get back out in Florence. And keep this dinner as short as possible.

"Then you should order the Margherita. It's pretty basic. Just tomato sauce, mozzarella, and basil."

"That sounds good."

"You're going to love the food here. Pizza here is in a whole different category from the stuff back home."

I set my menu down. "Why?"

"It's really thin and you get your own large pizza. And fresh mozzarella…" He sighed. "There's nothing like it."

He honestly had a dreamy look in his eyes. Did my more-than-a-friend love for food come from him? I hesitated. I guess it *would* be a good idea to at least sort of get to know him. He was my father after all.

"So … where's 'back home'?"

"I grew up in a small town in South Carolina called Due West, if you can believe it. It's about a hundred and fifty miles from Adrienne."

"Is Due West where you rearranged all the traffic barricades and caused a traffic jam?"

He looked at me in surprise. "Your mom told you?"

"Yeah. She told me lots of stories about you."

He chuckled. "There wasn't a lot to do in Due West, and unfortunately, I made the whole town pay for it. What other stories did she tell you?"

"She said you used to play hockey and that even though you're pretty even-tempered, you used to get in fights on the ice."

"Proof." He turned his head and ran his finger across a scar that disappeared under his jawline. "This was one of my last games. I couldn't seem to keep it under control. What else?"

"You guys went to Rome and the owner of a restaurant thought you were a famous basketball player and you guys got a free meal."

"I forgot about that! Best lamb I ever had. And all I had to do was take pictures with the kitchen staff."

Our server came over and took our order, then filled our glasses with fizzy water. I took a big swig and shuddered. Was it just me, or did carbonated water feel like liquid sparklers?

Howard crossed his arms. "Forgive me for stating the obvious, but I can't believe how much you look like Hadley. Did people tell you that all the time?"

"Yeah. People sometimes thought we were sisters."

"That doesn't surprise me. You even have her hands." My elbows were resting on the table, one arm crossed over the other, and Howard suddenly jerked forward a couple of inches, like he'd gotten snagged on a fishing hook.

He was staring at my ring.

I shifted uncomfortably. "Um, are you OK?"

"Her ring." He reached out and almost touched it, his hand hovering an inch above mine. It was an antique, a slim gold band engraved with an intricate scrolling pattern. My mom had worn it until she'd gotten too thin to keep it on. I'd been wearing it ever since.

"Did she tell you I gave her that?"

"No." I pulled my hand to my lap, my face heating up. Had she told me *anything*? "Was it like an engagement ring or something?"

"No. Just a present."

There was another long silence, which I filled with unprecedented interest in the restaurant's décor. There were signed photographs of what were probably very famous Italian celebrities hanging all around the restaurant, and several aprons had been tacked to the wall. "We All Live in a Yellow Submarine" was playing overhead. My cheeks were boiling like a pot of marinara sauce.

Howard shook his head. "So do you have a boyfriend at home who is missing you?"

"No."

"Good for you. Plenty of time to break hearts when you're older." He hesitated. "This morning I was thinking I should make a call to the international school to see if anyone in your grade is around for the summer. It might be a good way to see if you're interested in going to the school."

I made a noncommittal sound, then took a special interest in a nearby photograph of a woman wearing a tiara and a thick sash. Miss Ravioli 2015?

"I wanted to tell you, if you ever need someone to talk to here – someone other than me or Sonia, of course – I have a friend who lives in town. She's a social worker and she speaks English really well. She told me she'd be happy to meet with you if you ever need, you know…"

Great. Another counselor. The one I'd seen at home had pretty much just said mm-hmm, mm-hmm, over and over and asked me, *How did that make you feel?* until I thought my ears were going to melt. The answer was always "terrible." I felt *terrible* without my mom. The counselor had told me that things would slowly start to feel better, but so far she was wrong.

I started tearing up the edges of the paper tablecloth, keeping my eyes off the ring.

"Are you feeling … comfortable here?"

I hesitated. "Yeah."

"You know, if you need anything, you can always just ask."

"I'm fine." My voice was gravelly, but Howard just nodded.

After what felt like ten hours, our server finally walked out and set two steaming pizzas in front of us. Each of them was the size of a large dinner plate, and they smelled unbelievable. I cut a piece and took a bite.

All weirdness evaporated immediately. The power of pizza.

"I think my mouth just exploded," I said. Or at least that's what I tried to say. It came out more like "mymog jesesieplod."

"What?" Howard looked up.

I shoveled in another bite. "This. Is. The. Best." He was right. This pizza belonged in a completely different universe from the stuff I was used to.

"Told you, Lina. Italy is the perfect place for a hungry runner." He smiled at me and we both ate ravenously, "Lucy in the Sky with Diamonds" filling in for conversation.

I had just taken an enormous bite when he said, "You're probably wondering where I've been all this time."

I froze, a piece of crust in my hand. *Is he asking what I think he is?* This couldn't be the big unveiling moment – you don't go around telling your children why you weren't around while stuffing your face with pizza.

I snuck a glance up. He'd set his fork and knife down and was leaning forward, his mouth set in a serious line. *Oh, no.*

I swallowed. "Um, no. I haven't really wondered." Lie with a capital *L*. I stuffed the piece of crust into my mouth but couldn't taste it.

"Did your mother tell you much about our relationship?"

I shook my head. "No. Just, uh, funny stories."

"I see. Well, the truth is, I didn't know about you."

Suddenly it seemed like the whole restaurant got quiet. Except for the Beatles singing "Ticket to Ride".

I swallowed hard. I had never even *considered* that possibility. "Why?"

"Things were … complicated between us."

Complicated. That was exactly what my mom had said.

"She got in touch with me around the same time she started getting tested. She knew she was sick, just not with what, and I think she had a feeling. Anyway, I want you to know I would have been there. If I'd known. I just…" He rested his hand on the table, palm-side up. "I guess I just want a chance. I'm not expecting miracles. I know this is hard. Your grandmother told me you really didn't want to come here, and I understand that. I just want you to know that I really appreciate having this chance to get to know you."

He met my eyes, and suddenly I wished with all my heart that I could evaporate, like the steam still curling off my pizza.

I pushed away from the table. "I … I need to find the bathroom." I sprinted to the front of the restaurant, barely making it inside the restroom before the tears started rolling.

Being here was awful. Before today I'd known exactly who my mother was, and she certainly wasn't this woman who loved violets or sent her daughter mysterious journals or forgot to tell the father of her child that – *oh, by the way, you have a daughter!*

It took all three minutes of "Here Comes the Sun" to get myself under control, mostly deep breathing, and when I finally cracked the door open, Howard was still sitting at the table, his shoulders slumped. I watched him for a moment, anger settling over me like a fine dusting of Parmesan cheese.

My mother had kept us apart for sixteen years. Why were we together now?

Chapter 7

THAT NIGHT I COULDN'T SLEEP.

Howard's bedroom was upstairs too, and the floorboards creaked as he walked down the hall. *I didn't know about you.* Why?

The clock on my bedroom wall made an irritating *tick-tick-tick*. I hadn't noticed it the night before, but suddenly the noise was unbearable. I pulled a pillow over my head, but that didn't help, plus it was kind of suffocating. There was a breeze blowing through my window and my violets kept swaying like Deadheads at a concert.

OK. Fine. I switched on my lamp and took the ring off my finger, studying it in the light. Even though my mother hadn't seen Howard in more than sixteen years, she'd worn the ring he'd given her. Every single day.

But why? Had they really been in love, like Sonia had said? And if so, what had torn them apart?

Before I could lose my nerve, I opened my nightstand drawer and felt for the journal.

I lifted the front cover:

I made the wrong choice.

A chill moved down my spine. My mother had written in thick black marker, and the words sprawled across the inside cover like a row of spiders. Was this a message to me? A kind of precursor to whatever I was about to read?

I mustered up my courage, then turned to the front page. Now or never.

———

MAY 22

Question. Immediately following your meeting with the admissions officers at University of Washington (where you've just given official notice that you will not be starting nursing school in the fall) do you:

A. go home and tell your parents what you've done?

B. have a complete panic attack and run back into the office claiming a temporary lapse in sanity?

C. go out and buy yourself a journal?

Answer: C

True, you will eventually have to tell your parents. And also true, you purposely timed your appointment so the office would be closing as you walked out. But as soon as the dust settles I'm sure you'll remember all the reasons why you just did what you did. Time to walk yourself into the nearest bookstore and blow your budget on a fancy new journal — because as scary as this moment is, it's also the moment when your life (your real life) begins.

Journal, it's official. As of one hour and twenty-six minutes ago I am no longer a future nursing student. Instead, in just three weeks I will be packing up my things (aka, whatever my mother doesn't smash when she hears the news) and boarding a plane for Florence, Italy (ITALY!), to do what I've always wanted to do (PHOTOGRAPHY!) at the Fine Arts Academy of Florence (FAAF!).

Now I just have to brainstorm how I'll break the news to my parents. Most of my ideas involve placing an anonymous call from somewhere in Antarctica.

MAY 23

Well, I told them. And it somehow went even worse than I expected. To the casual observer, The Great Parental Fallout would have sounded something like this:

Me: Mom, Dad, there's something I need to tell you.

Mom: Good heavens. Hadley, are you pregnant?

Dad: Rachelle, she doesn't even have a boyfriend.

Me: Dad, thanks for pointing that out. And, Mom, not quite sure why you jumped straight to pregnant. [*Clears throat*] I want to talk to you about a recent life decision I've made. [Wording taken directly from a book called <u>Savvy Communication: How to Talk So They'll Agree</u>.]

Mom: Good heavens. Hadley, are you gay?

Dad: Rachelle, she doesn't even have a girlfriend.

Me: [*Abandoning all attempts at civilized conversation.*] NO. What I'm trying to tell you is that I'm not going to nursing school anymore. I just got accepted to an art school in Florence, Italy, and I'll be there for six months studying photography. And ... it starts in three weeks.

Mom/Dad: [*Prolonged silence involving two trout-like open mouths.*]

Me: So...

Mom/Dad: [*Continue gaping*]

Me: Could you please say something?

Dad: [*weakly*] But, Hadley, you don't even have a decent camera.

Mom: [*regaining voice*] WHATDOYOUMEANYOU'RENOT-
GOINGTONURSINGSCHOOO...

[*Neighborhood dogs start howling*]

I'll spare you the lecture that followed, but it basically boils
down to this: I am throwing away my life. I'm wasting
my time, my scholarship, and their hard-earned money for
six frivolous months in a country where the women don't
even shave their armpits. (That last tidbit was contributed
by my mother. I have no idea if it's true or not.)

I explained to them that I will pay for the entire thing.
I thanked them for their contributions to my education.
I assured them that I'll keep up on my normal grooming
routines. And then I went up to my room and bawled my
eyes out for at least an hour because I am SO SCARED. But
what choice do I have? The second I had that art-school
acceptance letter in my hand I knew I wanted it more
than I've ever wanted anything. I'm going because it feels
scarier not to!

I set the journal down. A straight-up monsoon was happening in the general vicinity of my face, and the words kept
running together in a big, blurry mess. *This* was why I couldn't
read her journals. They made me feel like I was overhearing
her talking on the phone to a friend and then when I looked
up from the page and she wasn't there...

Pull it together. I rubbed my eyes ferociously. She'd sent me this journal for a reason, and I had to find out what it was.

JUNE 13

It seems like a bad omen to be leaving on the thirteenth, but here I am. Chilly good-bye from Mom, then Dad dropped me off at the airport. Hello, unknown.

JUNE 20

I'M HERE. I could write fifty pages about my first week in Florence, but suffice it to say, I am <u>here</u>. FAAF is exactly what I pictured: tiny, cluttered, overflowing with talent. My apartment is right above a noisy bakery and my mattress might be made of cardboard, but who cares when the world's most gorgeous city is right outside my window?

My roommate is named Francesca, and she's a fashion photography student from northern Italy. She wears all black, switches effortlessly in and out of Italian, French, and English, and has been chain-smoking out our window since the moment she arrived. I adore her.

JUNE 23

First free day in Italy. I was looking forward to a lazy morning involving a fresh jar of Nutella and some bread from the bakery downstairs, but Francesca had other plans. When I came out of my room she instructed me to get dressed, then spent the next thirty minutes arguing enthusiastically with someone on the phone while I sat waiting for her. When she finally hung up she insisted I had to change my shoes. "No sandals. It's after eleven o'clock." She made me change twice more. ("No dark denim after April." "Never match your shoes to your handbag.") It was exhausting.

Finally we were out on the street and Francesca started giving me a speed-dating version of Florence's history. "Florence is the birthplace of the Renaissance. You <u>do</u> know what the Renaissance is, don't you?" I assured her that everyone knows what the Renaissance is, but she explained it anyway. "A third of the population died in the bubonic plague in the 1300s, and afterward Europe experienced a cultural rebirth. Suddenly there was an explosion of artistic work. It all started here before trickling out to the rest of Europe. Painting, sculpture, architecture — this was the art capital of the world. Florence was one of the wealthiest cities in history ..." and on and on and <u>on</u>.

She was weaving in and out of the streets, not even taking a second to make sure I was following, and then suddenly I saw it. THE DUOMO. Intricate, colorful, Gothic Duomo. I was completely winded, but even if I hadn't been, it would have taken my breath away.

Francesca put out her cigarette, then led me to the Duomo's side entryway and told me that we were climbing to the top. And we did. Four hundred and sixty-three steep stone stairs, with Francesca pogo-ing up the steps like her stilettos had springs. When we finally got to the top I couldn't stop taking pictures. Florence spreads out like an orange-tinted maze, towers and buildings jutting up here and there, but nothing as tall as the Duomo. There were green hills in the distance, and the sky was the most perfect shade of blue. Francesca finally stopped talking when she saw how in awe I was. She didn't even get mad when I reached my arms out wide, feeling the wind and this new feeling — this freedom. Before we headed back down I gave Francesca a giant hug, but she just peeled me off her and said, "All right, all right. You got yourself here. I just took you to see the Duomo. Now let's go shopping. I've never seen a sadder pair of jeans. Really, Hadley, they make me want to weep."

———————

"No way," I whispered to myself. What were the chances that I'd read this entry on the day *I'd* seen the Duomo for the first time? I ran my fingers over the words, imagining my twenty-something-year-old mom running to keep up with tyrannical, springy Francesca. Was this part of the reason my mom had sent her journal? So we could experience Florence together?

I marked my place and switched off the light, my chest

heavy. Yes, hearing her voice was the emotional equivalent of a damaged ship taking on water. But it felt good, too. She'd *loved* Florence. Maybe reading her journal would be like seeing it with her.

I'd just have to take it in small doses.

Chapter 8

I HAVE TO TELL ADDIE ABOUT THE JOURNAL. **THE NEXT** morning I tumbled down the stairs without even changing out of my pajamas. Ren had been totally wrong about the jet-lag thing. Once I'd finished reading the diary entries, I'd tucked the journal under the covers with me and then slept a solid thirteen hours. I felt like a well-rested hummingbird.

Right before I escaped up to my room, Howard had told me he'd leave his cell phone out for me, and I was ridiculously grateful that I didn't have to ask him for it. If last night's drive home were a book, it would have been titled something like *The Longest, Quietest, Most Miserable Ride Ever,* and I really wasn't looking forward to a sequel. The less interacting, the better.

Back in my room I closed the door, then powered up the phone. Country code first? Area code? Where were my instructions? After three tries, the phone finally started ringing. Ian answered.

"Hello?"

"Hey, Ian. It's Lina."

A video game blared in the background.

"You know ... the one who lived with you for five months?" I prompted.

"Oh, yeah. Hi, Lina. Where are you again? France?"

"Italy. Is Addie there?"

"No. I don't know where she is."

"Isn't it like two a.m. there?"

"Yeah. I think she stayed over at someone's house. We're sharing a phone now."

"I heard. Could you tell her I called?"

"Sure. Don't eat snails." *Click.*

I groaned. Ian's track record meant that my message had a less-than-zero chance of ever getting to Addie. And I *really* needed to talk to her – about the journal, about what Howard had told me, about ... everything. I paced around my bedroom like my grandma's OCD cat. I really didn't feel ready to go back to the journal again, but I also *really* couldn't just sit around thinking. I quickly changed into my running clothes, then went outside.

"Hi, Lina. How'd you sleep?"

I jumped. Howard was sitting on the porch swing with a stack of papers on his lap and dark circles under his eyes. I'd been ambushed.

"Fine. I just woke up." I propped my foot up on the banister and gave my shoelaces total and complete concentration.

"Ah, to be a teenager again. I don't think I saw the morning side of a sunrise until I was in my late twenties." He stopped swinging and sort of stumbled into his next sentence. "How are you feeling about what we talked about last night? I wonder if I could have told you that in a better way."

'I'm not upset," I said quickly.

"I'd really like to talk to you more about your mother and me. There are some things she didn't tell you that—"

I yanked my foot off the banister like I was a Rockette. "Maybe another time? I'd really like to start my run." *And I want to hear my mom's side first.*

He hesitated. "OK, sure." He tried to meet my gaze. "We'll take it at your pace. Just tell me when you're ready."

I hurried down the steps.

"You got a phone call at the visitors' center this morning."

I whipped around. "Was it Addie?" *Please be Addie.*

"No. It was a local call. His name was strange. Red? Rem? An American. He said he met you yesterday while you were out running."

A handful of confetti rained down on me. *He called?* "Ren. It's short for 'Lorenzo.'"

"That makes more sense. He said you're going to a party with him tonight?"

"Oh, yeah. Maybe." The whole Howard/journal thing had done an awesome job at crowding everything else out of my brain. Was I feeling gutsy enough to go?

Howard's forehead creased. "Well, who is he?"

"He lives nearby. His mom's American and he goes to the international school. I think he's my age."

His face lit up. "That's great. Except... Oh, no."

"What?"

"I started grilling him because I thought he was one of the guys who chased you when you were out running. I think I might have scared him."

"I met Ren behind the cemetery. He was playing soccer on the hill."

"Well, I definitely owe him an apology. Do you by chance know his last name?"

"Ferrari or something? They live in a house that looks like gingerbread."

He laughed. "Say no more. The Ferraras. How lucky that you ran into him. I didn't realize their son was your age or I would have tried to arrange for you guys to meet. Is the party with your other classmates?"

"*Potential* classmates," I said quickly. "I'm not sure if I want to go."

His smile just increased in wattage, like he hadn't heard me. "Ren wanted me to tell you that he can't make it until eight-thirty. I'll make sure dinner is ready before then so you have plenty of time to eat. And we should look into getting you a cell phone – that way your friends won't have to call at the visitors' center."

"Thanks, but that would probably be overkill. I only know one person."

"After tonight you'll know more. And in the meantime you can just give people my number so they don't have to call the cemetery line. Oh, and good news. Our Internet connection is finally sorted out, so FaceTime should work great." He set the papers on the porch. "I need to head down to the visitors' center, but I'll see you a little later. Enjoy your run." He turned and went into the house, whistling quietly to himself.

I squinted after him. Was *Howard* my mom's wrong

choice? And what about the party? Did I really want to go meet a bunch of strangers?

"What about this?" I walked up to my laptop and twirled around so Addie could see what I was wearing.

She leaned in, her face filling the screen. She'd just woken up and her smudged eyeliner was kind of making her look like a blond vampire. "Hmm. Do you want me to be nice or do you want me to be honest?"

"Is there a possibility that you could be both?"

"No. That shirt looks like it's been wadded up in the bottom of a suitcase for three days."

"Because it has."

"Exactly. My vote is the black-and-white skirt. Your legs are killer and that skirt is maybe the only thing you have that doesn't look awful."

"Whose fault is that? You're the one who talked me into binge-watching *America's Next Top Model* instead of doing my laundry."

"Listen, it's all about priorities. One of these days I'm going to grow ninety inches, and then I'm totally going to be on that show." She sighed dramatically, attempting to wipe some of the makeup off her eyes. "I can't believe you're going to a *party*. In *Italy*. I'm probably just going to wind up stuck at Dylan's again tonight."

"You like going to Dylan's."

"No, I don't. Everyone just sits around talking about all the stuff we could do, but then no one makes a decision and we end up playing foosball all night."

"Look on the bright side. He has that downstairs freezer full of burritos and churros. Those are pretty good."

"You're right. Eating mass-produced churros totally sounds better than going to a party in Italy."

I picked up my computer, then flopped onto my bed, setting it on my stomach. "Except I don't like going to parties, remember?"

"Don't say that. You used to."

"And then my mom got sick and no one knew what to say to me anymore."

She set her mouth in a line. "I honestly think some of that's in your head. People just don't want to say the wrong thing, you know? And you have to admit you shut people down a lot."

"What do you mean? I don't shut people down."

"Um, what about Jake?"

"Who's Jake?"

"Jake Harrison? Hot senior lacrosse player? Tried to ask you out for like two months?"

"He didn't ask me out."

"Because you kept avoiding him."

"Addie, I could barely go thirty minutes without talking about my mom and crying. Think he would have been into that?"

She frowned. "Sorry. I know it's been rough. But I think you're ready now. In fact, I'm making an official prediction: Tonight you will meet and fall in love with the hottest boy in all of Italy. Just don't fall so in love that you don't want to come home again. It's already been the longest three days of my life."

"Mine too. So, black-and-white skirt?"

"Black-and-white skirt. You'll thank me later. And call me as soon as you're home. I want to talk more about the journal. I think I'm going to hire a film crew to start following you around. Your life would make awesome TV."

"Lina! Dinner is ready."

I looked at myself in the mirror. I'd gone against Addie's advice and settled on my favorite jeans. And I was way too nervous to eat.

I guess there's a first for everything.

"Did you hear me?" Howard called.

"Coming!"

I put on some lip gloss and smoothed my hair one last time. I'd had to spend a solid forty-five minutes with a flat iron, but at least now my hair looked like a normal person's. Not that that was any sort of guarantee. If someone looked at it funny, it would assume its natural craziness in about half a second. *You're sort of like Medusa,* Addie had once told me helpfully.

Howard met me at the bottom of the stairs and handed me a giant bowl of pasta. I could tell he was making a big effort to make things feel less tense, and so far it was working.

"You look nice."

"Thanks."

"I'm sorry about dinner being so late. We had an issue with maintenance. I thought I was going to be working all night."

"That's OK." I set my bowl down. "And thanks for

dinner, but I'm actually not all that hungry."

He raised an eyebrow. "Not hungry? How many miles did you run today?"

"Seven."

"Are you feeling all right?"

"I guess I'm kind of nervous."

"I understand. Meeting new people can be nerve-wracking. But they're going to love you."

BEEP! We both looked out the window to see Ren riding up the road on a shiny red scooter. My stomach clenched. *Why did I agree to go?* Was it still possible to get out of it?

"That's the Ferrara boy?"

"Yes."

"He's early. He's not taking you on that scooter, is he?"

"Yeah, I think so." I shot Howard a hopeful glance. Maybe he'd say I couldn't go! That would solve everything. Except, are brand-new fathers allowed to tell you what you can and can't do?

Howard crossed the living room in three long strides, then opened the door. "Lorenzo?"

I hurried after him.

"Hi, Howard. Hi, Lina." Ren was wearing jeans and expensive-looking sneakers. He pulled the scooter back onto a kickstand, then bounded up the stairs, his hand extended to Howard. "Nice to meet you."

"Nice to meet you too. I'm really sorry about the mix-up on the phone earlier. I had you confused with someone else."

"That's OK. I'm just glad to know you're not going to come after me with a chainsaw anymore."

Oh, boy. Howard was really taking his new role seriously.

"Lina, you ready to go?" Ren asked.

"Um, I think so. Howard?" I looked at him hopefully. He was eyeing Ren's scooter, his face grim.

"You been driving that thing for a while?"

"Since I was fourteen. I'm a really safe driver."

"And you have an extra helmet?"

"Of course."

Howard nodded slowly. "All right. Drive carefully. Especially on the way back." He tilted his head toward me. "*È nervosa. Stalle vicino.*"

"*Si, certo.*"

"Um, excuse me. What was that?" I asked.

"Man talk," Ren said. "Come on. We're missing the party."

Howard handed me his cell phone and a twenty-euro bill. "Take this, just in case. The cemetery's number is in there. If I don't answer, Sonia will. What time will you be home?"

"I don't know."

"I can have her back whenever," Ren said.

"Let's say one."

I looked at him. *One?* He must really want me to make friends.

Howard settled himself on the porch swing and I followed Ren to his scooter, where he handed me a helmet from the compartment under the seat.

"Ready?" Ren asked.

"Ready." I clambered awkwardly onto the back, and suddenly Ren and I were zipping down the road, cool air flowing past us. I grabbed tight around Ren's waist, grinning like an idiot. It was like riding on a motorized armchair, superfast and supercomfortable. I glanced back to see Howard watching from the porch.

"Why do you call him 'Howard'?" Ren shouted over the noise of the scooter.

"What else would I call him?"

"'Dad'?"

"No way. I haven't known him long enough."

"You haven't?"

"Just … long story." I quickly changed the subject. "Where's the party?"

He paused to signal at the main road, then turned away from Florence. "At my friend Elena's house. We always go there because she has the biggest house. Her mom is a descendant of the Medici, and they have this giant villa. You can always tell when Elena's had too much to drink because she starts telling people that back in the day they would have been her servants."

"What's the Medici?"

"Really powerful Florentine family. They basically funded the Renaissance."

I had a sudden image of a teenage girl in flowing robes. "Did I dress up enough?"

"What?"

I repeated my question.

He slowed for a red light, then turned to look at me. "You look great. We're wearing the same thing."

"Yeah, but you look…"

"What?"

"Cooler."

He tipped his head back so our helmets *clacked*. "Thanks."

Chapter 9

THE DRIVE TO ELENA'S HOUSE TOOK FOREVER. For-*ev*-er. By the time Ren signaled to pull off the main road, my legs were going numb.

"Almost there."

"Finally. I thought we were driving to France or something."

"Wrong direction. Hold tight."

He accelerated and we sped up a long, tree-lined driveway. Where were we? I hadn't seen a single house or building in more than ten minutes.

"Just wait for it. Three … two…"

We rounded the corner and I exploded. *"What?"*

"I know. Crazy, right?"

"That's a house? Does anyone live in normal places here?"

"What? You don't know people who live in gingerbread houses back home?"

Elena's villa was a palace. The house was several stories high, and huge – like museum huge – with towers that rose on either side of a large arched doorway. I started to count all the windows, then gave up. It was that big.

Ren slowed down, navigating around a large circular fountain that sat in the center of the tennis-court-size driveway. Then we bumped off the pavement to park next to a bunch of other scooters. My mouth was as dry as the Sahara. Eating churros in Dylan's basement was really more my speed.

"You OK?" Ren asked, catching my eye.

I gave him the world's most unconvincing nod, then followed him past a wall of sculpted hedges to the sort of door you imagined angry villagers storming with torches and battering rams. I was about three seconds from throwing up.

Ren nudged me. "You sure you're OK?"

"Fine." I took a deep breath. "So ... how many people live here?"

"Three. Elena, her mom and her older sister, when she's home from boarding school. Elena told me there are rooms that she's never even set foot in, and she and her mom sometimes go days without even seeing each other. They have an intercom system so they don't have to walk across the house every time they want to talk to each other."

"Are you serious?"

"Totally serious. I've never even seen her mom. There are theories she doesn't actually exist. Also, this place is ridiculously haunted. Elena sees a ghost like once a day." He pushed hard on a brass doorbell and there was a loud *clang*ing noise.

"Do you believe that? About ghosts?"

He shrugged. "Elena does. She passes the ghost of her great-great-grandmother Alessandra on the stairwell every night."

Ghosts had never made sense to me. When my mom was

gone, she was just *gone*. I'd give anything for it to be otherwise.

Suddenly a loud *bang*ing noise made me shriek. I stumbled back and Ren caught me.

"Relax. It's just the door. It takes a long time to unlock it."

After what felt like ten minutes, the door slowly creaked open and I took a step back, half expecting to be greeted by Great-great-grandmother Alessandra. Instead, a casually dressed teenage girl stepped into the doorway. She was curvy, with a diamond stud in her nose and thick black hair.

"*Ciao*, Lorenzo!" She threw her arms around Ren and pressed her cheek to his, making a kissing noise. "*Dove sei stato? Mi sei mancato.*"

"*Ciao, Elena. Mi sei mancata anche tu.*" Ren stepped back, then gestured to me. "Guess who this is?"

She switched from Italian to English as quickly as Ren did. "Who? You must tell me immediately."

"Carolina."

Her mouth dropped open into a perfect *O*. "You're *Carolina*?"

"Yes. But I just go by Lina."

"*Non è possibile!* Come!" She grabbed my hand and pulled me inside, kicking the door shut behind her. The foyer looked like something out of a *Scooby-Doo* episode. The hall was dimly lit with a few electric sconces, and tapestries and old-looking paintings covered every inch of wall, and wait – was that a *suit of armor*? Elena was looking at me.

"Your house is really—"

"Yes, yes. Creepy. Spooky scary. I know. Now come with me." She linked her elbow with mine, then dragged me down the hall. "They will be so surprised. You wait."

At the end of the hallway she opened a set of double doors, then shoved me inside. The room was a lot more modern-looking, with a jet-size leather sectional, a big-screen TV, and a foosball table. Oh, and twenty people. Give or take. And they were all looking at me like something that had managed to escape from the zoo.

I gulped. "Um, hi, everyone."

Elena took my hand and held it triumphantly in the air. "*Vi presento*, Carolina. *Ragazzi*, she exists!"

A collective cheer went up in the room and suddenly I was being swarmed.

"You are here. You are really here!" A tall boy with a French accent patted my arm enthusiastically. "I am Olivier. Welcome."

"I won the bet! They all said you'd never show."

"Better late than never."

"*Che bella sorpresa!*"

"I'm Valentina."

"Livi."

"Marcello."

Half of them reached out to pat me. Did they think I was a hologram?

I stumbled backward. "Nice to … meet you all."

"Guys, quit mouth-breathing on her!" Ren shoved a couple of people back. "You're acting like you never meet anyone new."

"We don't," a boy with braces said.

They started raining questions.

"How long have you been here?"

"Are you going to AISF in the fall?"

"Why didn't you start school last year?"

"Was that really tall man your dad?"

I took another step back. "Um … which one do you want me to answer first?"

They all laughed.

"Where do you live? In Florence?" It was a redheaded girl on my left working on a big wad of gum. She sounded like she was from New Jersey or somewhere.

"My house is kind of near Ren's."

"It's in the American Cemetery," Ren clarified.

I shot him a look. *Way to make me the weirdo.*

He patted my arm. "Don't worry. Everyone here lives in weird places."

They all started chiming in.

"My family is renting a medieval castle in Chianti."

"We live in a farmhouse."

"William lives at the American Consulate. Remember when his sister ran over that foreign dignitary's foot with a Razor scooter?"

An Italian boy with shoulder-length hair stepped forward. "*Ragazzi*, she will think we are very strange. Sorry for all the questions."

"It's fine," I said.

"No, we're weird. We don't meet new people all that often. We're totally sick of each other," a Hispanic-looking girl on my left said.

Suddenly a pair of arms wrapped around me and I was lifted off my feet. "Hey!"

"Marco! Down, boy!" Ren yelled.

"Heel!" Gum Chewer said.

Was Marco a Rottweiler? I wriggled away and turned to see a muscly guy with short black hair.

"Ren, introduce me. Now!" he bellowed.

"Lina, this is Marco. Now forget you ever met him. Trust me, you'll be better off."

He grinned. "You're really here! I knew you would come. I knew it all along."

"Wait a minute. Are you my biology partner?"

"Yes!" He pumped his fist in the air, then put his arms around me again and gave me another one of his specialty python hugs.

"Can't. Breathe," I gasped.

"Let her go," Ren commanded.

Marco loosened his grip, shaking his head sheepishly. "Sorry. I'm normally not like this."

"Yes, you are," the dark-haired girl said.

"No, it's this beer." He held his can out to me. "I don't know who brought it, but it's disgusting. It tastes kind of like a urinal, you know?"

"Not really."

"That's OK. I'd offer you a drink, but I just told you it tastes like piss. By the way, you're really cute. Like way cuter than I thought you'd be."

"… Thanks?"

"Hey! Margo! Who's your papa?" He turned and loped away.

"Wow," I said.

Ren shook his head. "Sorry about that. I wish I could say it's because he's drunk, but he's actually worse when he's sober."

"Much, much worse," a short boy with glasses chimed in.

"There you are." A cool voice cut through the noise, and I turned and came face-to-face with an exquisitely pretty girl. She was tall and slim with big blue eyes and hair so blond it was almost white. She was looking straight through me.

"Hi, Mimi. Welcome back." Ren's voice was suddenly like three octaves lower.

"I was worried you weren't going to make it tonight," she said in an accented voice. Swedish? Norwegian? Someplace where everyone has good skin and silky, well-behaved hair?

"Everyone says you haven't been around much."

"I'm here now."

"Good. I missed you." She lifted her chin at me, her eyes still fixed on Ren. "Who's this?"

"Carolina. She just moved here."

"Hi. I go by Lina."

She slid her eyes at me for about a millimeter of a second, then leaned in to Ren and whispered something.

"*Si, certo.*" He glanced at me. "Just … later. Give me a few minutes."

She walked away, and it was like the whole group exhaled.

"Ice queen," someone whispered.

"She's really gorgeous," I said to Ren.

"Really? I hadn't noticed." He grinned like someone had just offered him a lifetime supply of pink Starbursts. I'd definitely misread that moment at the gingerbread house when he'd held my hand. If Mimi was what he was used to, then forget it.

"Hey, come on. I want to show you something."

"OK. So … see you around?" I said to the rest of the people.

"Ciao, ciao," one of them said.

Ren was already halfway across the room.

"Where are we going?"

"It's a surprise. Come on." He held the door open for me. "After you."

I walked out into a dark hall and Ren pulled the door shut behind us. We were standing in front of an enormous staircase.

"Oh, no. Is this where we go to see Elena's great-great-grandmother?"

"No, that's in the other wing. Come on. I want to show you the garden."

He started up the stairs, but I held back. "Um, Ren? It looks creepy up there."

"It is. Come on."

I looked back toward the door. Creepy staircase or overly friendly international teenagers? I guess I'd take my chances with Ren. I hurried after him, my footsteps echoing off the high ceiling. At the top of the stairs Ren pushed open a tall, skinny door and I reluctantly stepped in after him.

"This place is unbelievable," I muttered. The room was packed full of stuff, like the contents of ten rooms had been consolidated into one, and everything was covered in thick, dusty sheets. There was even a gigantic fireplace guarded by the portrait of a stern-looking man wearing a feathered hat.

"Is that for real?" I pointed to the portrait.

"I'm sure it is."

"It looks like something from a haunted house. Like I'm going to turn around and he'll have changed positions."

Ren grinned. "And that's coming from someone who lives in a cemetery."

"I don't think two days counts as 'living.'"

"Over here." He made his way over to a set of glass doors and unhooked a latch, then opened them to a balcony. "I wanted to show you the gardens, but mostly I wanted to give you a break from your adoring crowds."

"Yeah, they seemed kind of hyperactive about meeting me."

"A lot of us have been stuck together since elementary school, so we're crazy excited to meet new people. We should probably work on the whole playing-hard-to-get thing."

"Hey, the hedges are a maze." I leaned over the balcony. The hedges around the front door were actually part of a carefully sculpted pattern interspersed with old-looking statues and benches.

"Cool, right? They have this ancient gardener who has spent half his life pruning those things."

"It looks like you could actually get lost."

"You can. Once Marco wandered out there and we couldn't find him for like three hours. We had to come up here with a spotlight. He was sleeping on his shoes."

"Why his shoes?"

"I have no idea. You want to hear something really creepy?"

I shook my head. "Not really."

"Elena's older sister, Manuela, refuses to live here because ever since she was little she's had this ancestor appear to her. The spooky part is that whenever the ghost appears she's the same age as Manuela."

"No wonder she's at boarding school." I leaned against the railing. "This place is making me feel way better about living in a cemetery."

"Telling ghost stories?"

I jumped, practically toppling over the edge.

"Lina! You're like the Incredible Startled Girl," Ren said.

"Sorry, guys. Didn't mean to scare you." A boy sat up on one of the couches and stretched his arms over his head.

"Hi, Thomas. Spy much?"

"I have a headache. I was just trying to get away from the noise for a while. Who are you with?" He stood up and lazily made his way over to us.

OM… And then I couldn't remember how to end the acronym, because *who looks like this?*

Thomas was tall and thin with dark brown hair and thick eyebrows, and he had this strong-jaw thing going on that I'd heard about but never actually witnessed. And his *lips*. They were pretty much ruining any chance I had of forming words.

"Lina?" Ren was raising one eyebrow. *Crap. Did they ask me something?*

"Sorry, what'd you say?"

The boy grinned. "I just said that I'm Thomas. And I gather that you're the mysterious Carolina?" He had a British accent.

A British. Accent.

"Yes. Nice to meet you. I go by Lina." I shook his hand, doing my best to stay upright. Apparently "weak in the knees" was a real thing.

"American?"

"Yeah. Seattle. You?"

"All over. I've lived here for the past two years."

The door swung open and Elena and Mimi walked in. "*Ragazzi, dai*. My mom will *freak out* if she finds out you are up here. I had a forty-five-minute lecture after the last party. Some *idiota* left a piece of pizza on a two-hundred-year-old credenza. Come downstairs, *per favore!*"

"Sorry, El," Thomas and Ren said in unison.

"I was just showing Lina the garden," Ren said. "And Thomas was taking a nap."

"Who takes a nap at a party? It's lucky you look like a god, because you're *veramente strano*. Really, Thomas."

Like a god. I snuck another look at Thomas. Yep. Could totally imagine him lounging around on Mt Olympus.

Mimi linked arms with Ren and everyone walked out except for Thomas and me. Was I making this up, or was he staring at me, too?

Thomas crossed his arms. "A bunch of us made bets on whether or not you'd ever show. Looks like I'm going to be out twenty euro."

"I was supposed to move here earlier this year, but I decided to finish out the school year in Seattle."

"Still doesn't change the fact that you owe me twenty euro."

"I don't owe you anything. Maybe next time you should have a little more faith in me."

He grinned, raising one eyebrow. "I'll let you off the hook this one time."

My bones were roughly the consistency of strawberry jelly. He was so flirting with me.

"Did I hear you live in a cemetery?"

"My dad's the caretaker for the Florence American Cemetery. I'm staying with him for the summer."

"The whole summer?"

"Yes."

A slow smile spread across his face. I was smiling too.

"Thomas!" Elena shrieked from the doorway.

"Sorry." We both followed her out of the room.

So this is what it's like to be normal. Well, sort of normal.

"First concert you ever went to." Most everyone had moved outside to the pool and Thomas and I were sitting with our feet in the deep end. The water was glowing bright blue and either the stars had dropped down to our level or fireflies were everywhere.

"Jimmy Buffett."

"Really? Margaritaville guy?"

"I'm surprised you know who that is. And yeah, it was pretty much a sea of Hawaiian shirts. My mom took me."

We both ducked as a spray of water came our way. Half the party was playing a rowdy alcohol-fueled game of Marco Polo, and Marco kept getting stuck as, well, Marco. It was way funnier than it should have been.

"OK, favorite movie."

"You're going to make fun of me."

"No, I won't. I promise."

"Fine. *Dirty Dancing*."

"Dirty Dancing…" He tipped his head back. "Oh, right. That horrible eighties movie with Patrick Swayze as a dance teacher."

I splashed him. "It isn't horrible. And why do you know so much about it anyway?"

"Two older sisters."

He scooted in to me until our bodies touched from shoulder to hip. It was the exact sensation of licking a nine-volt battery.

"… So you're a runner, you're from one of the coolest cities in the U.S., you have horrible taste in movies, you once blacked out snowboarding, and you've never tried sushi."

"Or rock climbing," I added.

"Or rock climbing."

Addie, you were so right. I splashed my feet around happily, sneaking another glance at Thomas. I was never going to hear the end of it. Who knew that guys this good-looking even *existed*? And, side note, he'd just slipped his arm around me. Like it was no big deal.

"So why did you move here?" Thomas asked.

"I came to stay with my dad. He's, uh … sort of new in my life."

"Gotcha."

There was a *crash*ing noise, and suddenly Ren came careening out of the darkness behind us. "Lina, it's twelve-thirty!"

"Already?" I pulled my feet out of the water and Thomas dropped his arm. I stood reluctantly.

"We have to go now. He'll kill me! He'll *kill* me. " Ren clutched his hands to his chest and fell over on the grass.

"He's not going to kill you."

"Who's going to kill you?" Thomas asked.

"Lina's dad. The first time I talked to him he said he had a bullet with my name on it."

"No, he didn't." I looked at him. "Wait. Did he?"

"He might as well have." He rolled to his knees, then stood up. "Come on. We have to leave now."

"You have a bunch of grass in your hair," I said.

He shook his head like a dog, sending grass flying. "I was rolling down a hill."

"A Swedish hill?" Thomas asked.

"I didn't ask its nationality."

I groaned. "Is it really twelve-thirty? Maybe we could stay for just another twenty minutes or something."

Ren threw his hands in the air. "Lina. Don't you care whether I live or die?"

"Of course I care. I just wish we didn't have to leave."

Thomas stood too, then wrapped his arms around me, his chin resting heavily on my shoulder. "But, Lina, it's so early. I'll be so bored without you. Can't you get an extension?"

Ren raised an eyebrow. "I see things have *progressed* in the last couple of hours."

My mouth would not stop smiling. I turned my face so Ren wouldn't see. "Sorry, Thomas. I do have to leave."

He blew air out of his mouth. "Fine. Guess we'll just have to hang out again."

"*Ciao, tutti!*" Ren yelled to the group. "I have to take

Lina home. She has a curfew."

There was a chorus of "*Ciao, Lina*s."

"*Ciao!*" I yelled back.

"Wait!" Marcus pulled himself out of the pool. "What about the initiation? She has to do it."

"What initiation?" I asked.

"She has to walk the plank."

Ren groaned. "Marco, that's dumb. We stopped doing that in like seventh grade."

"Hey, you guys made *me* do it, and that was just last year," Olivier protested. "Also, it was November. I froze my balls off."

"Yes, she must do it," another girl chimed in. "It is tradition."

"She is wearing jeans," Elena said. "*È troppo* mean."

"Doesn't matter! Rules are rules!"

Thomas sidled up next to me. "If you jump, I'll jump too."

Cut to mental image of Thomas soaking wet.

I turned to Ren. "How much will you hate me if you have to drive me home drenched?"

"Not as much as you'll hate yourself."

I kicked off my sandals and headed for the diving board.

"New girl's going for it!" Marco whooped.

The whole party broke out in wild applause as I climbed up on the diving board, then bowed. *Is this me?* Too late to wonder. I sprinted down the board, bouncing high and tucking into the world's most perfect cannonball.

I felt the most alive I had in more than a year. Maybe ever.

Chapter 10

SO MAYBE SOGGY SCOOTER RIDING WASN'T MY most brilliant idea. By the time we pulled up to the house I was shaking like crazy. Also, the pool had reactivated my hair's natural crazy, and when I took off my helmet, my hair fluffed around my head like a cloud.

"Are you shivering because you're cold or because you're terrified?"

"Cold. Ren, come on. We're an hour late. What's he going to do?"

The front door burst open and Howard stepped into the doorway, his enormous silhouette illuminated against the light.

Now we were both shivering.

"Want me to come in with you?" Ren whispered.

I shook my head. "Thanks for the ride. I really had a lot of fun."

"Me too. See you tomorrow. Good luck."

I waddled up to the door, my jeans sticking to my legs. "Sorry I'm late. We lost track of time."

He squinted at me. "Is your hair wet?"

"They made me walk the plank."

"The plank?"

"It's their initiation ritual. I jumped into the pool."

A faint smile glimmered under his stern look. "So tonight was a success."

"Yes."

"I'm glad to hear it." He looked over my head. "Good night, Ren."

"Good night, Mr … Carolina's dad." He spun his scooter around and took off in a spray of gravel.

"Hello, hello," a woman said as I followed Howard into the house.

Sonia and four other people were sitting on the couches, wineglasses in hand. Jazz music was playing in the background and everyone looked a little tipsy. Apparently Howard was having a party too. Cemetery-style. Maybe later they'd all dive into the little pools in front of the memorial.

"Everyone, this is Lina," Sonia said. "Lina, everyone."

"Hi."

"*Che bella*. You are a beauty," an older woman in cat-eyed-glasses purred.

Howard grinned. "Isn't she?"

"We are old friends of your dad's," one of the men said in deliberate English. "We've known him since his wild stallion days. Oh, the stories we could tell."

"Yeah," the guy next to him chimed in. "He wasn't giving you a hard time about being late, was he? Because maybe I should tell you about the time we went backpacking through Hungary and he—"

"That's enough," Howard said quickly. "Lina went for a little swim, so I'm sure she wants to go upstairs and get changed."

"Pity," Cat Eyes said.

"Good night," I said.

"Good night," they all chorused back.

I clambered up the stairs. I was *freezing*.

"She's the photographer's daughter?" It was Cat Eyes. I froze.

"Yes. She's Hadley's."

Silence.

And ... yours, too, right? I waited for him to clarify, but someone just changed the subject.

What was *that* about?

I FaceTimed Addie as soon as I was in dry clothes. "You ready to say 'I told you so'?"

"I am *always* ready to say 'I told you so.' Oh my gosh! How was it? Amazing?" She started bouncing up and down on her bed.

I turned down the volume on my computer. "Yes. A-mazing."

"Please tell me you met the hottest of hot Italian guys."

"I did. But he's not Italian. He's British."

She squealed. "Even better! Is he online? I have to stalk him."

"I don't know. I didn't ask."

"I'll look him up. What's his name?"

"Thomas Heath."

"Even his name is attractive." She was quiet for a minute

as she typed in his name. "Thomas … Heath … Florence…" She inhaled sharply. "HOLY MOTHER OF HOTNESS. That is the best hair I have ever seen. He looks like a model. Maybe an underwear model."

"Right?"

"Have you seen him without his shirt on? You have to get online and see these pictures. Great. Now you'll never come back to Seattle. Why would you when *Thomas Heath* is—"

"Addie, slow down! It doesn't matter how hot he is. I'm not staying here."

"What do you mean it doesn't matter? You can have a summer fling, can't you? And wow. I mean, really, *wow*. That is one good-looking guy. What's your other friend's name?"

"Ren. But his full name is Lorenzo Ferrara."

"Yeah, you're gonna have to spell that for me."

"His mom said it's like 'Ferrari' but with an *a*."

"Ferrari with an *a*…" She bit her lip and typed into her keyboard. "Curly hair? Plays soccer?"

"That's him."

She grinned at me. "Well, Lina, you're two for two. Ren's adorable. So if Underwear Model doesn't work out, you're still in good shape."

"No, Ren's off the table. I met his girlfriend tonight. She's like Sadie Danes, only Swedish. And Photoshopped."

"Shut up. Did you run for your life?"

"Pretty much. She didn't seem all that happy that Ren brought some new girl along."

Addie sighed, falling back on her pillow. "I'm spending the rest of the summer living vicariously through you. And I know the cemetery thing is weird, but now I'm one hundred percent on board with you being there. You have to stay there for at least a little while. Do it for me. Please!"

"We'll see. How's Matt?"

"Still not getting the message that I'm interested. But who cares about him? On a scale of one to ten, how weird would it be if I printed out Thomas's profile picture and had it framed?"

I laughed. "Weird. Even for you."

"Or how about I make a Thomas calendar? 'Twelve Months of British Hotness.' Do you think you could get more pictures of him with his shirt off? Maybe you could spill Kool-Aid or something on him next time you're together."

"Yeah, definitely not doing that."

She sighed again. "You're right. That would be pretty weird. So how's the journal?"

"I'm just about to read more." I hesitated. "Last night was kind of hard, but it was nice, too. She really loved it here."

"And so will you. And so will I. Vicariously."

I shook my head. "We'll see."

"OK, you get back to the journal. I want to know what her wrong choice was. The suspense is killing me."

"Night, Addie."

"Morning, Lina."

JULY 2

Florence is exactly how I thought it would be and nothing like it at all. It is absolutely magical — the cobblestones, the old buildings, the bridges — and yet it's gritty, too. You'll be walking down the most charming street you've ever seen and suddenly get a whiff of open sewer or step in something disgusting. The city enchants you, then brings you right back down to reality. I've never been anyplace that I want to capture so much. I spend a lot of time photographing things that seem uniquely Italian — laundry hanging in alleyways, red geraniums planted in old tomato-sauce cans — but mostly I try to capture the people. Italians are so expressive; you never have to guess what they're feeling.

Tonight I watched the sun set at Ponte Vecchio. I think it's safe to say I have finally found the place that feels right to me. I just can't believe I had to come halfway across the world to find it.

JULY 9

Francesca has officially inducted me into her circle of friends. They were all at FAAF last semester too, and they're smart and hilarious, and I secretly wonder if they're being followed around by reality-TV cameras. How can this many interesting people be together in one spot? Here's our cast of characters:

> **Howard:** The perfect Southern gentleman (Southern <u>giant</u>, Francesca calls him), handsome, kind, and the sort of guy who will go marching into battle for

you. He's in a research program studying Florence history, and when he isn't teaching he sits in on a lot of our classes.

Finn: An Ernest Hemingway wannabe from Martha's Vineyard. He pretends to just happen to have a full beard and a penchant for turtlenecks, but we all know he spends half his time reading *The Sun Also Rises*.

Adrienne: French and probably the prettiest person I've ever seen in real life. She is very quiet and unbelievably talented.

Simone and Alessio: I'm grouping them together because they are ALWAYS together. They grew up together just outside of Rome and are constantly getting into fistfights — typically over the fact that neither of them has ever dated a girl that the other didn't immediately fall in love with.

And finally ...

Me: Pretty boring. American wannabe photographer who has been giddy since the moment her plane touched down in Florence.

Mine and Francesca's apartment has become the official hangout. We all crowd onto the tiny balcony and have long discussions about things like shutter speed and exposure. Is this heaven?

JULY 20

Turns out you can't learn Italian through osmosis, no matter how many times you fall asleep with <u>Italian for Dummies</u> propped open on your face. Francesca said that learning a language is the easiest thing in the world, but she said it while simultaneously smoking, studying aperture, and making homemade pesto, so she may not have a normal grasp on "easy." I signed up for the institute's beginner Italian class. It's held evenings in the mixed-media room and meets three times a week. Finn and Howard are in the class too. They're both much further along than I am, but I'm glad to have them for company.

AUGUST 23

It's been more than a month since I've written, but I have good reason. I'm sure it will come as no surprise when I say that I've fallen in L-O-V-E. What a cliché! But seriously, move to Florence and eat a few forkfuls of pasta, then stroll in the twilight and just TRY not to fall for that guy you've been ogling from day one! You'll probably fail. I <u>love</u> being in love in Italy. But truth be told,

I would fall for X anywhere. He's handsome, intelligent, charming, and everything I've ever dreamed of. We also have to keep things completely secret, which, if I'm totally honest, makes him all the more appealing. (Yes, X, I seriously don't think anyone would read my journal, but I'm giving him a new name, just in case.)

WHAT? I let the book fall onto my lap. It had taken only three pages for Howard to make the leap from squeaky-clean "Southern gentleman" to secret lover X. Apparently I hadn't been giving him enough credit.

I picked up my laptop and FaceTimed Addie again, and she answered almost immediately. Her hair was wrapped in a towel and she was holding a half-eaten freezer waffle. "What's up?"

"They had to keep their relationship a secret." I kept my voice down. It sounded like Howard's guests were on their way out, but there was still some backslapping and "Let's do this again soon" going on outside on the front porch.

"Howard and your mom?"

"Yeah. She talks about them being in the same group of friends, and then suddenly she's calling him by a new name because she's worried someone will pick up her journal and find out that they're secretly dating."

"Scandalous!" Addie said happily. "Why did they have to be secretive? Was he in the mafia or something?"

"I don't know yet."

"Call me back when you figure it out. Crap. I won't be here! Ian's driving me to the car dealership. I'm finally getting my car back."

"That's good news."

"Tell me about it. Last night Ian made me fold all his nasty laundry before he'd take me to Dylan's. Call me tomorrow?"

"Definitely."

<hr>

SEPTEMBER 9

Now that I've started writing about my <u>storia d'amore</u>, I might as well tell it from the very beginning. X was actually one of the very first people I met when I arrived in Florence. He gave one of the semester's opening lectures, and afterward I just couldn't stop thinking about him. He's obviously talented, and the kind of good-looking that makes you stumble over words like "hello" and "good-bye," but there was something else — he had this <u>depth</u> to him. It made me want to figure him out.

Lucky for me we were able to spend a lot of time together in and out of class. It's just that we were never alone. Ever. Francesca was either sitting in the corner rattling away on her phone or Simone and Alessio would ask us to weigh in on some ridiculous new argument, and our conversations just never seemed to get all that far. I had this big debate going on my head. IS HE OR ISN'T HE

INTERESTED? Some days I was positive he was, and others I was less sure. Maybe I was just reading too much into things?

But I kept catching him staring at me during class, and every time we talked, there was this <u>something</u> between us that I couldn't ignore. This went on for weeks. And then, finally, just when I thought I was imagining the whole thing, I saw him at Space. Francesca calls it the official nightclub of FAAF, but he'd never come with us before. I had stepped outside for a little air, and when I came back in, there he was, leaning against the wall. Alone.

I knew this was my chance, but as I started toward him I realized I had absolutely no idea what to say. "Hi. I hope this doesn't sound crazy, but have you noticed this weird chemistry thing between us?" Luckily I didn't even have to open my mouth. As soon as he saw me, he reached out and grabbed my wrist. "Hadley," he said. And the way he said it — I knew that I hadn't been imagining things.

SEPTEMBER 15

Met X at the Boboli Gardens so we could be alone for a while. It's a sixteenth-century park, kind of an oasis in the middle of the city. Lots of architecture and fountains and enough space to let you forget you're in a city. We both took our cameras, and when we'd captured everything we wanted to, we sat down under a tree and talked. He knows so much about art. And history. And literature. (And everything, really.) The grounds closed at seven-thirty, but when I stood up to pack my things, he pulled me back down and we kissed until a guard made us leave.

SEPTEMBER 20

The only hard part about being in love with X is not telling anyone about it. I know the school wouldn't be OK with us dating, but it's hard to keep something this big a secret. It's torture to spend half our days within ten feet of each other and not even touch.

I'm pretty bad at secret-keeping, and everyone seems to know I'm in love. Part of it is logistics. Most nights we meet up late, and I don't get home until three or four a.m. I told Francesca that I'm out working on my night photography, but she just rolled her eyes and told me she knows all about "night photography." Part of me wonders if everyone is just pretending not to know what's going on. Are they really that dense? Our relationship is taking place right under their noses!

OCTOBER 9

X and I are starting to get really creative about where we meet. We knew that everyone else would be staying in studying tonight, so we went to Space (one and the same) and after we'd danced until we were exhausted we wandered around the city. X told me he had a surprise for me and we started winding our way through the dark streets until I could smell something amazing — a mixture of sugar and butter and something else. Bliss?

Finally we turned a corner and saw a group of people gathered around a brightly lit doorway. It was a secret bakery — one of a few. Basically, commercial bakers work through the night to produce pastries for restaurants, and even though it's illegal, they'll give you a freshly baked pastry for a few euro. Only a few insiders know about it, but those who do, well ... let's just say they're in danger of becoming nocturnal.

Everyone in line was acting really quiet and nervous, and when it was our turn, X bought a chocolate-filled <u>cornetta</u>, a glazed croissant, and two stuffed cannoli. Then we sat down on a curb and devoured all of it. When I got home Francesca, Finn, and Simone were sprawled out on our tiny couches and they all teased me about what kind of night shots I'd gotten. I wish I could tell them.

Wow.

First of all, sign me up for a trip to the secret bakery. I didn't even know what a *cornetta* or cannoli was, and I was still practically salivating all over the pages. But most important, what was the deal with all this secrecy?

I flipped back through the entries. Did schools really have

policies on students not dating assistant teachers? I could see it being a rule for actual professors, but research students? And my mom had been *smitten*. How was it possible that someone this crazy about their boyfriend had ended up walking out and keeping their child a secret for sixteen years?

I marked my place in the journal, then walked over to the window. It was a gorgeous night. Clouds were drifting past the moon like ghost ships, and now that Howard's friends had cleared out, everything was still and quiet.

Suddenly a blur of movement caught my eye and I froze. What was *that*? I leaned out the window, my heart hammering against my rib cage. A white figure was moving toward the house. It looked like a person, but it was moving way too fast, like a… I squinted. Was that *Howard*? On a long board?

"What are you doing?" I whispered. He kicked off hard and went sailing past the driveway, like a seal gliding out to sea. Like it was something he did all the time.

I had to figure this guy out.

Chapter 11

"LINA, YOU AWAKE? PHONE'S FOR YOU." HOWARD knocked on my open bedroom door, and I shoved the journal under the bed. I'd been rereading the entries from the night before. And stalling. Because, yes, I wanted to know what had happened. But I also wanted to prolong the happy part. Sort of like the time I stopped *Titanic* halfway through and made Addie watch the first part over again.

"Who is it?"

"Ren. I've got to get you your own phone. You just hang on to my cell phone for now. I'll use the landline."

"Thanks." I got up and walked over to him. He looked wide-awake and very un-X-like. No evidence of his ghostly night riding. Or sketchy dating practices.

He handed me the phone. "Will you please tell Ren that he doesn't need to be afraid of me? He just set a world record for using 'sir' the most times in a single conversation."

"I can, but it probably won't do any good. You really messed with him that first time you talked."

"I had good reason." He smiled. "See you a little later? I should be off work around five."

"OK." I put the phone to my ear and Howard stepped out into the hallway. Ciao, *mysterious X*.

"Hi, Ren."

"*Ciao*, Lina. I'm so glad you're alive."

I leaned casually out the door and watched Howard walk down the stairs. He'd made out with my mom in a public park? Totally not the kind of thing you should have to know about your parents. And what had been so special about the way he'd said her name that first time they'd connected at Space? It sounded like a cheesy scene from one of those soap operas Addie's mom pretended not to watch.

"You there?" Ren asked.

"Yeah, sorry. I'm kind of distracted." I closed my bedroom door, then sat on my bed.

"So he wasn't mad?"

"No. He was having a party, and I don't think he even noticed we were late."

"*Fortunato*. Have you gone running yet?"

"No. I was just about to. Want to come?"

"Already on my way. Meet me at the cemetery gates."

I changed, then ran out to meet him. Ren was wearing a bright orange T-shirt and was jogging in place like an old man. As usual his hair was in his eyes and he looked sort of warm and glowy from the run over.

"How is *this* not American-looking?" I asked, plucking at his shirt.

"It's not American-looking when it's on an Italian."

"Half-Italian," I corrected.

"Half is enough. Trust me." We started up the road.

"So your mom won a LensCulture Award," he said.

I looked at him. "How'd you know?"

"There's this thing called the Internet. It's really helpful."

"Oh yeah, I vaguely remember that from back before I lived in Italy." I'd tried to FaceTime Addie about ten times that morning to update her on the night's reading, but so far I'd just gotten this annoying NO SERVIZIO message over and over. At least now I could use Howard's phone whenever I wanted.

"I found a bunch of articles on her. You didn't tell me she was a big deal."

"The LensCulture jump-started her career. That's when she started doing photography full-time."

"I liked the picture. I've never seen anything like it. What was it called? *Erased?*" He sprinted ahead of me, then wrapped his arms around himself, looking over one shoulder. The photograph had been of a woman who'd just had a tattooed name removed from her shoulder.

I laughed. "Not bad."

He fell back in line with me. "I also saw the self-portraits she did while she was sick. They were pretty intense. And I saw you in some of them."

I kept my eyes laser focused on the road. "I don't really like looking at those."

"Understandable."

The road dipped and I automatically sped up. Ren did too.

"So … you hanging out with your friends again soon?" I asked.

"You mean Thomas?"

I flushed. "And ... others." Priority number one was figuring out what had gone on between Howard and my mother, but that didn't mean I had to let my chance with Thomas go to waste, right?

"It's Marco, right? You really want to see him again, don't you?"

I laughed again. "Maybe."

"Didn't Thomas get your number?"

"I don't even have a number. You keep calling me at the cemetery, remember?" Also, he hadn't asked for it. Probably because he'd remembered his expensive watch *after* following me into the pool.

"I also called you on your dad's cell phone. Even though it was terrifying."

"How'd you even get that number?"

"Sonia. But it took me like an hour to get up the courage to use it."

I sighed. "Ren, you've got to get over that first bad conversation with Howard. I mean, he's a pretty nice guy. It's not like he's going to hurt you for being nice to me."

"Have you ever been yelled at by an ogre for something you didn't do? It's not that easy to get over."

"Ogre?" I laughed.

"People just aren't that tall here. I bet he gets stared at everywhere he goes."

"Probably."

The world's tiniest truck sped past us, sending out a series of staccato beeps. Ren waved. "Hey, do you want to go into town with me tonight? We could get some ice cream or just walk around or something. Maybe like eight-thirty?"

"Think Swedish Model would be OK with that?"

I meant it as a joke, but he looked at me seriously. "I think it will be all right."

When Ren arrived to pick me up, Howard and I were finishing dinner. He'd made a big bowl of pasta with fresh tomatoes and mozzarella, and I'd spent the whole meal staring at him like a complete weirdo. *X is handsome, intelligent, and charming.* Except for when you get pregnant with his baby? Then he's suddenly so terrible that you flee halfway across the world and avoid him for the next sixteen years? I'd picked up the journal three different times that afternoon, and each time I'd had to set it back down. It was just so overwhelming.

"Is everything all right?" Howard asked.

"Yes. I was just … thinking." Ever since we'd had that talk about *not* talking about my mom, things had been feeling a little better. He was actually pretty easy to be around. Sort of laid-back-beach-guy-meets-history-buff.

I stabbed another forkful of pasta. "This is really good."

"Well, that's in spite of the chef. It's pretty hard to mess up when you have such great ingredients. So what do you think about tomorrow? I can take the whole day off so we'll have plenty of time for sightseeing."

"OK."

"Where are you and Ren headed tonight?"

"He just said he wants to go into town."

"Lina?" Ren poked his head into the kitchen.

"Speak of the devil," I said.

"Sorry I'm late." He caught sight of Howard and startled. "And I probably should have knocked. Sir."

Howard smiled. "Hey, Ren. Would you like some dinner? I made *pasta con pomodori e mozzarella*."

"*Buonissimo*. But no thanks. I already ate. My mom tried to re-create a Kentucky Fried Chicken meal and she made this giant pot of potatoes that basically turned to glue. I'm still trying to get over it."

"Ewww."

Howard laughed. "Been there. Sometimes you just have to have KFC." He picked up his plate and walked into the kitchen.

Ren sat down next to me and grabbed a noodle from my plate. "So, where should we go tonight?"

"How should I know? You're the one from Florence."

"Yeah, but I get the feeling you haven't spent much time in the city. Anything you've been dying to see?"

"Isn't there like a leaning tower or something?"

"Linaaa. That's in Pisa."

"Relax, I'm joking. But actually, there is something I want to see. Come upstairs with me for a second." I took my plate to the kitchen, then Ren followed me to my bedroom.

"Is this really your room?" he asked when we stepped inside.

"Yeah. Why?"

"Haven't you unpacked anything? It's kind of bare in here." He opened one of my empty dresser drawers, then slowly rolled it shut.

"All my stuff's over there." I pointed to my suitcase.

Everything was piled on top of it, and it looked like there had been some kind of explosion.

"Aren't you going to be here awhile?"

"Just for the summer."

"That's like two more months."

"Hopefully it will be less." I shot a look at the open door. *Yikes.* Was it just me, or had my voice just reverberated through the whole cemetery?

"I don't think he can hear us."

"I hope not." I crossed the room, then knelt to get the journal from under the bed and started flipping through the pages. "I just read about this place ... Pont Ve-chee-o?"

"*Ponte Vecchio?*" He looked at me incredulously. "You're joking, right?"

"I know I said it wrong."

"Well, yeah, I mean you totally butchered it. But you've never *been* there? How long have you been in Florence?"

"Since Tuesday night."

"That means you should have seen Ponte Vecchio by Wednesday morning. Get dressed. We're leaving."

I looked down at what I was wearing. "I am dressed."

"Sorry. Figure of speech. Get your purse or whatever. We're going now. You have to see it. It's in my top ten most favorite places in the entire world."

"Is it open? It's almost nine."

He groaned. "Yes, it's open. Come on."

I grabbed the money Howard had given me the night before, then stuffed my mom's journal into my purse. Ren was already halfway down the stairs, but he stopped abruptly at the bottom and I crashed right into him.

Howard was sitting on the couch, his laptop balanced on his knees. "Where are you two headed in such a hurry?"

"Lina's never been to Ponte Vecchio. I'm taking her." Ren cleared his throat. "With your permission, sir."

"Permission granted. That's a great idea. Lina, you'll love it."

"Thanks. I hope so."

We headed for the door, and just as Ren stepped out on the porch Howard said, "I'm keeping my eye on you, Ren."

Ren didn't turn around, but he straightened up like someone had just sent a jolt of electricity down his spine. Howard caught my eye and winked.

Great. Now Ren was never going to relax.

It was a hot night, and Florence seemed twice as crowded as the night I'd gone with Howard. Traveling by scooter was a little faster because we could just drive around stopped cars, but it still took us a long time. Not that I minded. Riding the scooter was really fun, and the cool air whipping past us felt like my reward for surviving such a long, hot day. By the time Ren parked his scooter, the moon had risen round and heavy as a ripe tomato, and I felt like I'd taken a long, cool swim.

"Why's it so crowded tonight?" I asked, handing him my helmet to stow under the seat.

"It's summer. People like to go out. And tourists come in droves. Droves, I tell you!"

I shook my head. "Ren, you're kind of weird."

"So I hear."

"What are we going to see exactly?"

"A bridge. 'Ponte Vecchio' means 'Old Bridge.' It's on the

Arno. Come on, it's this way." I did my best to keep up with him as he elbowed his way across the street, and before long we were standing on a wide sidewalk running the length of the river. The Arno stretched black and mysterious in either direction, and the banks were lit up like a runway with strings of glittering lights that stretched and disappeared in either direction.

I gave myself a second to take it all in. "Ren … this is really pretty. I can't believe people get to actually live here."

"Like you?"

I glanced at him and he was smiling. Duh. "Well, yeah, I guess so."

"Just wait. What you see next is going to make you want to stay here forever."

People kept pushing us away from each other, so Ren linked arms with me and we headed up the river, stepping over a long-haired guy sitting with his back to the water. He was playing a banged-up guitar and singing "Imagine" in a heavy accent.

Ren sang along. "My dad has this book that's supposed to teach English song lyrics to Italian speakers. I think that guy back there could really use it."

"Hey, at least he got the feeling right. He sounds really nostalgic." My arm was kind of heating up where Ren's was interlocked with mine, but before I could think about it, he pulled away and put both hands on my shoulders.

"Ready to swallow your gum?"

"What?"

"Ready to see Ponte Vecchio?"

"Of course. That's why we're here, right?"

He turned and pointed. "This way."

The sidewalk had led us to a small commuter bridge. It was paved with asphalt, and a bunch of tourists were milling around blankets set up with displays of knockoff bags and sunglasses. *So* not impressive.

"This is it?" I asked, trying not to sound disappointed. Maybe it was cooler at sunset.

Ren guffawed. "No. Not *this* bridge. Trust me, you'll know it when you see it."

We headed toward the center of the bridge, and a dark-skinned man stepped out in front of his blanket of stuff, blocking our way. "Young man. You want nice Prada handbag for girlfriend? Five hundred euro in store, but ten euro for you. Make her fall in true love."

"No thanks," Ren said.

I nudged him. "I don't know, Ren. That sounds like a pretty good deal. Ten bucks for true love?"

He smiled, stopping in the center of the bridge. "You didn't see it, did you?"

"See wha – oh."

I ran over to the railing. Stretched across the river, about a quarter mile ahead of us, was a bridge that looked like it had been built by fairies. Three stone arches rose gracefully out of the water, and the whole length of it was lined with a floating row of colorful buildings, their edges hanging over the water. Three mini-arches were cut out of the center, and the whole thing was lit golden in the darkness, its reflection sparkling back up at itself.

Gum officially swallowed.

Ren was grinning at me.

"Wow. I don't even know what to say."

"I know, right? Come on." He looked to his right, then his left, then launched himself over the side like a pole vaulter.

"Ren!"

I leaned over, fully expecting to see him dog-paddling toward Ponte Vecchio, but instead came face-to-face with him. He was crouching on a table-size ledge that jutted out about five feet below the side of the bridge and he looked ridiculously pleased with himself.

"I was waiting for a splash."

"I know. Now come on. Just make sure no one sees you."

I looked over my shoulder, but everyone was too involved in the whole fake-Prada-bag thing to pay me any attention. I climbed over, dropped down next to him. "Is this allowed?"

"Definitely not. But it's the best view."

"It's amazing." Being just a few feet lower somehow cut out the noise of the people above us, and I swear Ponte Vecchio was glowing even brighter and more regal. It gave me a solemn, awestruck kind of feeling. Like going to church. Only I wanted to stay here for the rest of my life.

"So what do you think?" Ren asked.

"It makes me think of this time my mom and I drove to a poppy reserve in California. The flowers all bloom at once and we timed our visit just right. It was pretty magical."

"Like this?"

"Yeah."

He shimmied back next to me and we both rested our heads against the wall, just looking. *I have finally found the place that feels right to me.* It was like she was waving at me from just across the water. If I squinted I could almost see her. My eyes fogged up a little, turning Ponte Vecchio's lights into big gold halos, and I had to spend like thirty seconds pretending to have some mysterious Arno dust in my eye.

For once, Ren was being totally quiet and once the crying jag had passed I looked over at him. "So why is it called 'Old Bridge'? Isn't everything old here?"

"It's the only bridge that survived World War II, and it's really, really old, even by Italian standards. Like medieval old. Those house-looking things used to be butcher shops. They'd just open the windows and dump all the blood and guts into the river."

"No way." I glanced at the windows again. Most of them had green shutters and they were all closed for the night. "They're way too pretty for that. What are they now?"

"High-end jewelry shops. And you see those windows spaced out across the very top of the bridge?"

I nodded. "Yeah?"

"Those go to a hallway. It's called the Vasari Corridor and it was used by the Medici as a way to get around Florence without having to actually walk through the city."

"Elena's people."

"*Esattamente*. That way they didn't have to mix with us commoners. Cosimo Medici was the one who kicked out all the butchers. He wanted the bridge to be more prestigious." He looked at me. "So what was that book you were reading? The one you had under your bed."

You trust him. The words elbowed their way into my head before I even had a chance to wonder. So what if I'd known

Ren for only two days? I did trust him.

I took the journal out of my purse. "This is my mom's journal. She was living in Florence when she got pregnant with me and it's all about her time in Italy. She sent it to the cemetery before she died."

He glanced at the book, then back up at me. "No way. That's pretty *heavy*."

Heavy. That was exactly it. I opened to the front cover, looking again at those ominous words. "I started reading it the day after I got here. I'm trying to figure out what happened between Howard and my mom."

"What do you mean?"

I hesitated. Was it possible to condense the whole messy story into a couple of sentences? "My mom met Howard when she was here going to school, and then when she got pregnant, she left Italy and never told him about me."

"Seriously?"

"Once she got sick she started talking about him a lot, and then she made me promise I'd come live here with him for a while. She just never actually told me what went wrong between them, and I think she left me the journal so I could figure it out."

I turned and met Ren's stare. "So last night when you said you don't know Howard very well, it was like a huge understatement."

"Yeah. I've officially known him for…" I counted on my fingers. "Four days."

"No way." He shook his head incredulously, sending his hair flying. "So let me get this straight. You're an American, living in Florence – no, living in a *cemetery* – with a father you just found out about? You're even stranger than I am."

"Hey!"

He bumped his shoulder against mine. "No, I didn't mean it that way. I just meant we're both kind of different."

"What makes you different?"

"I'm sort of American, sort of Italian. When I'm in Italy I feel too American, and when I'm in the States I feel too Italian. Also, I'm older than everyone in my grade."

"How old are you?"

"Seventeen. My family lived in Texas for a couple of years when I was really young, and when we moved back I didn't speak Italian very well. I was already kind of old for my grade, and they had to hold me back a year so I could catch up. My parents ended up enrolling me at the American school a few years later, but the school wouldn't allow me to skip forward to the grade I'm supposed to be in."

"When will you be eighteen?"

"March." He looked at me. "So you're really only staying for the summer?"

"Yeah. Howard and my grandma want me to stay longer, but the circumstances are obviously pretty weird. I barely know him."

"But maybe you'll get to know him. Chainsaw aside, I kind of like him."

I shrugged. "It just seems so bizarre. If my mom hadn't gotten sick, I probably still wouldn't know anything about him. She'd always just told me that she'd gotten pregnant young and decided it was best to keep my father out of the picture."

"Until now."

"Until now," I echoed.

"Where will you live when you leave Florence?"

"Hopefully with my friend Addie. I stayed with them for the rest of sophomore year, and she's going to ask her parents if I can stay with them next year too."

He looked at the journal. "So what have you been reading about in there?"

"Well, so far I know that they had to keep their relationship a secret. He was an assistant teacher at the school she was going to, and I guess the school wouldn't have liked it. And she was hard-core about keeping it a secret. Like after they started dating, she stopped writing his name because she was afraid someone would read her journal and find out about them. She just calls him 'X.'"

He shook his head. "Scandalous. Well, that's probably your answer right there. Seems like most secret romances have a shelf life."

"Maybe. But when I first got here Sonia told me that my mom lived with Howard at the cemetery for a while, so that's not exactly secretive. And she said that one day my mom just left. She didn't even say good-bye to Sonia."

"Wow. Something must have happened. Something big."

"Like … my mom got pregnant?"

"Oh. I guess that would be a big deal." He chewed on his lower lip thoughtfully. "Now you have me curious. Keep me in the loop, would you?"

"Sure."

"So she loved Ponte Vecchio. What other places did she write about?"

I took the journal from him and started flipping through it. "She talks about this club a couple of times, Space."

"Space Electronic?" He laughed. "No way. I was there like two weeks ago. Elena loves it. She knows one of the DJs, so we usually get in for free. Where else?"

"The Duomo, Boboli Gardens... He also took her to a secret bakery. Do you know where one is?"

"A secret bakery?"

I handed him the journal. "Read here."

He scanned the entry. "I've never heard of this, but it sounds awesome. Too bad she didn't write down the address – I could totally go for a fresh *cornetta*."

His phone started ringing and he pulled it out of his pocket and hesitated for a second, then hit SILENCE. It started ringing again right away and he hit SILENCE again.

"Who is it?"

"No one."

He shoved the phone back in his pocket, but not before I saw the name on the screen. *Mimi*.

"Hey, do you want to get a gelato?"

I wrinkled my forehead. "What's that?"

He groaned. "Gelato. Italian ice cream. The greatest thing that will ever happen to you. What have you been *doing* since you arrived?"

"Hanging out with you."

"And you're telling me I only have one summer." He shook his head, then stood up. "Come on, Lina. We've got work to do."

Chapter 12

SO ... ITALIAN GELATO. TAKE THE DELICIOUSNESS OF a regular ice-cream cone, times it by a million, then sprinkle it with crushed-up unicorn horns. Ren stopped me after my fourth scoop. I probably would have kept going forever.

When I walked in the front door Howard was watching an old James Bond movie with his bare feet propped up on the coffee table. There was an industrial-size bucket of popcorn sitting next to him.

"Movie just started – want to watch?"

I glanced at the screen. James Bond was swimming toward a building, wearing a disguise that consisted of a stuffed duck attached to a helmet. Normally I was all over cheesy old movies, but tonight I had other things on my mind. "No thanks. I'm going to get some rest." *And hopefully some answers.*

NOVEMBER 9

Tonight was the best night of my life, and I have a statue to thank for it.

X and I were standing in Piazza della Signoria looking at a statue by Giambologna called "The Rape of the Sabine Women". The name confused me because it doesn't match what's going on. It's of three figures: a man holding a woman up in the air and a second man crouching down on the ground looking up at her. There's obviously something distressing going on, but the three of them are graceful, harmonious even.

I told X that I thought the woman looked like she was being lifted up, not hurt, and as usual he knew the story. When Rome was first settled, the men realized their civilization was missing one very important ingredient: women. But where to find them? The only women within striking distance belonged to a neighboring tribe called the Sabines, and when the Romans went to ask for permission to marry some of their daughters, all they got was a big fat no. So in a particularly Roman move, they invited the Sabines to a party, then, partway through the night, overpowered the men and dragged all the women kicking and screaming back to their city. Eventually the Sabines managed to break into Rome, but by that time they were too late. The women didn't want to be rescued. They'd fallen for their captors and it turned out life in Rome was actually pretty great. The reason I was confused by the statue's title is that it is mistranslated in English. The Latin word "raptio" sounds like "rape" but actually means "kidnapping." So really the sculpture should be called "The Kidnapping of the Sabine Women".

It was already late and I told X that I needed to head home, but suddenly he turned to me and told me he loved me. He said it casually, like it wasn't the first time he'd said it, and it took a moment for the words to seep in. Then I made him repeat it. He LOVES me. Carry me off. I'm invested.

NOVEMBER 10

Went to class this morning on about two hours of sleep. X arrived late, and even though I knew he'd probably gotten even less sleep than I had, he somehow looked perfect. He broke our act-like-friends-in-school rule and gave me a big shiny smile that anyone could see. I wish I could pause this moment and live in it forever.

NOVEMBER 17

Sometimes I feel like my time is divided into two categories: time with X, and time spent waiting to be with X. Since that night in Piazza della Signoria, things have been up and down between us. Some days we get along perfectly, and other days he acts like I really _am_ just a friend. Lately I feel like he's been overly cautious about keeping things secret. Would it be that big of a deal if everyone knew? I think they'd be happy for us.

NOVEMBER 21

When I left for Italy in June, six months sounded like

an eternity. Now it feels like it's slipping through my fingers. I only have a month left! The school director, Signore Petrucione, told me they'd love to admit me for another semester, and I would kill for a little extra time to study and be with X, but how would I make that work financially? And would it completely devastate my parents? Every time I talk to them, they bring up nursing school and I can hear that I'm disappointing them.

When I got home from class today there was a letter waiting for me from my parents. They'd enclosed two letters from the university telling me that if I don't return for spring semester I will lose my spot in the program. I basically just skimmed the letters, then shoved them in my closet. I secretly wish it would just be over with.

Uh-oh. First signs of trouble. Like those minishakes you feel before an earthquake hits. What were they called? Tremors? I was definitely feeling them in these entries. He told her he loved her, but he wouldn't let her tell their friends about their relationship? Why was he so adamant about keeping things a secret? She didn't seem all that worried about it.

I lay back on my bed and covered my eyes with my arm. Young Howard seemed pretty hot and cold. Had he used the whole secrecy thing as an excuse for not really committing? Had she been way more into him than he was her? That was *crazy* depressing. My poor mom. But then how did that fit in with what Sonia told me about

Howard being crazy about her?

I glanced at the photograph on my nightstand. I couldn't stop thinking about that feeling I'd gotten at Ponte Vecchio. After she died a bunch of people had told me my mom would stay close to me, but I'd never actually felt that. Until tonight.

I rolled off the bed and grabbed Howard's cell phone from the dresser.

"Pronto?" Ren sounded groggy.

"Sorry, are you asleep?"

"Not anymore. I saw Howard's number on my phone and had a panic attack."

I smiled. "I've commandeered his phone. He said I can keep it until further notice. So I have a question for you."

"You want to know if I'll take you to Space?"

I blinked. "Uh ... yeah. How'd you know what I was going to ask?"

"I just had a feeling. And I'm way ahead of you. I texted Elena when I got home. She thinks her DJ buddy is working this week, which means we'll get in for free. Want to go tomorrow? I can see if other people from the school want to go too."

Yes. "Ren, that's perfect. And thanks again for taking me to Ponte Vecchio."

"And for introducing you to your new best friend? I think you set a new world record for most gelato ever eaten in one sitting."

"I want to try for another record tomorrow. What was that last kind I had? With the chocolate chunks?"

"Stracciatella."

"I'm naming my first daughter after it."

"Lucky her."

DECEMBER 6

Got an e-mail from the nursing school stating that they have officially revoked my spot in the program. I tried to file an extension after I got those letters from my parents, but if I'm honest, I didn't try that hard. My parents are upset, but all I feel is relief. Now there's nothing holding me back. When I told X the news, he seemed surprised. I guess he didn't know I was serious about wanting to stay.

DECEMBER 8

Amazing news! The school has offered to let me stay for a second semester at half tuition. Petrucione said I'm one of the most promising students they've ever had (!!) and that he and the other faculty think another semester of study will really help my future career. FUTURE CAREER. Like it's a given! I can't wait to tell X. I almost told him over the phone, but decided to wait to tell him in person. The soonest we can meet up is tomorrow night. I hope I can last that long.

DECEMBER 9

Told X. I think the news kind of caught him off guard, because for a second he just stared at me. Then he lifted me off my feet and swung me around. I'm so happy.

DECEMBER 27

X went home for the holidays, and Francesca saved me from what was almost the longest, saddest Christmas by inviting me to go to Paris to stay in her friend's vacant apartment.

Paris is a photographer's dream. When we weren't out shooting, we hung out on the apartment's balcony, wrapped up in blankets and eating giant boxes of chocolates we claimed to have bought for our families. On Christmas Eve I talked Francesca into going to the ice-skating rink on the first level of the Eiffel Tower, and even though she just sat on the sidelines and complained about the cold, I skated for more than an hour, giddy about how magic it all was.

The only downside was how much I missed X. Francesca brought him up a couple of times, and it took every ounce of willpower I had not to tell her what's been going on between us. It's like we're living a double life — friends in public, lovers in private. I hated spending Christmas away from him. And I'm also feeling worried. How is our relationship supposed to progress if we can't even tell anyone that we're together? Can I survive another six months of secrecy?

JANUARY 20

School is back in full swing, and now that the initial excitement of staying for another semester has worn off, I'm stuck with reality, which basically means calculating and recalculating. Every night I get out my notebook and try out different scenarios. How long can I afford to stay in Italy if I take fewer classes? What if I eat only spaghetti and tomato sauce? What about if my student loan gets approved? (Fingers crossed.) All the answers are pretty grim. I can stay, but just barely.

FEBRUARY 4

Student loan finally cleared today. PHEW. Had a dinner party to celebrate. Weather was perfect (cold and clear), and the food was divine. Even Simone and Alessio were on their best behavior — they had only one argument (a record), and it was just over who got to eat the last piece of caprese. Finn didn't end up coming back for the semester. He was on the fence about it, and at the last minute decided to accept a teaching position at the University of Maine. Francesca put a copy of <u>The Old Man and the Sea</u> in the chair where he usually sat, so at least he's here in spirit. I felt that old familiar weirdness about my friends still not knowing about X and me, but I'm kind of coming to peace with it. He doesn't seem to mind, and it is what it is. It feels out of my control.

MARCH 15

Something weird happened tonight.

Adrienne hasn't been hanging out with us much this semester. She stays in most nights and lately it seems like she avoids us even when we're in class, so tonight a few of us ambushed her at her apartment and took her out to dinner. Afterward, everyone headed over to our apartment, but when we got to the building, she hung back. I finally went looking for her, and when I stepped out of the apartment I saw her standing in the stairwell, talking on the phone and sobbing like her heart had just been snapped in half. I tried to sneak away, but the floorboards creaked, and when she saw me, she gave me a look that froze me to the core. She left without saying good-bye.

MARCH 20

By some horrible stroke of luck, Adrienne and I were paired up for an "Out in Florence" assignment. And I say "horrible" because things have been pretty uncomfortable since the other night.

My idea for the project was to head down to the Arno to photograph fishermen, but Adrienne told me she already had the perfect subject in mind. The way she said it left absolutely no room for discussion, so I just packed up my camera and followed her out into the street. I tried to ask her if she was all right, but she made it pretty clear she didn't want to talk about the other night. Or anything else for that matter. Finally I gave up on conversation and just followed her into the city.

We walked for at least ten minutes in silence and then she turned off onto a side street and went into a small tourist shop. There were two middle-aged men sitting in the corner of the shop playing cards, and when they saw Adrienne, they nodded at her and she just headed for the back of the shop. Behind the register was a doorway with a beaded curtain, and on the other side was a small apartment with a kitchenette and a twin bed. A woman wearing a flowered housedress was sitting in front of a black-and-white TV, and when she saw us she raised her hand and said, "Aspetta. Cinque minuti." (Translation: "Wait. Five minutes." See, I am learning some Italian.)

While I tried to figure out what we were doing there, Adrienne pulled out her camera and started taking photos of the room and the woman, who didn't seem to notice. Finally Adrienne turned to me and said in her deliberate English, "This is Anna. She is a psychic. Her sons own the shop out front, and during the day she reads cards. No one else will be photographing a Florentine psychic. It is a unique subject."

I had to hand it to her. It was unique. And the setting couldn't have been more interesting: dingy back room, the beaded curtain, smoke from Anna's cigarette curling at the ceiling. So I pulled out my camera and started taking pictures as well. Finally the show ended and Anna got up to turn off the TV, then shuffled over to a table pushed up against the wall, gesturing for us to take a seat. After we'd crowded around the table, she picked up a stack of cards and began laying them out one by one in front of her, muttering to herself in Italian. Adrienne set her camera down and was absolutely silent. After a few minutes Anna looked up at us and said with a thick accent, "One of you will find love. Both of you will find heartache."

I was a little bit stunned. I hadn't realized we were getting an actual reading. But my reaction was nothing compared to Adrienne's. She looked devastated. Once she regained her composure she started firing off questions in Italian until Anna got annoyed and cut her off. Finally Adrienne gave her some money and we left. She didn't say a word to me the entire way back.

MARCH 23

All of us went to a lecture at the Uffizi. Howard offered to walk me home, and I found myself telling him about Adrienne and the psychic. For several minutes he didn't say anything. Then he started walking faster and asked if he could show me something. We headed to Piazza del Duomo, and when we got there he led me to the left side of the cathedral and told me to look up. The sun had just started to set and the Duomo's shadow was covering half the piazza. I had no idea what I was looking for — all I could see were the beautifully detailed walls — but he just kept trying to get me to see something. Finally he took my finger and guided it so I was pointing at something jutting out of the cathedral's wall. "There," he said. And then I saw it — right in the middle of all that beautiful stonework and statues of saints is a sculpture of a bull's head. Its mouth is open and it stares down at the ground like it's looking at something.

He told me that there are two stories about the bull's head. The first is that animals were critical to the building of the Duomo, and the bull was added as a way to honor them. The other story has a bit more Italian flair.

When the Duomo was being constructed a baker set up shop near the building site, and he and his wife sold bread to the stonemasons and workers. The baker's wife and one of the master stonemasons ended up meeting and falling in love, and when the baker found out about their affair he took them to court, where they were humiliated and sentenced to life away from each other. To get revenge, the stonemason carved the bull and placed it on the Duomo in a spot where it would stare down at the baker in his stall as a constant reminder that his wife loved another man.

I <u>love</u> how much he knows about Florence, and it definitely took my mind off the whole Adrienne thing, but now I keep wondering about the timing of the story. Was he trying to tell me something?

———————

Howard. The place where she'd written his name was practically glowing. Why had she not called him X? Was it a slipup, or were they on their way to making their relationship public? And was there some kind of connection between Adrienne and the timing of Howard's story?

I stood up and walked over to the window. It was still warm out, almost hot, and the moon was flooding the cemetery like a spotlight. I scooted my violets over, then leaned out, resting my elbows on the windowsill. It was funny, but less than a week in and already the headstones weren't bothering me all that much. They were kind of like people you pass on the street – there, but not really. Like background noise.

A set of headlights appeared over the edge of the trees and I watched as the car snaked its way down the windy road. Why had Adrienne taken my mom to a psychic reading about their love lives? Was it possible she'd been interested in Howard too? Was it maybe him she'd been talking to in the stairwell?

I sighed. So far the journal wasn't clearing anything up. It was just making things more confusing.

Chapter 13

"THERE ARE SO MANY PLACES I WANT TO SHOW YOU in Florence, it's hard to know where to start."

I glanced at him. Howard and I were headed for the city again, and I was having a really hard time deciding how to feel about him. Maybe because he was blasting Aerosmith's "Sweeeeeeeet Emooooootion" with all the windows rolled down, and his occasional drum-playing on the steering wheel made it really hard to think of him as the mysterious heart-breaker X. Also, he couldn't sing worth anything.

I leaned against the door, letting my eyes close for just a second. I'd stayed up really late thinking about Howard and my mom, and then an incredibly exuberant group of what appeared to be Italian Boy Scouts had come galumphing through the cemetery at the crack of dawn. I'd gotten approximately four minutes of sleep.

"Would you mind if we started at the Duomo again? We could climb to the top and you'd see the whole city at once."

"Sure." I opened my eyes. What if I brought up the baker and the bull? Would he remember?

"I thought you'd probably invite Ren to tag along."

"I didn't know that was an option."

"He's always welcome."

"Except he's petrified of you." Which was ridiculous. I gave him a quick look. Regardless of his shady past, Howard looked like he was trying to emulate the perfect 1950s dad. Freshly shaved face, clean white T-shirt, winning smile.

Check, check, check.

He sped up to pass a semi. "I shouldn't have given him a hard time last night. I can tell he's a good kid, and it's nice to have someone I feel safe sending you out with."

"Yeah." I shifted in my seat, suddenly remembering our phone call the night before. "He actually invited me to go somewhere tonight, too."

"Where?"

I hesitated. "This, uh, club. A bunch of people from the party will be there."

"For someone who's been here less than a week, you've sure got quite the social calendar. Sounds like I'll have to restrict all our outings to daytime." He smiled. "I have to say, I'm really glad that you're getting to know students from the school. I called the principal a few days before you arrived, and she said she'd be happy to give us a tour. Maybe Ren would come with us. I'm sure he could answer any questions you have."

"That's all right," I said quickly.

"Well, maybe another time. It doesn't have to be right away." We circled through a roundabout, and then he pulled over in front of a row of shops.

"Where are we?" I asked.

"Cell phone store. You need your own."

"Really?"

He smiled. "Really. I miss talking to people. Now come on."

The shop's windows were coated with dust and when we walked inside, a tiny old man who looked like a direct descendant of Rumpelstiltskin looked up from his book.

"Signore Mercer?" he asked.

"*Si.*"

He hopped nimbly off his stool and started rummaging around on the shelf behind the desk. Finally he handed Howard a box. "*Prego.*"

"*Grazie.*" Howard handed him a credit card, then passed the box off to me. "I had them get it all set up, so we're ready to roll."

"Thanks, Howard." I pulled out the phone and looked at it happily. Now I had my very own number to give Thomas. Just in case he asked. *Please let him be at Space tonight. And please let him ask.* Because really? Even with all my parents' drama, I couldn't stop thinking about him.

Howard parked in the same area he had the night of the pizzeria, and when we got to the Duomo he groaned. "The line is even worse than normal. You'd think they're giving away free Ferraris at the top."

I eyed the line leading into the Duomo. It was made up of about ten thousand sweaty tourists and half of them looked like they were on the verge of a nervous breakdown. I tilted my head back to look up at the building, but there was no sign of the bull. I probably wouldn't be able to find it on my own.

He turned to me. "What do you say we get a gelato first,

see if we can outwait the line a bit. Sometimes it's more crowded in the morning."

"Do you know any place with *stracciatella* gelato?"

"Any *gelateria* worth its salt will have *stracciatella*. When did you try it?"

"Last night with Ren."

"I thought you seemed different. Life-changing, right? Tell you what, let's go get a cone. Start the day off right. Then we'll brave the line."

"Sounds good to me."

"My favorite place is a ways away. Do you mind a walk?"

"Nope."

It took us about fifteen minutes to get to the *gelateria*. The shop was roughly the size of Howard's car, and even though it was pretty much breakfast time, the shop was packed to the brim with people happily devouring what I now knew was the most delicious substance on earth. They all looked rapturous.

"Popular," I said to Howard.

"This place is the best. Really."

"Buon giorno." A bell-shaped woman waved at us from behind the counter and I made my way to the front. This place had a huge selection. Mountains of colorful gelato garnished with little bits of fruit or chocolate curls were piled high in metal dishes, and every single one of them looked like they had the ability to improve my day by about nine hundred percent. Chocolate, fruit, nuts, pistachio... How was I going to choose?

Howard came up next to me. "Would you mind if I ordered for you? I promise I'll get you another one if you don't like my choice."

That solved things. "Sure. Bad flavors of gelato probably don't exist, right?"

"Right. You could probably make dirt-flavored gelato and it would turn out all right."

"Ew."

He looked up at the woman. *"Un cono con bacio, per favore."*

"Certo."

She took a cone from the stack on the counter, piled it high with a chocolate-looking gelato, then handed it to Howard, who handed it to me.

"This isn't dirt-flavored, right?"

"No. Try it."

I took a lick. Super rich and creamy. Like silk, only in gelato form. "Yum. Chocolate with ... nuts?"

"Chocolate with hazelnuts. It's called *bacio*. Otherwise known as your mom's favorite flavor. I think we came here a hundred times."

Before I could catch it, my heart slammed straight down to my feet, leaving me with a massive hole in my chest. It was amazing how I could just be going along, doing OK, and then suddenly – *wham* – I missed her so much even my fingernails hurt.

I looked down at my cone, my eyes stinging. "Thanks, Howard."

"No problem."

Howard ordered his own cone, and then we made our way out onto the street and I took a deep breath. Hearing Howard talk about my mom had kind of thrown me, but it was summertime in Florence and I was eating *bacio* gelato.

She wouldn't have wanted me to be sad.

Howard looked down at me thoughtfully. "I'd like to show you something at Mercato Nuovo. Have you ever heard of the *porcellino* fountain?"

"No. But did my mom by chance swim in it?"

He laughed. "No. That was a different one. Did she tell you about the German tourist?"

"Yes."

"I don't think I've ever laughed that hard in my life. I'll take you there sometime. But I won't let you swim."

We made our way down the street. Mercato Nuovo was more like a collection of outdoor tourist shops – lots of booths set up with souvenir stuff, like T-shirts printed with funny sayings:

I AM ITALIAN, THEREFORE I CANNOT KEEP CALM.

I'M NOT YELLING, I'M ITALIAN.

And my personal favorite:

YOU BET YOUR MEATBALLS I'M ITALIAN.

I wanted to stop and see if I could find something ridiculous to send to Addie, but Howard bypassed the market and led me to where a ring of people stood gathered around a statue of a bronze boar with water running out of its mouth. It had a long snout and tusks and its nose was a shiny gold color, like it had been worn down.

" '*Porcellino*' means 'boar'?" I asked.

"Yes. This is the Fontana del Porcellino. It's actually just a copy of the original, but it's been around since the seventeenth century. Legend is that if you rub its nose you'll be guaranteed to come back to Florence. Want to try?"

"Sure."

I waited until a mom and her little boy cleared out of the way, then stepped forward and used my non-gelato hand to give the boar's nose a good rub. And then I just stood there. The boar was looking down at me with his beady eyes and creepy little molars and I knew without asking that my mom had stood right here and gotten gross fountain water splashed all over her legs and hoped with all her heart that she'd stay in Florence forever. And then look what had happened. She'd never even come back to *visit*, and she never would again.

I turned around and looked at Howard. He was watching me with this kind of sad/happy look in his eyes, like he'd just had the exact same line of thoughts and now he suddenly couldn't taste his gelato all that well anymore either.

Should I just ask him?

No. I wanted to hear it from her.

Conditions at the Duomo had not improved. In fact, the line had gotten even longer, and little kids were crying left and right. Also, Florence had decided we could all handle a little more heat, and makeup and sunscreen and all hope of ever cooling off was pretty much dripping off of people's faces.

"Maybe we should have just stayed hoooooome," the little boy behind us wailed.

"Fa CALDO," the woman in front of us said.

Caldo. I'd totally recognized an Italian word.

Howard met my eye. We'd both been pretty quiet since the *porcellino*, but it was more of a sad quiet than an awkward quiet. "I promise it's worth it. Ten more minutes, tops."

I nodded and went back to trying to ignore all the sad feelings sloshing around my stomach. Why couldn't Howard and my mom just have had a happy ending? She'd totally deserved it. And honestly, it seemed like he did too.

Finally we were at the front of the line. The Duomo's stones had some kind of miraculous ability to generate cold air, and when we stepped inside it took effort not to lie down on the stone floor and weep from happiness. But then I caught a glimpse of the stone staircase everyone was filing up and suddenly I wanted to weep for a whole different reason. My mom had described walking up lots of stairs, but she'd left out the tiny detail that the staircase was narrow. Like gopher-tunnel narrow.

I shifted nervously.

"You OK?" Howard asked.

No. I nodded.

The line fed slowly into the staircase, but when I got to the base of it my feet stopped moving. Like *stopped*. They just straight-up refused to climb.

Howard turned around and looked at me. He kind of had to hunch over to even fit in the staircase. "You're not claustrophobic, are you?"

I shook my head. I'd just never faced the possibility of being squeezed through a stone tube with a bunch of sweaty tourists.

The people behind me were starting to bottleneck and a man muttered something under his breath. My mom had said the view was amazing. I forced one foot onto the stairs.

Wasn't a staircase this narrow a fire hazard? What if there was an earthquake? And, lady snorting nasal spray behind me, could you please give me some *room*?

"Lina, I didn't tell you the whole story of the *porcellino*." I looked up. Howard had walked back down to the stair just above me and was looking at me encouragingly. He was going to try to distract me.

Well played, Howard. Well played.

"Tell me the story." I looked down at the stairs again, focusing on my breathing and finally beginning to climb. There was a smattering of applause from behind me.

"A long time ago there was a couple who couldn't have a child. They tried for years, and the husband blamed the wife for their bad luck. One day after they'd gotten into a fight, the woman stood crying at the window and a group of wild boars ran past the house. The boars had just had piglets and the woman said aloud that she wished she could have a child just like the boars did. A fairy happened to be listening in, and decided to grant her wish. A few days later the woman found out she was pregnant, but when she gave birth she and her husband were shocked because the baby came out looking more like a boar than a human. But the couple was so happy to have a son that they loved the child anyway."

"That story doesn't sound true," a woman behind me said.

I winced. Four hundred more steps?

Chapter 14

THE CLIMB WAS TOTALLY WORTH IT. THE VIEW OF
Florence was just as stunning as my mother had described it,
a sea of red rooftops under an unblemished blue sky and soft
green hills circling everything like a big, happy hug. We sat up
there roasting for about a half hour, Howard pointing out all
the important buildings in Florence and me working up the
courage to climb back *down* the staircase, which turned out to
be way easier. Afterward we stopped for lunch at a café and I
left Florence with an unsettling realization. Regardless of what
I was reading in the journal, I kind of *liked* Howard. Was that
traitorous?

Ren's scooter pulled up just after nine.

"Ren's here!" Howard yelled from downstairs.

"Will you tell him I'm still getting ready? And don't scare
him!"

"I'll do my best."

I looked in the mirror. As soon as we'd gotten home I'd
figured out how to use Howard's arthritic washing machine,
then hung a bunch of stuff to dry on the porch. Luckily it
was still sweltering outside, so my clothes had been dry in no

time. No more crumpled-up T-shirts for me. If Thomas was going to be there, I wanted to look amazing. No matter what my hair insisted on doing. I'd tried the flat iron again, but my curls were feeling extra-rebellious and had basically spat in its face. At least they were mostly vertical.

Please, please, please let him be there. I twirled around. I was wearing a short jersey dress my mom had found for me more than a year ago at a thrift shop. It was kind of amazing and I'd never really had anything to wear it to. Until now.

"Looking sharp tonight, Ren," Howard boomed scarily from downstairs.

I groaned. Ren answered, but I couldn't make out the rest of their conversation except for a couple of "yes, sirs."

After a few minutes there was a knock on my bedroom door. "Lina?"

"Hang on." I finished putting on my mascara, then gave myself one last look in the mirror. This was the longest I'd spent getting ready in ages. *You'd better be there tonight, Thomas Heath.*

I flung the door open. Ren's hair was wet, like he'd just taken a shower, and he was wearing an olive-green T-shirt that set off his brown eyes.

"Hey, Lina. Have you—" He stopped. "Whoa."

"Whoa what?" My cheeks flushed.

"You look so…"

"So what?"

"*Bellissima.* I like your dress."

"Thanks."

"You should wear dresses more often. Your legs are really…"

My blush spread like a wildfire. "OK you should totally stop talking about my legs. And quit staring at me!"

"Sorry." He gave me one last look, then made this stiff forty-five-degree turn to the corner, like he was a penguin that had just been put on time-out.

"I like your hair better curly."

"You do?"

"Yeah. Last night I thought you didn't really look like yourself."

"Huh." My cheeks were on *fire*.

He cleared his throat. "So … how's the journal? Have they crashed and burned yet?"

"Shh!"

"He just left to check on something at the visitors' center. He can't hear us."

"Oh, good." I pulled him into the room, then shut the door. "And no. Their relationship is still secret and he seems kind of hot and cold, but for the most part I'm still reading about the good stuff. It's all pretty lovey-dovey."

"Do you mind if I read it?"

"The journal?"

"Yeah. Maybe I could help you figure out what went wrong. And I could find more places to take you to in Florence."

I hesitated for approximately three-tenths of a second. This was *way* too good of an offer to pass up. "Sure. But you have to promise, *promise* me you won't tell Howard. I want to finish reading it before I talk to him about it."

"Promise. So Space doesn't really open until about ten. How about I start reading now?"

"Good idea." I fished the journal out of my nightstand. "It's pretty much half writing and half photographs, so it should go pretty fast. I marked where I left off, so don't read past that." I turned around and he was staring at my legs again. "Ren!"

"Sorry."

I walked over to him, flipping open the front cover. "Look what she wrote on the inside cover."

He made a low whistling noise. "'I made the wrong choice'?"

"Yeah."

"That sounds ominous."

"I think she wrote it as a message to me."

He flipped through the pages. "This should only take me like a half hour. I'm a really fast reader."

"Great. So ... do you by chance know who is going to Space with us?"

"You mean, will Thomas be there?"

"And, um, other people."

"I don't know. All I know is that Elena sent out a mass text." He looked up at me. "And I think Mimi is coming."

"Nice."

There was a pause, and then we both looked away at the exact same second.

"So ... I'll be on the porch." I grabbed my laptop and ran out of the room. I sort of hadn't been able to stop staring at him, either.

Weird.

* * *

Ren met me on the porch. I'd hoped that the Italian Internet gods would smile upon me and I'd be able to check my e-mail or watch a YouTube cat video or something, but I'd had no such luck. Instead I was lying on the swing, kicking off the banister every so often to keep me moving.

"Your mom reminds me of you."

I sat up. "How so?"

"She's funny. And brave. It's cool that she took such a big risk, dropping out of nursing school and everything. And her photographs are really good. Even though she was just starting out, you can tell she was going to be a game changer."

"Did you see the series of portraits of Italian women?"

"Yeah. That was cool. And you totally look like your mom."

"Thanks."

He sat down next to me. "It's nine-thirty. Ready to go to Space?"

"Ready."

"I told Howard we'd honk on our way out. We had a good conversation earlier. I think we really made some progress."

"I told him to be nice."

"Is that why he kept smiling at me? It kind of freaked me out."

LINA'S RULES OF SCOOTER RIDING:

1. Never ride a scooter sopping wet.

2. Never ride a scooter wearing a short skirt.

3. Try to pay attention to light signals.

Otherwise, every time the driver accelerates you'll smash into him and you'll have this awkward untangling moment and then you'll worry he's thinking you're doing it on purpose.

4. If by chance you aren't abiding by rule number two, be sure to avoid eye contact with male drivers. Otherwise they'll honk enthusiastically every time your skirt flies up.

Ren turned down a one-way street, then pulled up next to a two-story building with a long line of people wrapped around its perimeter. "This is it." Music pulsed from the windows.

My stomach sank down to my sandals. "This is like a *club* club."

"Yeah."

"Do I actually have to *dance*?"

"Ren!" Elena was attempting to run across the street to us, but her high heels were making it difficult. The effect was sort of Frankenstein-ish. "Pietro put us on the list. *Ciao*, Lina! It is nice to see you again." She pressed her cheek against mine and made a kissing sound. "Your dress is very beautiful."

"Thanks. And thanks for getting us in. I really wanted to see Space."

"Oh, yes. Ren said something about your parents coming here? They're not here tonight, are they?"

I laughed. "No. Definitely not."

"Who's coming tonight?" Ren asked.

"Everyone says they are coming, but we'll see who actually shows up. Don't worry, Lorenzo. I'm sure a certain someone will make it. *Vieni*, Lina." She linked arms with me, then dragged me across the street to the front of the line. Dragging me around was kind of her thing.

"*Dove vai?*" a man in line yelled as we cut ahead of him.

She tossed her hair. "Ignore him. We are much more important. *Ciao*, Franco!"

Franco wore a black T-shirt and was disproportionately muscular on top, like he'd skipped leg day way too many times. He unhooked the velvet cord from a stanchion that blocked the entrance and let us inside.

We stepped into a dimly lit hallway with big racks of clothing. Was this a coatroom?

"Continue," Elena said. "The party is this way."

I kept going, my arms stretched out in front of me, blind as a bat. It was *really* dark. And loud. Finally we emerged in a rectangular room with a long bar on one side. Two different songs were playing – one in English, and one in Italian – and on the far side of the room people sang group karaoke to a third. Everyone was either not talking or shouting to be heard.

"Lina, do you want a drink?" Elena asked, gesturing to the bar.

I shook my head.

"We will wait here for everyone. Once we get in the actual club there is no way to find each other."

"This isn't the club?" I asked.

She laughed like she thought I was being cute. "No. You'll see."

I looked around. Was *this* the room where Howard had uttered his first infamous "Hadley..."? I half expected to see him lounging against the wall, a good two heads taller than everyone else. Except this totally didn't seem like his scene. They probably wouldn't let him wear his flip-flops here.

Ren nudged me. "Want to sing karaoke with me? We could pick something in Italian, and I could pretend I don't speak Italian either. It would be hilarious. How about... ?"

He trailed off because Mimi and Marco were making their way toward us. Mimi was wearing a miniscule skirt and her hair was pulled back in a long, loose braid. Not a stray Medusa hair in sight. I shot a look at Ren. Did he like her legs too?

OK, yeah, he did. Someone needed to teach him the art of discretion.

"Hi, guys!" Marco yelled. He had exactly one volume. "Lina!" He came at me with his arms outstretched, but I ducked. "Too fast for me, I guess."

"Are you going to try to pick me up every time you see me?"

"Yes." He turned and picked up Elena. "Ask Elena."

"Marco, *basta*! Put me down or I'll feed you to a pack of wild dogs."

"That's a new one." Marco grinned at me. "She's kind of creative with her threats."

Mimi was yelling to be heard over the music. "Ren, why didn't you call me back? I didn't know if you were going to be here or not."

I couldn't hear his response, but she smiled at him and then started playing with the buttons on his shirt, which shouldn't have bugged me, but kind of did. Just because she was into him didn't mean she had to spread her Swedish PDA all over the place.

"Lina?"

I slowly turned around. *Please let it be* … "Thomas!"

He was wearing a royal-blue T-shirt that said BANNED FROM AMSTERDAM and somehow looked even better than I remembered. If that was possible. I forgot all about Mimi's button playing.

"Elena said you'd be here. I tried to call Ren to—"

"Hello, stalker." Ren suddenly side checked him, sending him stumbling.

"Ren, what the hell?" he said, straightening up.

"I had like ten missed calls from you."

"All you had to do was answer one."

Ren shrugged. "Sorry, man. I've been busy."

Mimi sidled up next to Ren, staring at me like she had no idea who I was.

"Hi, Mimi," I said.

"Hey." She squinted.

"I'm Lina. We met the other night at Elena's?"

"I remember."

Elena launched herself into the middle of our weirdly tense little circle. "*Ragazzi*, no more talking! I want to dance."

"Do you dance?" Thomas asked me.

"Not really."

"Me neither. We could just hang out. We could go walk

around by the Arno or something. I know this cool place that—"

"No way!" Ren grabbed my hand. "Thomas, you can't rob her of this experience. She's at Space. She wants to get her dance on."

"I don't have that much dance to get on," I protested.

"Sure you do." He lowered his voice. "And come on. This is where it all started, right?"

I nodded, then looked at Thomas. "I'd better stay. I would hate to miss the chance to embarrass myself."

"Worst case you just bust out your *Dirty Dancing* moves. Nobody puts baby in the corner, right?"

"I'm telling you, you know *way* too much about that movie."

"*Ragazzi!*" Elena yelled. "I mean it, let's go!"

We followed her through a narrow doorway, Thomas resting his hand on the small of my back and causing all sorts of ecstatic feelings, and then we were all shoving our way up a ramp into a large room. For a second I couldn't see anything solid – everything was flailing. Then a spotlight washed over us and OMG.

We were in a gigantic room with a ceiling that was at least twenty-five feet high, and it was *crawling* with people, like an anthill, only with designer clothes. There was a bunch of platforms set up throughout the floor, so some people were standing like five feet above everyone else. And they were all dancing. And I don't mean The Shopping Cart or The Sprinkler or any of the other moves that always seemed to dominate the proms back home. They were *really* dancing.

Like having-sex-on-the-dance-floor dancing.

Mom, what have you gotten me into?

"Welcome to Space!" Ren yelled into my ear. "This is the most crowded I've ever seen it. Probably because it's tourist season."

"Guys, follow me!" Marco put his arms in front of him like a diver, then started cutting through the crowd, all of us trailing behind.

"Ciao, bella," a man hissed in my ear. I yanked my head away. Everyone I brushed past was sweaty. This place was kind of gross.

Finally we were in a little pocket of space somewhere in the middle of the floor and everyone started dancing. Immediately. I guess no one else needed a little warm-up period before they got their groove on?

My palms started sweating. Time for some positive self-talk. *Lina, you are a confident woman and you've totally got this. Why don't you try out a sexy version of the Running Man? Or the Hokey Pokey? Just quit standing still. You look ridiculous.* And then I made the fatal mistake of looking at Mimi, which made things about a million times worse. She had her arms up over her head and she looked awesome. Like cool-sexy-European awesome. I wanted to crawl into a hole.

"You've got this!" Ren yelled, giving me a thumbs-up.

I cringed. *OK, start moving. Maybe copy Elena? Sway back and forth. Move hips. Pretend not to feel like a total idiot.* I glanced at Thomas. He was doing this awkward back-and-forth step that kind of made me want to melt into oblivion, because *how cute was he?* He couldn't dance either. Maybe I could take him up on a walk through Florence later.

And then something crazy happened. The music was so loud it was like it was pounding and rattling through my bones and teeth and everyone was having such a *good time* and suddenly I was dancing. Like actually dancing. And actually having fun. Well, maybe not as much fun as Ren, who was dirty dancing with Mimi, but *still*. The DJ pulled a microphone close to his mouth and shouted something in Italian and everyone cheered, raising their drinks over their heads.

"He is my friend! *È mio amico!*" Elena shouted.

"Lina, you're doing great!" Ren shouted. Mimi was doing this crazy hip-rolling thing that looked like it required intense concentration, but when she heard Ren she looked up, sending me the polar vortex of all looks.

I was getting the feeling she didn't like me.

Thomas nudged me with his shoulder. "Have you ever been someplace like this before?"

"No."

"It's weird, you'd have to be twenty-one to get into a club like this in the States." We were so close I could see the tiny droplets of sweat in his hair. Even his *sweat* was sexy. I was officially disgusting.

Ren disentangled from Mimi, then came up on my other side. "Having fun?" He was out of breath.

"Yes."

"Good. I'll be back in a few." Mimi grabbed his hand and they disappeared into the crowd.

Thomas made a face. "He's kind of protective of you, isn't he?"

"It's because of my dad. He keeps messing with him, so Ren's afraid that something will happen to me and he'll be the one to blame."

"Nothing will happen to you – you're with me."

Sort of cheesy, but I grinned. Idiotically. Thomas pretty much obliterated any control I had over my facial muscles.

He raised his chin, looking over the crowd. "There he is. Looks like he and Mimi are *talking*."

I stood on my tiptoes, taking the opportunity to rest my hand on his shoulder. Ren and Mimi were leaning against a wall and she had her arms crossed in front of her chest and looked pissed. But maybe that was just her regular face.

"So they're together, right?"

"Yeah. He's been into her for like two years. Guess persistence pays off, right?"

I nodded. "Right."

"Hey, I have to go call my dad, and then I'm going to get a drink. You want one?"

"Sure, thanks."

He flashed me one of his bone-melting smiles, then disappeared into the crowd.

"Lina, dance with me!" Elena grabbed my hands and twirled me around. "What is happening with you and Thomas? Is it *amore*?"

I laughed. "I don't know. This is only the second time I've ever seen him."

"Yeah, but he likes you. I can tell. He is never interested

in anyone, and last night after you left he asked me if I'd gotten your number."

"Ooh la la!" Marco said. "New girl and Thomas."

Elena rolled her eyes at him. "You sound like a child."

"Oh, yeah? Could a child do this?" He bent his arms at the elbows and started doing the robot.

"Marco, *basta!* You are awful at that."

"Want me to do the worm?"

"No!"

The song faded into a faster-paced one, and soon the three of us were holding hands and jumping up and down like little kids. No wonder my mom had liked it here. It was pretty fun. Except for the fact that the temperature kept rising. Didn't this place have AC?

"Where's Thomas?" Elena asked. Her bangs were plastered to her forehead with sweat.

"He went to get a drink."

"He's been gone for a long time." She fanned herself. *"Fa troppo caldo.* I am sweating like a pig."

Suddenly the room tilted from under me and I stumbled. Elena grabbed me by the arm. "You OK?"

"I just got dizzy. It's too hot."

"What?"

"I'm too hot."

"Me too!" Marco yelled. "I'm so hot!"

"I need to sit down for a minute."

"Lina, there are couches. There." She pointed to where Ren and Mimi had been standing. "Want me to come with you?"

"No, it's OK."

"I will tell Thomas where you are."

"Thanks." I made my way over to the side of the room. The couches looked like breeding grounds for some kind of infectious disease, but I was desperate. I suddenly felt like I might pass out.

The first couch was mostly taken up by a scrawny guy sprawled out on his back. He was wearing gold chains and an enormous pair of sunglasses and every few seconds he'd twitch, like a fly had landed on him or something. An older-looking man sat smoking at the other end and when he saw me he smiled and said something in Italian.

"Sorry, I don't understand." I pushed my way past. My head was pounding along with the music. Hopefully there was an open seat somewhere. Otherwise I was going to have to buddy up with the passed-out wannabe rapper.

There's one! I rushed for an open spot, but just as I got there I stopped, because there was a pair of hands on my butt. And not in an accidental way. I whirled around. It was the older guy from the couch. His hair was long and greasy and he smelled, amongst other things, like a dead muskrat pickled in vodka. Or at least, that's what I'd imagine one would smell like.

"Dove vai, bella?"

"Leave me alone."

He reached out and ran his fingers along my bare shoulder and I sprang away. "Don't touch me."

"Perche? Non ti piaccio?" One of his front teeth was gray. And he was way older than I'd originally thought. Like ten years older than anyone here.

Forget the couch. I turned to run, but he lunged at me and then grabbed me by the arm. Hard. "Stop it!" I yanked my arm back, but he just tightened his grip. "Elena! Marco!" I couldn't even see them anymore. Where was Ren?

I tried to pull away again, but the man grabbed me by the waist and pulled me in to him until my pelvis was smashed up against his. "Let. *Go*." Head butt? Knee him in the crotch? What were you supposed to do when you got attacked? He grinned, sidestepping every desperate move I made.

How was I going to get out of this? There were people everywhere, but absolutely no one was paying attention. "Help me!"

Suddenly someone grabbed me by the shoulders, pulling me back, and the man loosened his grip long enough for me to wrench my body away. It was Mimi. Looking like some kind of beautiful, pissed-off warrior.

"Vai via, fai schifo!" she yelled at the man. *"Vai."*

He put both hands in the air, then grinned and walked away.

"Lina, why didn't you just tell him to go away?"

"I tried. He wouldn't let go of me."

"Try harder next time. Just call them a *stronzo*, then push them off you. I have to do it all of the time."

"Stronzo?" I was shaking all over. It felt like I'd just been dragged through a Dumpster – that had been *revolting*.

She crossed her arms. "What is happening between you and Ren?"

I tried to focus my brain. "I'm sorry, what?" I rubbed at

my arms, trying to get the feel of Gray Tooth's skin off of me.

"What's going on between you and Lo-ren-zo?" She spoke slowly, exaggerating her words like she thought I couldn't understand her.

"I don't know what you're talking about." Where *was* he?

She looked at me for a moment. "You know Ren and I are together, right? He's only hanging out with you because he feels bad for you because your mom died."

Maybe it was leftover adrenaline from my run-in with Creepy McCreeperson, but suddenly I blurted out the first thing that came to mind. "Is that why he was ignoring your calls last night?"

Her eyes widened and she stepped toward me murderously. "He was home with his little sister."

"No, he was at Ponte Vecchio with me." *Please let me have pronounced that right.*

"There you are!" Thomas stepped between us, holding a soda in each hand. He took one look at Mimi and wilted. "Whoa. What did I miss?"

"Shut up, Thomas." She turned and flounced away.

"What just happened?" Thomas asked.

"I have no idea."

"Lina!" Ren was shoving his way toward me. "There you are. Do you want to leave? It's like a thousand degrees in here. I think the AC might be broken."

Relief flooded through me and suddenly I was holding back a boiling lake of tears. "Where have you *been*?"

"Looking for you." He leaned in. "Are you OK?"

"I want to leave. Now."

"I need to leave too," Thomas said. "I'll walk out with you guys."

It took us what felt like an hour to get out of there, and when we finally burst onto the sidewalk we all gulped in the cool air like we'd just emerged from the depths of the ocean.

"Freedom!" Thomas said. "That was like being slowly smothered."

I leaned back against the wall and shut my eyes. I was never going there again. Ever.

Ren touched my arm. "Lina, are you OK?"

I did a half shake, half nod. *OK?* I could still smell pickled muskrat.

"So, what did you think of Space? Perfect place for a relationship to start?"

"What relationship?" Thomas asked. "Mine and Lina's?" He gave me a meaningful look, but I barely noticed.

"He means my parents." I took a deep breath. "This old guy attacked me. He grabbed me and wouldn't let go."

"What do you mean? In Space?" Ren whirled around like he thought he could see through the walls. "When?"

"Right before you found me. Mimi rescued me."

"*That's* what was going on," Thomas said. "Are you OK? What a creep."

"Are you hurt?" Ren asked.

"No. It was just awful."

Ren looked furious. "Why didn't you yell for me? I would have destroyed him."

"I had no idea where you were."

Thomas's phone started ringing and he looked down at it

and groaned. "My dad keeps calling. We have family in town and I told him I wouldn't stay out long." He looked up at me. "But I'm not leaving without getting your number."

"Oh. Sure." I'd practiced for this, but when I went to tell him my new number, I forgot and had to look at the paper I'd written it on.

"Great. I'll call you tomorrow." He gave me a big hug, then clapped Ren on the shoulder. "See you around."

"Later." Ren turned to watch Thomas walk away and I used the opportunity to wipe my eyes. My mascara was everywhere.

"His shirt was really stupid, don't you think?"

"What?"

"'Banned from Amsterdam.' No one gets banned from Amsterdam. That's the point."

"I wouldn't know."

"I'm really sorry about what happened in there. I shouldn't have left you alone." He looked at me closer. "Wait a second. Are you crying?"

"No." A giant tear rolled down my face. And then another.

"Oh, no." He put his hands on my shoulders and looked me in the eyes. "I'm so sorry. We'll never go there again."

"I'm sorry. I feel really stupid. That guy was just so disgusting." But that was only half the reason I was crying. I took a deep breath. "Ren, why did you tell Mimi my mom died?"

His eyes widened. "I don't know. It just came up. She was asking why you moved here and I just told her. Why? Did she say something?"

"You know, you don't have to feel sorry for me. It's not

like I need you to read the journal and drive me around everywhere. I can figure this out on my own. I get that you have a life."

"Whoa, what? I don't feel sorry for you. I mean, it's sad that you lost your mom and everything, but I hang out with you because I like to. You're ... different."

"Different?"

"You know, like we talked about last night. We're alike, you know?"

I ran my arm across my face. Because that was totally going to help the mascara situation. "Promise?"

"Yeah, I promise. What brought that on?"

"Mimi—" I stopped. Did it matter? She was just a jealous girl. And every time Ren saw her he acted like he'd just won the lottery.

"Mimi what?"

"Never mind. Can we go to Piazza Signoria? I want to see that statue."

Chapter 15

WE WERE QUIET ON THE DRIVE TO THE PIAZZA. IT WAS after eleven and the city felt different. Sort of emptied out. Like me, after an embarrassing postclubbing cry fest. Ren pulled his scooter up to a curb and we both got off.

"This is it?"

"This is it. Piazza Signoria." He was looking at me like I was a box of highly fragile dishes, but I *was* still covered in snot, so I guess he was justified.

I walked out into the piazza. One side was lined by a large fortress-looking building with a clock tower, and in front of that was a fountain with a statue of a man surrounded by smaller figures. A handful of people were milling around, but for the most part it was empty.

"What's that building?" I asked.

"Palazzo Vecchio."

"Old something… Old palace?"

"*Esattamente.* You're getting good."

"I know. I recognized the word 'old.' I'm practically fluent."

We smiled at each other. My eyes felt like water balloons, but at least I wasn't sniveling anymore. Sheesh. I was lucky

Ren hadn't abandoned me at the nearest taxi stand.

"So what happened here again?" Ren asked.

"This is the first place he told her he loved her. They were looking at a statue. Something with 'rape' in its name."

"Oh, right. 'The Rape of the Sabine Women.' I think it's under that roofed area."

We made our way across the piazza, passing a bunch of other statues along the way, then walked under an arched entryway into what was basically a large patio filled with sculptures.

I recognized it right away. "There it is."

"The Rape of the Sabine Women" was made of white marble and sat high on a pedestal, the three figures intertwined in one tall column. I walked around it slowly. My mom was right. No one looked *happy* per se, but they were all connected and they definitely complemented one another. They were also all naked and their muscles and tendons were bulging out all over the place. Giambologna hadn't been kidding around.

Ren pointed. "Look how the woman is looking back at the other man. She definitely didn't want to go. And that guy on the ground looks totally spooked."

"Yeah." I folded my arms, looking up at the statue. "Is it just me, or is this a weird spot for Howard to tell my mom he loved her?"

"Maybe it just kind of happened. He got caught up in the moonlight or whatever."

"But he was studying art history and he'd just told her the whole backstory. I'd be surprised if it didn't have some kind of significance to him."

Ren hesitated. "Speaking of Howard ... I have to tell you something."

"What?"

He took a deep breath. "I sort of asked him about the secret bakery."

I whirled around. "Ren! You told him about the journal?"

"No, of course not." He pushed his hair out of his eyes, avoiding my gaze. "It was when you were getting ready. I made up this whole story about my mom finding a secret bakery when she first moved here, and then I asked him if he knew where one was. I was going to surprise you and take you there tonight after Space."

Finally he looked up at me with big, soulful eyes, and I sighed. It was like trying to be mad at a baby seal. "Did he tell you where it was?"

"No. That was the weird thing. He said he'd never been to one."

I squinted at him. "What? And you described it to him?"

"Yeah. I tried to be vague so he wouldn't know I was talking about his date with your mom, but he acted like he had no idea."

"So he didn't remember taking her there?"

He shook his head. "No, it was more than that. It was like he'd never even heard of Florence's secret bakeries."

"*What?* That doesn't seem like something you'd forget."

"I know, right?"

"Was he lying?"

"Maybe. But why would he?" He shook his head again. "For the past couple of hours I've been trying to come up with a reason why he'd forget about the bakery, but so far I have nothing. No offense, but your parents' story is kind of sketchy."

I put my back to one of the columns, then slid to the ground with a *thud*. "You're telling me. Why do you think I'm reading the journal?"

He sat down next to me, then leaned in until our arms touched. "I really am sorry, though."

I exhaled. "It's OK. And you're right. Something *is* weird. I've been thinking that all along."

"Maybe you should ask him about something else from the journal. Like a test."

"Like 'The Rape of the Sabine Women'?" We looked up at it.

"Yeah. See what he does when you ask him about that."

"Good idea." I looked at the ground. Now it was my turn to hesitate. "So … I did something I should probably apologize for too."

"What?"

"Back at Space, Mimi and I kind of got into this … argument, and I told her that you were ignoring her calls when we were at Ponte Vecchio."

His eyes widened. "*Cavolo*. I'm guessing that's why she called me a *cretino* and left?"

"Yeah. I mean, I don't know what a *cretino* is, but I'm sorry. Thomas told me you've liked her for a long time, and I hope I didn't mess things up."

"I'll call her when I get home. It'll be OK." He sounded like he was trying to convince himself.

I took a deep breath. "Hey, you know if you can't hang

out with me anymore, I understand. It seems like it's kind of complicating things for you."

"No. It's good complicated." He pulled out his cell phone. "It's almost eleven-thirty. Back to the cemetery?"

"Yeah. I should get back to the journal."

"And the man of mystery."

When I got home Man of Mystery was, inexplicably, taking a pan of muffins out of the oven.

"You're baking?"

"Yes."

"It's almost midnight."

"I specialize in late-night kitchen disasters. Also, I thought you might want a snack when you got home, and my blueberry muffins are legendary. And by 'legendary,' I mean 'edible.' Sit down."

It was a command. I pulled out a chair and sat.

"So where did you go tonight?"

I hesitated for a second, then plunged in. "Space. It's a club near the Arno."

He chuckled. "That place is still around?"

Phew. At least he remembered Space. "Yes. Have you been there?"

"Lots of times. Your mother too."

I leaned forward. "So you guys like ... went together?"

"Many times. Usually on nights we should have been studying. I don't know what it's like now, but it used to be the place to go for international students. Lots of Americans." He transferred a couple of the muffins to a plate, then set it on the table, pulling up a chair.

"Space was kind of grimy. I didn't like it very much."

"I never really did either. And I'm not much of a dancer."

So I had him to thank for my dancing skills.

I took a muffin and broke it open, steam curling up toward my face. *Now or never.* "So, Howard, I have a question for you. You know a lot about art history, right?"

"Yes." He smiled. "That's one thing I know plenty about. You knew I was teaching art history when your mom and I met, right?"

"Right." I looked down at my muffin again and took a deep breath. "Well, Ren and I went for a drive after Space, and we stopped in this piazza. Piazza della Signoria? Anyway, there was an interesting statue, but we didn't know the history of it."

"Hmm." He stood up and grabbed a butter dish off the counter, then sat down again. "Lots of statues there. Do you know who it was by?"

"No. It was in this open-air gallery. Kind of like a covered patio. You can just walk in."

"Oh, right. Loggia dei Lanzi. Let's see … there are the Medici lions, and the Cellini… What did it look like?"

"It was of two men and a woman." I held my breath.

"Woman being carried away?"

I nodded.

He smiled. "'The Rape of the Sabine Women.' That one is actually pretty interesting, because the artist – Giambologna – didn't even think of it as a real piece. He just made it as an artistic demonstration to show that it was possible to incorporate three figures into one sculpture. He didn't even bother to give it a name, and then it ended up being the work he's best known for."

OK. Interesting, but not quite the story he'd told my mom. I tried again. "Do you know if my mom ever saw it?"

He cocked his head. "I don't know. I can't remember ever talking to her about Giambologna. Why? Did she tell you about it?"

I can't remember. His face was as smooth as a fresh jar of Nutella. He definitely wasn't lying, but was it really possible that he'd forgotten? Had he suffered some kind of head trauma or have a mental block that kept him from remembering details about his relationship with my mom?

Suddenly a new thought tiptoed out of the corner of my mind. What if he *wasn't* forgetting? Or denying? What if … ? I sprang to my feet, crumbling the muffin in my hand. "I need to go upstairs."

I ran out of the room before he could ask why.

My mother's words spun through my mind as I climbed the stairs: *Yes, X. I seriously don't think anyone would read my journal, but I'm giving him a new name, just in case.*

As soon as I was in my room I locked the door behind me and fumbled for the journal. I switched on my lamp and started flipping through it.

> **Howard:** The perfect Southern gentleman (Southern giant, Francesca calls him), handsome, kind, and the kind of guy who will go marching into battle for you.

I <u>love</u> being in love in Italy. But truth be told,
I would fall for X anywhere.

Howard offered to walk me home, and I found myself
telling him about Adrienne and the psychic.

"No way," I breathed.

There was a reason Howard didn't know about the
secret bakery or the significance of Giambologna's statue,
and why my mom had slipped up and called him by his
real name.

He wasn't X.

"Addie, pick up, pick up!" I whispered.

"Hey, this is Addie! Leave a message and I'll—"

"Argh!" I tossed the phone on my bed and started pac-
ing around. Where *was* she? I went and stood at the window.
My mom had been in love with someone who wasn't Howard.
She'd had this take-over-everything passionate love affair and
then she'd ended up pregnant with *someone else's baby*. Howard's.
Was *that* her wrong choice? That she'd gotten pregnant with
Howard when really she'd been in love with someone else?
Was that what had made her flee Italy?

I fell heavily into my chair, then popped back up. Ren
would answer! I dove onto my bed, fishing my phone out of
the covers and dialing his number.

He answered on the second ring. "Lina?"

"Hey. Listen, I did what you suggested. I asked him about
the statue."

"What did he say?"

"He knew all about it, the history and everything. But then I asked him if he'd ever seen it with my mom and he couldn't remember."

"What is his deal? Either he has the worst memory in the world or—"

"Or he was never there," I interrupted impatiently.

"What?"

"Ren, think about it. Maybe he doesn't know about the secret bakery or the confession of love at the Sabine statue because *he isn't X*."

"Oh."

"Right?"

"Ohhh. Well … *yeah*. OK, walk me through it."

"I'm thinking it went something like this: My mom moves to Italy and makes a bunch of friends, Howard included. Then a few months in she falls for this guy X. Something happens, maybe they fight too much, or there's too much pressure because the school has some kind of weird rule about dating, and they break up. Then my mom rebounds with this nice Southern gentleman who probably had a thing for her all along. She gives it a try, but she can't get X off her mind. Then one day she finds out she's pregnant and panics, because she's having a baby with someone she isn't in love with."

"That totally makes sense!"

"I know. And that would explain why we stayed away from him all these years. I mean, he is a nice guy, and from all the stories she told, he was definitely a good friend to her, but you can't just *pretend* to be in love with someone. It would hurt them too badly."

"Poor, scary Howard," Ren breathed.

"And that's why she wrote 'I made the wrong choice.' Maybe that was her big regret. She had a baby with someone she wasn't in love with."

"Except you're that baby. So do you really think she'd have written that in the front of her journal?"

"Oh. Probably not." I sat down. "But, Ren, it's so sad! I mean, the way Howard talks about her, you can tell he really loved her. And she told me all these stories about how much fun they used to have together. But it just wasn't enough – she loved someone else!"

"It's like that old song 'Love Stinks.'"

"Never heard of it."

"You haven't? It's in a bunch of movies. It's about how whenever you fall in love with someone it turns out they're in love with someone else. And it's this big messed-up cycle where no one ends up with the person they want."

"Ugh. That is so depressing."

"Tell me about it." He paused. "Are you going to tell Howard that you know? About X?"

"No. I mean, I'm sure we'll talk about it eventually. But not until I finish the journal. I have to make sure my theory is right."

APRIL 5

Another night of drama. Simone got tickets to a new club near Piazza Santa Maria Novella and our group plus a few other students met up around eleven. I'd been working late at the studio, so I showed up on my own and when I got there the first two people I saw were Adrienne and Howard. They were to the side of the building, and Adrienne was standing with her back to the wall and Howard was leaning in to her, saying something in a low voice. The scene was so intimate that for a moment I didn't understand what I was seeing. I've never seen the two of them even talk one-on-one. What _was_ this?

I went into the club without them noticing and found the rest of the group, and then the two of them came in separately, acting like nothing had happened. Then things really got weird. Partway through the night Adrienne called Alessio a liar — something about him breaking his promise to go with her to an art exhibit — and for some reason that really set Howard off. He told her that she was the last person on earth who should call someone a liar, and that if she had any shred of dignity she'd come out with the truth. Adrienne hissed back that it was none of his business. Then Simone stepped in and told them to both calm down.

Guess I'm not the only one with secrets.

APRIL 19

X has been out of town for a full week, but he gets home tomorrow. TOMORROW. I haven't been able to think about anything else. After class I told Francesca that I needed to find The Dress. You know, the once-in-a-lifetime dress guaranteed to make anyone fall in love with you. (Or in my case, make me look amazing when I tell him my big news.)

Francesca was the perfect person to ask, because when it comes to shopping she has the patience of a saint. It took us five hours, but we finally found it. It's an off-white sundress, very feminine, with a sweetheart neckline and a skirt that falls just above the knee. Francesca even talked me into getting a haircut. Who knew cutting off a few inches of useless hair could give you cheekbones?

And what's my big news, you ask? Earlier this week Petrucione asked me if I'd be interested in staying on through August to assist with the upcoming semester. I'll be paid and get an extension on my student visa, which means I will be here until the end of the summer!!

APRIL 20

Woke up early this morning ecstatic to see X and there was a message on my phone. He decided to extend his time at the conference he's attending and won't make it until Monday. That's when I had a brilliant idea — I'll surprise him in Rome! Even if he's attending seminars all day, at least we'll be in the same city. I can spend my days touring. Express trains take only ninety minutes, so if I catch the four p.m. train this afternoon, I'll be waiting for him at his hotel when he's done for the day. I can't wait to see the look on his face!

APRIL 21

This is my third attempt to sit down and write about what happened in Rome. I can't believe I'm writing this, but it's OVER.

I was never able to find X's conference online, so when I arrived I called his cell phone and told him I was at the train station with some great news. Right then an announcement started on the station's overhead speakers, and when things finally quieted down, I realized that something was wrong. He told me to wait right where I was.

A half hour later he came charging into the train station, and something was definitely wrong. I asked him if he wanted to sit in one of the station's cafés, and for the next twenty minutes I just listened to him talk. Bottom line: He feels like his work has gotten stagnant, he needs some new creative space, and he's decided to leave the school and pursue another job in Rome. Oh, and we're over.

Over.

I just sat there, his words swirling around me. It was like my mind couldn't process it. And then it all hit me. This was the end. He was breaking up with me.

Suddenly I couldn't hear his excuses anymore, only the hard truths. I'd spent nine months lying to my friends. I'd strained ties with my family. I'd completely changed my life to be closer to him, and our relationship had never been to him what it was to me. I had the fleeting thought that I could talk him out of it — tell him that I'd figured out a way to stay in Florence even longer — but even in that brief moment of denial I knew it was useless. When someone walks out of a relationship, there's nothing you can do to keep them there.

X was still talking when I stood. I said good-bye to him in a normal voice, like I hadn't just been shattered into a million pieces, then went to the counter and bought a return ticket on the very next train. I hadn't even been in Rome for an hour. I never even got to wear my dress.

APRIL 22

Woke up this morning thinking I'd had some kind of nightmare, but just like the last few days, reality was waiting for me to get my bearings so it could knock me down again. My eyes were so swollen from crying myself to sleep that I had to sit with a cold washcloth over them before I looked acceptable enough to go to class. The whole weekend I'd been holding on to a tiny shred of hope that X would be in class this morning, but of course he wasn't. Can it really be over? Nothing has ever hurt this badly. Nothing.

APRIL 25

It turns out that Francesca knew all along. Last night after dinner she put her arm around me and told me that X wasn't worth it, and he never had been. I was so surprised. Did everyone know?

MAY 2

This morning Petrucione announced that X has resigned from his position. I felt a huge relief — not because he's officially gone, but because someone said his name. I didn't let people in on the relationship, and so now I can't let them in on my heartache. I feel so alone. Talking to Francesca doesn't help. If I bring him up, she says bad things about him, and I end up feeling worse. Florence is the perfect place to fall in love, which means it's also the worst place to be heartbroken. Some days I just want to go home. Should I even stay through summer?

"Mom," I whispered. Her sadness was smeared across the journal like paint that had never had the chance to dry. How was it possible that she'd had her heart smashed to smithereens in a Rome train station and never even *mentioned* it to me? Had I even known this woman?

I scanned through the last few entries again. No doubt about it, X had been a serious jerk. I especially hated that he'd told her he needed "new creative space." What kind of a line was that? And it was *awful* that she hadn't seen the end coming, especially when it was so obvious from the outside that the relationship wasn't going anywhere. Reading those last few entries had been like watching a train wreck in slow motion.

And then there was Howard. I rested my finger on the entry about him and Adrienne. He'd definitely had something going on behind the scenes too. Had he and Adrienne been dating and broken up just before my mom and X? Had both my parents been interested in other people and just sort of fallen together for a while? Is that why they hadn't lasted? And what had been so special about X, anyway?

I wanted to keep reading, but my eyelids insisted on doing this slow downward drag. Finally I gave up, tucking the journal into the nightstand and switching out the light.

Chapter 16

"I NEED YOUR HELP." I'D WOKEN THAT MORNING WITH a brilliant idea, and even though I'd waited until a socially acceptable hour, I'd still had to practically drag Ren out of his bed. Now we were sitting on his front porch and he looked only about thirty percent awake.

"Couldn't it have waited?" He was wearing black sweatpants and a faded T-shirt and, like usual, had to keep shaking his hair out of his face. It was probably just the morning light, but he looked cute. Like way cuter than someone with bed head should.

He caught me staring. "What?"

I quickly looked away. "Nothing. I just need your help with one last thing."

"Listen, you know I'm all about this Howard-Hadley mystery. But can't I take a nap first?"

"No! Ren, why are you so tired?"

"I was on the phone with Mimi until like three."

The sun was suddenly way too bright. "Was she really mad about what I said last night?"

"Yeah. It was pretty ugly." He sighed. "But let's not talk

about that. What do you need help with?"

"Could you give me a ride to FAAF?"

"Your mom's school?"

"Yes. I called them this morning. They moved to a new location a few years ago, but I want to go and see if I can get any info on Francesca."

"Fashion police Francesca?"

"I think she's my best bet for tracking down X. Turns out she knew about him all along."

"Whoa, slow down. We're tracking down X? Why?"

"Because my mom had this whole life I didn't know about, and I want to know what was so great about X that she couldn't get over him and had to break Howard's heart."

"But wait. That's still just a theory, right? What if that isn't the reason she left Italy?"

I groaned. "Ren, come on. Don't you want to know who the mysterious X is? He was so awful when he broke up with her. It totally destroyed her. I just want to know what the big deal was. I think it will help me understand it all better."

"Hmm." He yawned and dropped his head onto my shoulder.

"So will you help me?"

"Of course I will. When do you want to go?"

"As soon as possible." His skin was warm and he had that puppy-dog sleeping boy-smell.

"You smell good," he said, echoing my thoughts.

"No, I don't. I ran six miles this morning and haven't showered yet."

"You still smell good."

Apparently that tiny little butterfly was alive and well. And it was definitely making the rounds. I quickly moved away.

Don't. Think. About. Ren.

I ran hard back to the cemetery. I had enough to think about without complicating things with some stupid crush on one of the best friends I'd ever had. Also, he was dating a Swedish supermodel. With anger issues. And let's not forget that I'd just given my number to the best-looking guy I'd ever met.

When I got to the house my heart practically fell out of my chest. Howard was sitting on the porch swing with a cup of coffee, looking like *such a nice guy*. It was cosmically unfair that the whole "Love Stinks" cycle had left him alone in a cemetery with his terrible muffins and old music. It made me want to buy him balloons or something.

"Good morning, Lina."

"Morning."

He gave me a funny look. Probably because I was looking at him like he was an injured baby duck.

"I was just at Ren's," I offered.

"Do you two have any plans today?"

"Yeah, he's coming to get me in a little bit."

"For what?"

"Uh, I think we're just going to get some lunch or something." *Should I invite him?* Wait. We weren't actually going to lunch.

"Fun. Well, I was thinking that if you two are up for it, we could go to a movie tonight. One of the nearby towns has an outdoor theater that plays films in their original language, and this week they're showing one of my favorites."

"That sounds great!" I cringed. All I needed were pom-poms and a megaphone. *Tone it down. It's not like his heart was broken recently.*

He squinted at me. "Glad you like the idea. I'll ask Sonia, too."

"Sure."

I hurried into the house, and when I snuck a glance back at him, pity welled up in me so fast it almost overflowed from my eyeballs. He'd loved my mom. Was it too much to ask that she just love him back?

"You said 'Piazzale Michelangelo,' right?" Ren yelled to me.

"Right. They said park there and then head south."

"OK, it's just up ahead."

It had been a quick scooter ride and I'd been careful to sit an extra inch or two back so we weren't brushing legs or anything. Or at least not that often.

"Someone's going to meet with us at FAAF, right?" he asked.

"Right. I didn't tell them why we're coming in, but they said someone from admissions would be in the office."

He started following behind a line of tour buses, one of them so big it probably moonlighted as a cruise ship. Piazzale Michelangelo was a whirlpool of tourists. They all looked hell-bent on getting their money's worth.

"Why are so many people here?"

"Best view in the city. As soon as this bus gets out of our

way you'll see it." The bus slowed and Ren zipped around it and suddenly we had this big panoramic view of Florence including Ponte Vecchio, Palazzo Vecchio, and the Duomo. I mentally patted myself on the back. Five days in and I already recognized half the city.

Ren veered off the road and pulled into a parking spot roughly the size of my suitcase. We squeezed our way out.

"Where to?" he asked.

I handed him the directions. "The woman at the school said it's easy to find."

Famous last words. We spent the next thirty minutes wandering up and down the same streets, mostly because everyone we asked gave us entirely different sets of directions.

"First rule of dealing with Italians," Ren growled, "they love giving directions. Especially if they have no idea what they're talking about."

I was noticing that Ren sort of had an *I'm only Italian when I feel like it* policy.

"And they use lots of hand gestures," I added. "I thought the last guy was directing a plane. Or maybe an orchestra."

"You know how to get an Italian to stop talking, right?"

"How?"

"Tie their arms down."

"This is it!" I stopped walking and Ren plowed into me. We'd passed by the building at least five times already, but this was the first time I'd noticed the miniscule gold sign above doorway. FAAF.

"Did they think people would be reading their sign with binoculars?"

"You're grumpy."

"Sorry."

I hit the buzzer and there was a loud ringing noise followed by a woman's voice.

"Pronto?"

Ren leaned in. *"Buon giorno. Abbiamo un appuntamento."*

"Prego. Terzo piano." The door unlocked.

Ren looked at me. "Third floor. Race you."

We simultaneously tried to shove each other out of the way, then went pounding up the stairs, bursting into a large, well-lit reception area. A woman wearing a tight lavender dress startled and stood up from behind her desk. *"Buon giorno."*

"Buon giorno," I answered back.

She glanced at my sneakers and switched to English. "Did you call about meeting with our admissions officer?"

"I beat you," Ren said quietly.

"No, you didn't." I caught my breath and took a step forward. "Hi. Yes, I did call. But I was actually hoping to ask you about one of your past students."

"I'm sorry?"

"My mom was a student here about seventeen years ago and I'm trying to track down one of her old classmates."

She raised her eyebrows. "Well, I certainly can't give out any personal information."

"I just need to know her last name."

"And like I said, I really can't help you."

Argh.

"What about Signore Petrucione? Could he help us?" Ren asked.

"Signore Petrucione?" She folded her arms. "Do you know him?"

I nodded. "He was the director when my mom was attending."

She stared at us for a moment, then turned and skulked out of the room.

"Wow. She was a real ray of sunshine," Ren said. "Think she's coming back?"

"I hope so."

A moment later the woman walked back into the room, followed by an energetic-looking old man with wiry white hair. He was dressed stylishly in a suit and tie, and when he saw me, he did a double take. *"Non è possibile!"*

I glanced at Ren. "Um, hi. Are you Signore Petrucione?"

He blinked. "Yes. And you are…"

"Lina. My mom was a student here and—"

"You're Hadley's daughter."

"… Yes."

"I thought I was seeing things." He crossed the room, extending his hand. "What a surprise. Violetta, do you know who this girl's mother is?"

"Who?" She looked determined to be unimpressed.

"Hadley Emerson."

Her mouth dropped open. "Oh."

"Lina, come with me." He glanced at Ren. "And bring your friend."

Ren and I followed Petrucione down a hallway into a small office cluttered with photographs. He sat down, then gestured for us to do the same. I had to move a box of negatives off of my chair.

"Lina, I was so sorry to hear about your mother. It was so tragic. And not just because of her contributions to the art world. She was a wonderful person, too."

I nodded. "Thank you."

"Who is this?" He gestured to Ren.

"This is my friend Lorenzo."

"Nice to meet you, Lorenzo."

"You too."

Petrucione leaned forward, resting his elbows on his desk. "How lovely that you're here visiting Florence. And what a delight that you stopped at FAAF. Violetta said something about you asking for information about your mother's classmates?"

I took a deep breath. "Yes. Well, I've been trying to learn a little bit about my mom's time at school, and I was hoping to get in touch with one of her old friends."

"Absolutely. Which one?"

"Her name is Francesca. She was studying fashi—"

"Francesca Bernardi. She's another one who made quite a name for herself. Had a spread in *Vogue Italia* last spring." He tapped his head with two fingers. "I never forget a name. Let me have Violetta check our alumni records. I'll be right back." He got up and rushed out of the office, leaving the door cracked a few inches.

"How old is that guy?" Ren whispered. "Didn't your mom say he was like two hundred years old? And that was back then."

"Yeah, she did. So I guess that makes him two hundred and seventeen?"

"At least. And he's superenergetic. He'd better slow down on the espressos."

"Should I ask him about X? They kept it a secret from the school, but I could ask if they had anyone quit their job partway through my mom's second semester."

"Yeah, do it."

I glanced over at the wall and my eye snagged on a photograph of an old woman looking directly into the camera. I stood up and walked over to it. "My mom took this."

"Really? How do you know?"

"I just do."

Petrucione bounded back into the room. "Ah, I see you found your mother's photograph."

"I can usually recognize her work." By the way it made my heart hurt.

"Well, it's certainly unique. She had a real gift for portraits." He handed me a piece of paper, and we both sat back down. "I've written down Francesca's full name and included the number to her company. I'm sure she'll be very happy to talk to you."

"Thank you; this is really helpful."

"You're so very welcome." He beamed at me.

I'd thought I'd just get the info and get out, but suddenly I didn't want to leave. "What was my mom like? When she was here?"

Petrucione smiled. "Like an exclamation mark in human form. I'd never seen anyone so excited to be doing what they were doing. This school is very selective, but even so we'll occasionally have a floater slip through – that's what we call students who are kind of lukewarm but have enough natural talent to get accepted. Your mother wasn't like that. She was full of talent – drenched in it, really – but that's only one part of the equation. You have to be talented *and* driven. I think she could have been successful by her drive alone." He smiled. "All of the students liked her. I remember her being very popular. And once she played a joke on me. She took this very abstract photograph of a section of Ponte Vecchio and turned it in as an assignment. I'd seen enough photographs of Ponte Vecchio to last me a lifetime by then, and I'd warned the class that if anyone dared to use that bridge as their inspiration I'd fail them on the spot. But she did it, and of course I loved the photograph, and only afterward she told me what it was…" He chuckled, shaking his head.

A warm, gooey feeling bubbled up inside of me. I *loved* it when people who really knew my mom talked about her. It was like holding her hand for one tiny second.

Ren met my gaze. *X*, he mouthed.

"Oh." I took a deep breath. "Mr Petrucione? I have one more question."

"Prego."

"My mom mentioned that there was a … male faculty member or teacher or something who resigned partway through her second semester. Do you know who that could be?"

The room's happy vibe evaporated with a *poof*. Petrucione suddenly looked disgusted, like someone had just offered him a plate of dog poop or something.

"No. I don't."

Ren and I exchanged a look. "Are you sure?"

"Positive."

I shifted in my seat. "OK. Well, he might not have been around for long. I think he ended up taking another job in Rome and—"

He stood, raising his arm to cut me off. "I'm sorry, but we've had a lot of faculty come and go. I don't remember." He nodded at us. "It was such a pleasure to meet you. If you're ever in town again, please stop by and say hello." His voice was still kind, but final. Definitely final.

He wasn't going to talk about X.

"Thanks for your help," I said after a moment, getting to my feet.

As Ren and I passed by Violetta's desk, she jumped up and gave us a smile as wide as the Arno. "It was *such* an honor meeting you, and I'm so happy we could help. Have a *wonderful* day."

"... Thanks."

As soon as the glass door sealed shut behind us, Ren raised an eyebrow. "What was that about?"

Chapter 17

"PETRUCIONE DEFINITELY KNEW WHO WE WERE talking about. Did you see that look on his face?"

Ren nodded. "Yeah, couldn't miss it. And he'd said like five seconds before that he doesn't forget people's names. He just didn't want to tell us."

"Hopefully we'll have more luck with Francesca." I dialed her number, then pressed the phone to my ear. "It's ringing."

"*Pronto?*" It was a man.

"Um, Francesca Bernardi?"

He answered in rapid Italian. "Um, Francesca?" I said again.

He *tsk-tsked*. Then the phone started ringing again and a woman picked up. "*Pronto?*" Her voice was low and smoky.

"Hello, Francesca?"

"*Si?*"

"My name is Carolina. You don't know me, but you knew my mom. Hadley Emerson?"

Silence. I made a face at Ren.

"What?" he whispered.

"Carolina," she said slowly. "What a surprise. Yes. I

knew your mother. She was a dear friend."

My heart sped up. "I'm just trying to learn a little bit more about her … studies in Florence. You were her roommate, right?"

"Yes. And a messier woman never lived! I thought I was going to be buried alive in her rubble."

"Yeah … that was always kind of an issue. Could you maybe answer some questions for me about her life in Florence?"

"I'm sure I could, but why are you asking me? Hadley and I haven't been in touch in ages."

"Well…" I hesitated. I never knew how to break the news to people. It was like opening a dam. You never knew what they were going to hit you with. "She died. A little over six months ago."

Francesca gasped sharply. "*Non ci posso credere.* How?"

"Pancreatic cancer. It was pretty sudden."

"Oh, my poor dear. *Era troppo giovane, veramente.* I would be happy to talk about your mother. After she finished her program she dropped off the side of the world. None of us were able to get in touch with her."

"Do you… ?" I grimaced. "This will sound weird. But do you remember if she was dating anyone?"

"Oh, the love life of Hadley Emerson. It was like a romance novel. Your mother was in love, yes, and I think half of Firenze was in love with her. I always knew who was right for her – we all did – but then there was that Matteo causing a mess and ruining things."

"Matteo?" I croaked. I hadn't even had to push; she'd just dropped his name into my lap.

Ren looked up sharply.

"Yes. Our professor."

"Professor," I whispered to Ren. Well, that cleared up the whole secrecy thing.

"… He had her very confused, and I was so angry that she'd hurt our friend…" She trailed off. "I feel like I'm telling old secrets."

"What's Matteo's last name?"

She paused. "I believe it was Rossi. Yes, that sounds right. But I shouldn't even mention him. That man was a waste of time for everyone, especially your mother." She sighed. "We all wanted to save her from him. He was charming. Very handsome. But controlling. He thought he could find talent and take it on as his own. It was quite the scandal when he was fired."

"Fired?" *So much for "creative space."*

"Yes. But that's all old news." Her voice lifted. "Do you know who would be a great person for you to talk to? Howard Mercer. He was another classmate of ours, and he works at a cemetery just outside of Florence. He and your mother were very close. Would you like his phone number?"

"No, that's OK," I said quickly. "So, Matteo Rossi. Any idea where he is these days?"

"None whatsoever. And I like it best that way. But how old are you, Lina? I have a daughter as well."

"I'm sixteen."

"*Sixteen?* Hadley was hardly old enough to have a daughter your age. So let's see, that means you were born in…" She trailed off. "*Aspetta.* Sixteen years old?"

"Um, yes."

Her voice sharpened. "Lina, are you calling because—"

"Got to go," I said hastily. "Nice talking to you." I quickly pressed END.

Ren was leaned up against me, his ear a couple of inches from the speaker. He stepped back. "What was that all about?"

"She was putting together who my dad is. Sounds like they might still be in touch, and I don't want this to get back to Howard."

"What did she say X's name is?"

I smiled triumphantly. "Professor Matteo Rossi. We are so going to find him."

Ren and I ran to the nearest Internet café, which apparently is a thing. I was expecting a bunch of trendy cappuccinos or at least a case full of those giant sugar-dusted muffins, but all the café consisted of was a bunch of ancient-looking desktop computers and a group of angry people waiting in line for a turn to delete their junk mail. It was crazy disappointing.

Ren shifted from one foot to the other. "Sure you don't want to just go home and use my computer?"

"No. I want to find Matteo right away." My phone chimed and I pulled it out of my purse.

> Want to go to a party with me tomorrow night?
> It's for a girl who graduated last year. Band, bar,
> fireworks …
> – Thomas

I braced myself for a stampede of stomach butterflies, but

nothing happened. In fact, I think a tumbleweed might have blown by. I looked at Ren furtively. *Lina, you've got to pull it together.* Why did he look so good to me today? Was it just because he was the only person I knew who'd be willing to join me on a wild-goose chase for my mom's ex-boyfriend?

"Who is it?" Ren asked.

"No one."

"So, Lina…" His mouth drew down in a cute worried look. *No, not cute.* "Petrucione obviously didn't want to talk about Matteo, and Francesca wasn't a fan of him either. Do you really think it's a good idea to track him down? What if he's a jerk?"

"He was definitely a jerk. But yes, I want to meet him. He was a huge deal in her life, and she must have wanted me to know about him – otherwise, why would I have her journal? I just feel like finding him is a big part of figuring all this out."

He nodded, still looking unconvinced. "OK. But 'Matteo Rossi' is a pretty common name. It's like looking for Steve Smith in the States."

"We'll find him," I said confidently. "Think: We've already been pretty lucky today. Number one, we found the school—"

"That was a miracle."

"… And number two, once we were in there, you thought to mention Petrucione. If you hadn't, I think Violetta would have thrown us out on the street." On the other side of the room a woman stood up from her computer. "Hey, look! I think one just opened up."

I sprinted over to the computer, Ren at my heels, and we both squished into the chair.

"Want me to search sites in Italian?" he asked.

"Yes. Last we know he moved to Rome, so he's probably still here."

"What should I search for?"

I pulled the journal out of my purse and started flipping through it. "Matteo Rossi Fine Arts Academy of Florence? Matteo Rossi photographer Rome? Just mash up everything we know about him."

He typed it all in, then started scrolling down the screen, pausing every few seconds to read. I tried to read too, but none of my five Italian phrases made an appearance.

"Nothing. Nothing. Nothing... Something? What about this?"

"What?"

He clicked one of the search results. "Looks like an ad. In English."

COMBINE YOUR LOVE OF TRAVEL WITH YOUR PASSION FOR PHOTOGRAPHY.

Join renowned photographer and gallery owner Matteo Rossi on a journey through Rome that will change the way you see the world. Offering several photography workshops throughout the year, Rossi will take your hobby to the next level.

"Ren, you found him! That's got to be him."

"Let's look at his website." He clicked on the link at the bottom of the ad and the website loaded piece by excruciatingly slow piece.

"Ugh. This is taking for ever," I groaned. It was like watching the ice age in slow motion.

"*Pazienza,*" Ren said.

Finally the website dragged itself onto the screen. It was monochromatic with a big gold banner at the top that read ITALY THROUGH THE LENS.

I grabbed the mouse from Ren, then scrolled down to read the huge amount of text on the site. Every paragraph was translated into both English and Italian, and it was pretty much all a bunch of mumbo jumbo about how unbearably happy and successful you'd be once you paid Matteo a bunch of money for the opportunity to sit at his feet. This guy was unbelievably annoying.

Ren pointed to a link at the bottom. "Bio page. Try that."

I clicked. Then we waited. And waited. Another full ice age came and went. Finally a black-and-white headshot of Matteo loaded and I leaned in to take a look.

And that's when I stopped breathing.

Chapter 18

THE ROOM SUDDENLY FELT EXACTLY LIKE THE WOOL
sweaters that my great-aunt used to send me every Christmas.
Hot. Itchy. Asphyxiating.

My hands were shaking, but I managed to click on the
image to make it bigger. Olive skin. Dark eyes. Hair that
had been cut short and then gelled within an inch of its life,
because otherwise he was going to have to spend half his day
trying to keep it under control.

I would know.

"Oh my gosh. Ohmigoshomigoshomigosh. I think
I'm going to throw up." I started to stand up, but the room
whirled around and Ren grabbed me and pulled me back into
the chair.

"Lina, it's OK. Everything's OK." His voice sounded
like it was coming from underwater. "This is probably just
a coincidence. I mean, you look a lot like your mom, too.
Everyone says so."

"Ren, she never said that he was my father."

"What?"

I spun around. "My mom never said that Howard was

my father. All along she talked about him like he was just her best friend."

His eyes widened. "*Davvero*? So why did you think he was?"

"Because of my grandma. She said that Howard's my father, and my mom never told me that because she wanted me to give him a chance without being mad at him." I put my hand to my heart – it was trying to knock down my ribs. "Obviously I don't look anything like Howard, and Ren, *look*." We both looked at the screen again.

"There's got to be some kind of explanation. Maybe..." He trailed off.

There was absolutely no room for "maybe."

"And ever since I got here people have been telling me I look Italian. You said so when we met on the hill. Oh my gosh. I'm Italian. I'm *Italian*!"

"Half-Italian. And, Lina, calm down. Being Italian isn't the end of—"

"Ren, do you think he knows? Do you think Howard knows?"

He hesitated, looking at the picture again. "I don't know. He has to, right?"

"Then why is he going around introducing me to people as his daughter? Oh, no." I doubled over. "The night we went to Elena's he had people over and I overheard one of them ask if I was 'the photographer's daughter' and he said yes. He didn't say I was his, too."

"But he told me he's your dad. That first time we talked. And Sonia says he is too, right?"

"So either they're all lying or they believe it." I put my

head in my hands. "Ren, what if only my mom knew? What if that's the reason she sent the journal? So that I would know the truth even if no one else did?"

Ren grimaced. "Would she do that? That seems pretty..."

Mean? Insensitive? Pick one.

I shook my head. "I don't know anymore. Ever since I started reading the journal I've been wondering if I even really knew her." I looked at the screen again. "Just last night I was thinking that she and Howard had to get together really soon, because my birthday is in January. But I guess there's no rush. She must have already been pregnant when she moved in with him."

"So now what?"

I took a deep breath. "We have to call Matteo. I have to meet him."

"Whoa, Lina, that sounds like a bad idea. Why don't we go talk to Howard first? Or at least finish the journal."

"Ren, please! I think it's what my mom wanted me to do. And I can't face Howard like this. I can't. Is that Matteo's number at the bottom?" I grabbed my phone and tried to dial it, but my hands were shaking too badly.

"I'll do it." He took the phone from me. "Should I just call the number to his gallery?"

"Yes. See when it's open. And where it is. How will we get there? Can we drive your scooter to Rome?"

"No, we'll take a train. They run all day." He leaned forward, the phone pressed to his ear. It was ringing.

Ren drove as fast as he could all the way to the train station, me clinging to him like a lunatic monkey. We'd looked up the train schedule online and had found an express train leaving in twenty-six minutes. We'd made it there in twenty-four.

"We made it. We made it," I panted.

Ren collapsed into an empty seat. "I've … never … run … that fast."

I pressed my fingers into my ribs. I had a horrible side ache. "What … were the chances … that a train … was running right now?"

He took a second to catch his breath. "They go all day, but this is one of the fast ones. And we need fast. Because if my parents find out I'm taking you to Rome to meet some random guy, they'll kill me. And Howard will drop me in a vat of boiling oil."

"Matteo isn't some random guy. And Howard…" I groaned. "This is so awful. He's already had his heart broken by my mom, and now he's going to find out he doesn't have a daughter, either."

Just then the intercom came on at an earsplitting decibel, and we both clamped our hands over our ears as a man made a long announcement in Italian. Finally the announcement stopped, then there was a screeching sound, and the train slowly began to move out of the station. *This is happening. This is really happening.*

"You have the journal, right?" Ren asked.

"Right." I pulled it out of my purse. "I'm going to read the whole way. How long until we get there?"

"Ninety minutes. Read fast." He propped his feet up on the seat across from us, then leaned back, shutting his eyes.

"Ren?"

He opened his eyes. "Yeah?"

"I promise I'm normally boring."

"I doubt that."

MAY 9

The semester is wrapping up. Simone and Alessio finished early. They managed to get jobs working together at a museum in Naples, and we're all just relieved they won't have to split up. Who would they fight with? Adrienne finished early too, but she left without saying good-bye.

Now that our group has dwindled to just the three of us, Francesca, Howard, and I spend so much time together that we joke that Howard should just save money and move in with us. Classes are done, but we technically have a couple of weeks before we have to turn in our final projects, and I've already started assisting Petrucione.

I feel like I've come to the end of an era. The past year has held some of my best moments but also some of my worst. I haven't heard a single word from X since that day in the train station, and now that the sharp edges of that day have dulled, I keep asking myself the same question: How could our relationship have meant so much to me and so little to him?

MAY 12

For the past few weekends Howard and I have been renting a car and dragging Francesca on outings to Tuscan hill towns. We have very specific roles: Howard drives and DJs, I read aloud from a travel book, and Francesca sits in the back and complains. We have so much fun, and I'm so glad to have them for a distraction. Sometimes I even forget about X for a while.

MAY 13

Francesca was just offered a position as an assistant to a prominent fashion photographer in Rome. If she takes it (and she will) she'll start in less than a month. Howard has been interviewing for jobs too. He told me he'll do whatever it takes to stay in Italy. Janitor with a PhD in art history, anyone? We've always been kindred spirits about Florence. While the rest of our friends sat around complaining about the city's tourists and how expensive everything is, we were the ones pointing out stained glass windows and trying every strange flavor of gelato we came across.

I hate to admit it, but even though I still love Florence with my whole heart, it has become a sad place to me as well. Everywhere I go I see places I went with X, and it's like I can hear echoes of our conversations. I spend hours wondering why our breakup was so sudden. Did the school find out? Did he meet someone else? But it's useless to think about. I could wonder for ever.

MAY 14

Only about a week left on my project. Petrucione has recommended a few art schools for portrait photography, and he said that if I can round out my portfolio I'll have my pick of any program I want. Trying to feel as enthusiastic as I should about it. Part of me is ready for the next phase, and part of me wishes I could just stay in this city for ever.

MAY 15

Howard must be sick of me blowing him off to work on my portfolio, because he blindsided me on my way out of the studio and told me he was taking me to see the Florence American Cemetery and Memorial. He's been working there as a volunteer for the past few months (add WWII history to his long list of interests) and was recently approached about applying for the position of live-in superintendent. The current superintendent had a stroke earlier this month, and they're scrambling to find someone to replace him. I can't imagine a more perfect person for the job — or a more perfect place for Howard. He said it's a long shot and tried to act nonchalant about it, but I could tell how badly he wants the job.

MAY 18

What is wrong with me?? One day I feel like I'm moving along just fine, and other days I'm so weepy and emotional I may as well be standing in that train station in Rome. I stay up late working most nights, but even if I don't I still can't sleep. Every time I close my eyes I just think about X. I know I should be getting over him by now, but I just wish we could have one more conversation. In a moment of weakness I tried his phone number, but it had been disconnected. I know it was for the better, but I was still so disappointed.

MAY 20

Howard was offered the job! Francesca and I took him out to his favorite pizza place to celebrate, and when we got back to our apartment, Francesca scurried up the stairs, leaving Howard and me standing outside. I was about to say good night, but he started hemming and hawing and then out of nowhere invited me to stay with him at the cemetery for the rest of the summer. He made it sound so easy: Finish up your grad school applications. Stay in my spare bedroom. Spend a little more time in Florence. What an offer! I said yes before he even finished asking.

MAY 22

Today was my last official day as a student at FAAF. I'm

planning to take the weekend off. Then I'll start assisting Petrucione on Monday. Francesca and I spent the afternoon packing up our apartment. I never thought I'd say this, but I'm going to miss my cardboard mattress and all those noisy bakery customers. So many good things happened to me here!

Francesca left an hour ago. Her internship starts in two weeks, and she's going to visit her parents first. I helped drag all nine of her bags down to the street, and then we just hugged. She claims she never cries, but when she pulled back, her eyeliner was a tiny bit smudged. Hopefully she makes good on her promise to visit Howard and me soon.

MAY 24

Well, it's official. I am now a resident of the Florence American Cemetery and Memorial. All the stress of ending the school year must have hit me, because yesterday I was so exhausted that I could barely even get out of bed. The previous superintendent left the place fully furnished, so Howard's been able to jump right into the job. The spare bedroom is perfect for me, and Howard said he doesn't mind if I cover the walls with photographs.

MAY 26

The cemetery is gorgeous, and even though I should be spending all my free time working on my grad school applications. I keep taking breaks to wander through the headstones. The Wall of the Missing is especially interesting. How is it that they were living, breathing people and all of a sudden they were just gone? This morning I was photographing it and the assistant superintendent, Sonia, joined me and we had a nice long talk. She's a lovely woman. Smart, like Howard, and so dedicated to working here.

MAY 30

This has been such a great week. After we're done working for the day, Howard and I cook, watch old movies, and go for long walks, and it just feels so _perfect_. Sometimes Sonia joins us, and we sit around playing cards or watching movies or just talking. I don't know how to explain it exactly, but for years I've felt like I was looking for something — like I wasn't quite in the right place. But here with Howard, that feeling has evaporated. I don't know if it's the city, or the peacefulness of the cemetery, or having so much time to work on my photography, but I've never felt more at ease. There's something very healing about this place.

MAY 31

This morning I showed Petrucione some of the photos I've taken at the cemetery. There's one spot in the northwest corner that gives a perfect view of the grounds, and I've been taking pictures there at different times of day. It's amazing to see the change in light and color as the day progresses.

I guess it makes sense, but living in a cemetery has me thinking often about death. There's an order here that doesn't exist in real life, and I find it strangely comforting. Maybe that's the beauty of death. Nothing is messy anymore. Everything is sealed up and final.

Sealed up and final.

"Ugh," I said aloud. She was so *wrong* about that. How could anything be final when you left people behind and didn't even tell them your secrets?

"What's up?" Ren asked. "Anything new?"

"She moved in with Howard at the cemetery. But they're just friends. She had to have been pregnant by then." I shook my head. "Matteo has to be the one."

"Can I catch up?"

I handed him the journal, then leaned back, watching the scenery fly past our window. We were driving through a postcard of green countryside and rolling hills, and it was so pretty and picturesque I wanted to scream.

Why had she told me this way?

Chapter 19

BY THE TIME THE TRAIN CAME TO A STOP I HAD ENOUGH adrenaline running through me to power a small island. Not that any of the other passengers cared. They were taking their sweet time gathering up their magazines and laptops, and I stood blocked in the aisle, jiggling nervously.

Ren nudged me with his shoulder. "You sure you want to do this?"

"I have to."

He nodded. "When we get out let's head straight for the curb. If we beat the rush we can get a cab and be there in like ten minutes."

Ten minutes.

Finally the line started moving and Ren and I hurried off the train. The station had a high ceiling and was even more crowded than the one in Florence.

"Which way?" I asked.

He turned around in a circle. "I think … that way. Yeah."

"You up for running again?"

"Let's do it."

He grabbed my hand and we sprinted toward the exit,

dodging people like they were pitfalls in a video game. *Ten minutes. Ten minutes.* My life was about to change. *Again.* What happened to normal, boring days?

There were a bunch of cabs waiting out on the street next to the taxi stand, and Ren and I jumped into the first one available. Our cabdriver had a thick mustache and a cologne problem.

Ren read him the address.

"Dieci minuti," the cabdriver answered.

"Ten minutes," Ren translated.

Breathe. Breathe. Breathe. He was still holding my hand.

Word to the wise. Unless you have no choice – like maybe you're being chased by a pack of rabid spider monkeys, or you've run away to a foreign city to track down your mysterious father – never, ever get into a cab in Rome. Ever.

"Ren, I think this guy is going to kill us," I whispered.

"Why? Because we almost just got into our second head-on collision? Or because he keeps trying to pick fights with other drivers?"

"Dove hai imparato a guidare?" our driver yelled at another driver. He leaned out the window and made a gesture that I'd never seen but definitely got the gist of.

"I think my life is flashing before my eyes," I said.

"How is it?"

"Exciting."

"Mine too. Although I have to admit, it got way more exciting five days ago when you ran up to me on the hill."

"I didn't run up to you. I was actually trying to avoid you."

"Really? Why?"

"I thought it would be awkward. And then it was."

He grinned. "And look at us now. Spending our last few minutes on earth together."

The driver swerved over to a curb, then threw the car into park before coming to a complete stop. Ren and I flew into the seats in front of us.

"Ow!" I rubbed my face. "Do I have a nose anymore?"

"A flat one," said Ren. He was crunched up on the floor like a balled-up piece of paper.

"Siamo arrivati," the cabdriver said pleasantly. He glanced at us in the rearview mirror, then pointed to his meter. *"Diciassette euro."*

I dug some money out of my purse and passed it forward, and then we climbed out onto the sidewalk. The second I closed the door, the cab screeched back into traffic, causing about four other cars to slam on their brakes and contribute to what was basically a grand orchestra of honking.

"That guy shouldn't be allowed to drive."

"Pretty standard. He's actually one of the better cab-drivers I've had. Look, there's the gallery."

I whirled around. We were standing in front of a gray stone building with gold lettering on the door:

ROSSI GALLERIA E SCUOLA DI FOTOGRAFIA
ROSSI GALLERY AND PHOTOGRAPHY SCHOOL

Rossi. Lina Rossi. Was that actually my name? Crap. It had an Italian *R.* I wouldn't even be able to pronounce it.

"Come on." Before my nerves could get the better of me,

I marched over to the door and pressed the buzzer.

"*Prego,*" a man's voice said through the speaker. *Matteo?* The door unlocked with a loud *click*.

I looked at Ren. "You ready?"

"Who cares about me? Are *you* ready?"

"No."

Before I could think, I shoved the door open, launching myself into a large, circular-shaped foyer. The room was made of shiny tile, and there was a huge light fixture with about ten different pendant lights jutting out of it like jellyfish tentacles. A blond man wearing a dress shirt and tie sat behind a curved silver desk. He was young and American-looking. Definitely not Matteo.

"*Buon giorno.* English?" he said in a bored voice.

"Yes." My voice echoed.

"I'm afraid you've missed the class. It started more than a half hour ago."

Ren stepped up next to me. "We're not here for the class. I called a couple of hours ago about meeting with Matteo? My name is Lorenzo."

"Lorenzo Ferrara?" He studied us for a moment. "I guess I didn't realize that you were quite so young. Unfortunately, Mr Rossi is upstairs teaching a class. His class times vary, and I can't promise that he'll have the time to meet with you afterward."

"We'll wait anyway," I said quickly. *Mr Rossi.* For all I knew he was standing right above me.

"And what is your name?" the man asked me.

"Lina…" I hesitated. Would Matteo recognize my last name? "My name is Lina Emerson."

Ren shot me a look, but I just shrugged. The point was to tell Matteo who I was, right?

"Very well. I can't make any promises, but I'll let him know you're here."

His phone rang with a loud *brrrrnng*, and he snatched it from the desk. "*Buon giorno. Rossi Galleria e Scuola di Fotografia.* Good morning, Rossi Gallery and Photography School."

"Let's look around," I said to Ren. I was crazy jittery. Maybe a tour of the gallery would keep my mind off of what was about to happen.

"Sure."

We walked under an arched doorway into the first room. The room was made of exposed brick, and all four walls were covered with framed photographs. A large one caught my eye and I walked over to it. It was a shot of an old graffiti-covered building in a big city, like New York City or somewhere, and one wall read, TIME DOESN'T EXIST, CLOCKS EXIST. There was a big looping handwritten signature in the bottom right corner: M. ROSSI.

"That's pretty cool," Ren said.

"Yeah, my mom would have loved his style." Correction. She *had* loved his style. My sweat glands immediately went into overdrive.

Ren wandered ahead a few feet, and I headed in the other direction. Most of the photographs were by Matteo, and they were really good. Like *really* good.

"Lina? Could you come here for a second?" Ren's voice was purposely calm, like when you need to tell someone they have a massive spider on their back but don't want them to freak out.

"What?" I hurried over to him. "What is it?"

"Look."

It took me a second to realize what I was looking at, and then I practically jumped out of my skin. It was a photograph of *me*. Or at least, the back of me, and I even remembered when my mom had taken it. I was five years old and I'd piled up a stack of books so I could watch out the window for our neighbor's pony-size dog, with whom I'd had an intense love/fear relationship. I was wearing my favorite dress. I looked at the tag. *Carolina*, by Hadley Emerson.

"How did he get this?" Suddenly I felt light-headed. "He knows about me. This isn't going to be a surprise."

"Are you sure you want to stay?"

"I don't know. Do you think he's been waiting for me to show up?"

"Excuse me." It was the man from the foyer. He was looking at us like he thought we might try to shove one of Matteo's massive photographs into my purse. "Do you two have any questions?"

About a million. "Um, yeah…" I gave the room a desperate glance. "Are all of these … for sale?"

"Not all of them. Some are part of Mr Rossi's private collection."

"Does he have anything else by Hadley Emerson?" I pointed to the photograph.

"Hmm." He walked over and took a look at *Carolina*. "I can check, but I believe this is the only one. Are you familiar with Hadley Emerson's work?"

"Uh, yeah. Sort of."

"Let me check our system and I'll let you know."

He walked out of the room and Ren raised his eyebrows. "Not exactly the most observant, is he?"

"What am I going to say to Matteo? Do I just tell him straight out who I am?"

"Maybe you should wait to see if he recognizes you."

A door opened overhead and suddenly there was a thundering of voices and footsteps. Class was out. My breathing went into overdrive. This was a mistake. It was too fast. What if he didn't want to be a part of my life? What if he did? Would he be as awful as the guy in my mom's journal?

I grabbed Ren's arm. "I changed my mind. I don't want to meet him. You're right. We should talk to Howard first. At least I know my mom trusted him."

"You sure?"

"Yes. Let's get out of here."

We raced out of the room. About a dozen people were making their way into the foyer, but we quickly skirted around them, and I reached for the doorknob.

"You two. Wait there!"

Ren and I froze. *Oh, no.* Part of me wanted to walk right out onto the street, but another even bigger part wanted to turn around. So I did. Slowly.

A middle-aged man stood at the top of the staircase. He wore an expensive-looking shirt and slacks, and was shorter than I'd thought, with a carefully groomed beard and mustache. His dark eyes were fixed on me.

"Come on, Lina, let's go," Ren said.

"Carolina? Please come up to my office."

"We don't have to go," Ren said quietly. "We can just walk out of here. Right now."

My heart was pounding in my ears. Not only had he called me "Carolina," but he'd pronounced it right. I grabbed Ren's hand. "Please come with me."

He nodded. Then we slowly made our way toward the staircase.

Chapter 20

"PLEASE, HAVE A SEAT." MATTEO'S VOICE WAS polished, with only a hint of an accent. He walked behind a half-moon desk and gestured to two chairs that looked exactly like hard-boiled eggs. Actually, come to think of it, *everything* in his office looked like something else. A large clock shaped like a cog ticked noisily in the corner, and the rug looked like it was supposed to be a map of the human genome or something. The whole room had this overly colorful modern vibe that didn't seem to mesh with the man standing in front of us.

I lowered myself uneasily into one of the hard-boiled eggs.

"What can I do for you?"

OK. Just tell him? How do I start?

"I—"I made the mistake of glancing at Ren, and suddenly my throat sealed up like a Ziploc bag. He gave me a worried look.

Matteo cocked his head. "You two speak English, correct? Benjamin told me you wanted to meet me. I'm assuming you have questions about my programs?"

Ren cast a glance at my frozen expression, then jumped in. "Uh … yes. Questions about your programs. Um, do you have any classes for beginners?"

"Of course. I teach several entry-level courses throughout the year. The next one begins in September, but I believe it is already full. All of that information is available on my website." He leaned back. "Would you like to be put on the waiting list?"

"Yeah, that sounds good."

"All right. Benjamin can help you with that."

Matteo slid his eyes at me, and suddenly I could feel every nerve ending. Was he pretending not to know, or did he not see it? I felt like I was standing in front of a mirror. An older, male mirror, but a mirror just the same. His eyes lingered on my hair for a moment.

"Can you recommend a good camera for a beginner?" Ren asked.

"Yes. I prefer Nikons. There are several good camera shops in Rome, and I'd be happy to give you the owners' contact information."

"Nice."

Matteo nodded and there was a long silence.

Ren cleared his throat. "So … those must be pretty pricey."

"There's a range of prices." He crossed his arms and glanced at the cog clock. "Now if you'll excuse me…"

"Do you collect a lot of photographs from other photographers?" I blurted out. Both of them looked at me.

"Not many. But I travel a lot, and I make it a point to visit studios and galleries everywhere I go. If I find something especially moving, I buy it and display it in my gallery, along with mine and my students' work."

"What about the Hadley Emerson photograph? Where did you buy that?"

"That one was a gift."

"From who?"

"Hadley." He looked straight into my eyes. Like a challenge.

All of the air whooshed out of me.

He pushed back from his desk. "Lorenzo, why don't we go to the reception area and ask Benjamin about placing you on the waiting list. Carolina, before you leave I'd be happy to show you the other Emerson photograph I have in my possession."

I rose clumsily from my chair and Ren grabbed my arm. "Why isn't he recognizing you?" he whispered.

"He is. He knew my real name and he's saying it right." No one ever said my name right. Unless they'd heard it before.

We followed him down the stairs, my heart pounding in my throat, and Matteo stopped at the desk. "Benjamin, will you please assist Lorenzo in being added to the wait list for the next beginners' course?"

"Of course."

"Carolina, the photograph is in the next room. Lorenzo, we'll meet you back here."

We looked at each other. *OK?* he mouthed.

OK.

OK, OK, OK.

"Right this way." Matteo walked briskly into the next

room and I followed after him, my mind scrambling like a bad TV connection. What was happening? Did he just want to talk in private?

He walked up to the far wall, then pointed to a photograph of a young woman, her face half in shadow. Definitely my mom's.

"You see?"

"Yes." I took a deep breath, keeping my eyes focused on the photograph for courage. "Matteo, I'm here because I'm—"

"I know who you are."

My head snapped up. He was looking at me like something that had attached itself to the bottom of his shoe. "You're your mother in a pair of skinny jeans and Converse sneakers. The real question is, what are you doing here?"

"What am I ... doing here?" I took a step back, fumbling to pull the journal out of my purse. "I read about you in my mom's journal."

"So?"

"She was ... in love with you."

He laughed bitterly. "In *love*. She was a stupid child, in love with her instructor. She'd had no exposure to life outside of that small town she came from, and when she got here she thought her life would be transformed into some sort of fairy tale. But regardless of what her fantasies were, I was her teacher, nothing more. And whatever ideas you have in your mind, you'd better erase them immediately, Carolina." He spat out my name like a rotten piece of fruit.

Heat spread through my body. "It wasn't *nothing*. You dated. You kept it a secret from everyone and then you broke up with her when she went to visit you in Rome."

He shook his head slowly. "No. Those are lies. She spun an elaborate fantasy about us being in a relationship and then went so far as to believe it herself." His lips curled in an ugly smile. "Your mother was unbalanced. A liar."

"No, she wasn't." My voice echoed through the room. "She wasn't delusional. She didn't make up your relationship."

"Oh, really." His voice rose. "Ask anyone who was there. Did any of them ever see us together? Have you ever spoken with anyone who confirmed her story?"

"Francesca Bernardi."

He rolled his eyes. "Francesca. She was your mother's best friend. Of course she believed her. But did she ever actually see us together? Did she have anything more to go on than your mother's ridiculous fairy tale?"

Did she? A merry-go-round of thoughts started whirling through my head. Francesca had *sounded* sure…

"I didn't think so. But since you've made the effort of coming here, I'll tell you exactly what happened. Your mother was struggling with her course work and asked if I would tutor her outside of school. At first I was happy to help, but then she started calling me at strange hours. During class she would stare at me, then leave things on my desk for me to find. Sometimes it was lines of poetry; other times it was photographs of herself." He shook his head. "At first I thought it was just a crush, harmless. But then she became more intense. One night she came to my apartment and told me she'd fallen in love with me. She said her life would have no meaning if we weren't together.

I tried to be kind. I told her that as her teacher a relationship simply would not be allowed. I told her she'd be happier dating people closer to her own age. Like that Howard Mercer."

Howard. I flinched, but Matteo didn't notice. He was looking past me, like he was watching the scene unfold on a big-screen TV.

"That's when she snapped. She started screaming, telling me that she was going straight to the school director to tell him I'd taken advantage of her. I told her that no one would believe her. And then she pulled out a journal – *that* journal, I'm guessing – and told me that it was all there. She'd filled it with a fantasy – a vision – of what she'd wished had happened between us, and told me she would give it an unhappy ending and offer it up as proof.

"The next day I requested a meeting with the school director, and we agreed that even though I'd committed no fault, it was best for me to resign. Later I heard she began sleeping with any man who looked her way. I'm guessing you're a product of that." He met my eyes, and a cold burst of air moved through me. "I wanted nothing to do with your mother, and I want nothing to do with you."

"You're a *liar.*" My voice trembled. "And a complete coward. Look at me. I look just like you."

He shook his head slowly, a pained smile on his face. "No, Carolina. You look just like *her*. And whatever poor man she suckered into her pathetic imaginations." In one quick motion he stepped forward, snatching the journal out of my hands.

"Hey!" I tried to grab it back, but he whipped around, blocking me with his shoulder.

"Ah, yes. The famous journal." He began flipping through it. "I guess she called me X? Clever, wasn't she? 'The only hard part about being with X is not telling anyone about it' ... 'Sometimes I feel like my time is divided into two categories: time with X, and time spent waiting to be with X'..." He turned around, fanning the pages lazily. "Carolina, you seem like a smart girl. Does this sound real to you? Does it seem likely that your mother was in a relationship that she managed to keep entirely secret?"

"She didn't make it up."

He glanced down at the book. It had fallen open to the front cover, and he held it up to me. 'I made the wrong choice.' You see? Even in her craziness she knew that faking this journal was wrong. She was so talented, but *folle*. I hate to tell you this, Carolina, but science has proven that the parts of the brain responsible for creativity and madness are the same. At least you can take comfort in the fact that it wasn't really her fault. Your mother was a genius, but her mind was weak."

Suddenly all I could see was hot, boiling red. Before I could think, I lunged at him, twisting the journal out of his hands and running for the foyer.

"Lina?" Ren looked up from the desk. He had a clipboard in front of him. "Are you OK?"

I pulled the door open and burst out onto the sidewalk, Ren chasing after me. I turned and ran up the street, my legs heavy as sandbags. *Her mind was weak.*

Finally Ren caught up to me, grabbing my arm.

"Lina, what happened? What happened in there?"

A wave of nausea washed over me and I ran over to the edge of the street and started dry heaving. Finally the feeling passed and I sank to the ground, the pavement hard under my knees.

Ren was kneeling next to me. "Lina, what just happened?"

I turned and pressed my face into his chest and suddenly I wasn't just crying. I was *sobbing*. Like splitting-at-the-seams, exploding-into-a-million-pieces, falling-*apart* crying. The weight of the last ten months was dumping down on me, and I couldn't do a thing about it.

I cried and cried and cried. Hot, noisy tears that didn't care who was watching. The kind of crying I'd never done in front of anyone.

"Lina, it's OK," Ren said over and over, his arms wrapped around me. "It's going to be OK."

But no, it wasn't. And it never would be. My mom was gone. And I missed her so much I sometimes wondered how I was breathing. Howard wasn't my father. And Matteo...
I don't know how long I cried for, but finally I felt my feet reach the bottom, my last few sobs coming out in shudders.

I opened my eyes. We were both still kneeling on the ground, and I was smooshed into Ren, my face buried in his neck, his skin hot and sticky. I pulled back. Ren's shirt had a giant soggy puddle on it, and he looked mortified.

This was *so* much more than he'd bargained for.

"I'm sorry," I said hoarsely.

"What just happened?"

I wiped my face, then pulled him up to standing. "He said

my mom made it all up. She was obsessed with him and she wrote a fake journal to get him in trouble with the school."

"*Che bastardo.* That's not even that good of a story." He looked at me closer. "Wait. You didn't believe him, did you?"

I hesitated for a moment, then shook my head hard, my hair sticking to my wet cheeks. "No. At first it scared me. But that wasn't her. She never would have hurt someone she loved."

He exhaled. "You scared me for a minute."

"I just can't believe that she loved *him*. He was horrible. And Howard is so…" I looked up.

Ren's face was like six inches away from mine, and suddenly we locked eyes and I wasn't thinking about Matteo and Howard anymore.

Chapter 21

IT WASN'T A LITTLE KISS. NOT LIKE YOUR FIRST PECK or like the time you made out with your junior high boyfriend behind the movie theater. It was throw-your-arms-around-his-neck, bury-your-fingers-in-his-hair, why-haven't-we-done-this-before kissing straight through all the salt on my face. Ren circled his hands around my waist and for five seconds everything was perfect, and then –

He pushed me off him.

Pushed.

Me.

Off.

Him.

I wanted the sidewalk to swallow me up.

He wouldn't look at me.

Seriously, why hadn't it swallowed me up yet?

"Ren … I don't know what just happened." He'd been kissing me back, hadn't he? *Hadn't* he?

He was staring at the ground. "No, no. It's OK. I just don't think that the timing's the best, you know?"

TIMING. My face went up in flames. Not only had he

just had to peel me off of him, but he was being *nice* about it. *Lina, fix this.* Words started pouring out of my mouth.

"You're right. You're totally right. I think I just got carried away after what happened in there – it was really emotional, and I think I just redirected and…" I squeezed my eyes shut. "We're just friends. I know that. And I've never, ever, ever thought of you as anything more."

Does it count as a lie if you're denying something you've only fully admitted to yourself for about a minute? Also: One too many "evers" there. But I was going for believable.

Ren's gaze shot up, meeting mine with literally the most unreadable expression on the planet. And then he was gone again. "It's OK. Don't worry about it."

Why, why, why did I do that? I slumped against my door of the taxi. Ren was sitting as far away from me as was physically possible, and he was staring out the window like he was trying to memorize the streets or something.

Couldn't I have a repeat? Go back twenty minutes to when I hadn't already lost my head and kissed my best friend who had a girlfriend and clearly didn't want *me*? Back before I'd noticed how much I loved his shaggy hair and sense of humor or the fact that even though I'd known him for less than a week I somehow felt comfortable sharing all my crazy history with him?

Oh my gosh. I was so in love it hurt.

I pressed my fingers into my chest. *You've known him like five days. There's no way you can be in love with him.* Totally rational.

Totally not true.

Of course I was in love with Ren. He was exactly himself, and I was exactly *my*self when I was with him. And all of that would be perfect if he felt even close to the same. But he didn't. I glanced over at him, and a flash of pain moved through me. Was he even going to talk to me again?

The cabdriver was eyeing us in his rearview mirror. *"Tutto bene?"*

"Si," Ren answered.

Finally the driver swerved to pull up to the train station and Ren handed him a wad of cash, then practically jumped out of the cab, me following miserably after him.

We still had to get back to Florence. A whole train ride, and then the scooter ride, and then… *Oh, no.* After that I'd be back in the cemetery. With Howard. I couldn't let myself think ahead that far. It made me feel like I was going to hyperventilate.

Ren slowed down for a second so I could catch up. "Our train leaves in forty-five minutes."

Forty-five minutes. Aka for ever. "Do you want to sit down?"

He shook his head. "I'm going to go get something to eat." *Alone.*

He didn't say it, but I heard it.

I nodded numbly, then walked over to a nearby bank of chairs, falling down in one of the seats. What was *wrong* with me? For one thing, you don't sob all over someone and then immediately try to kiss them. For another, you don't kiss someone who has a girlfriend. A gorgeous one. Even if you thought he *might* be into you.

Had I completely misread him? Had he really been

spending all this time with me because he was just a good friend? What about all the times he'd held my hand or told me he liked me because I was different? Didn't that mean something?

And what about *Matteo*? My father was literally the worst person I'd ever met. I had no doubts my mom had kept me away from him on purpose, so why had she sent me all the clues I needed to find him?

I needed a distraction. I pulled the journal out of my purse, but when I opened it, the words wriggled across the page like bugs. There was no way I'd be able to concentrate. Not when things felt like this.

Ten excruciating minutes later Ren walked up carrying a big bottle of water and a plastic sack. He handed them both to me. "Sandwich. It's prosciutto."

"What's that?"

"Thinly sliced ham. You'll love it." He sat down next to me and I unwrapped the sandwich and took a bite. Of course I loved it. But it was nothing compared to how I felt about Ren.

And yes. I'd totally just compared the only guy I'd ever felt this way about to a ham sandwich.

Ren reclined back in his chair, stretching his legs in front of him and crossing his arms over his chest. I tried to catch his eye, but he just kept staring at his feet.

Finally I exhaled. "Ren, I don't know what to say. I'm really sorry I put you in that situation. It wasn't fair."

"Don't worry about it."

"I mean, I know you have a girlfriend and—"

"Lina, really. Don't worry about it. It's OK."

But it definitely didn't *feel* OK, and there was maybe a cyclone right in the center of my chest. I leaned back in my chair too and closed my eyes, sending him telepathic messages. *Sorry I dragged you to Rome. Sorry I kissed you. Sorry I messed this up.*

Thirty-five minutes without talking.

No, thirty-one. Because we'd had that one horrible exchange and then I'd gone to the bathroom and stared hatefully at myself in the mirror for like two minutes. My eyes were all puffy and I looked destroyed. I *was* destroyed. I'd lost Ren and I was about to lose Howard, too. There was no other choice. I had to make sure Howard knew he wasn't my father, no matter how badly I wished that he were.

"Train's here," Ren said, standing up. He headed for the platform and I followed after him. *Ninety more minutes.* I could do this, right?

The train was crowded, and it took us several minutes to find a seat. Finally we found two empty spots across from a large older woman who'd put a bunch of plastic bags in the space between us. A man took the seat next to her and Ren nodded at them, sliding into the window seat, then closing his eyes again.

I took the journal out of my bag and wiped it on my jeans, hoping to get rid of any lingering Matteo cooties. Time to dive back into the story. I had to get my mind off of Ren.

JUNE 3

Tonight Howard let me know in his gentle way that he knew about X all along. It made me feel ridiculous. Here I thought we were so sneaky, but it turns out most everyone knew. I found myself telling him everything about the relationship — even the bad parts. And there were a lot of bad parts. The problem was that when things were good with X, they were SO good that I forgot about all the rest. It was such a relief to talk about it, and afterward Howard and I went out onto the porch and talked about other things until the stars came out. I feel the most peaceful that I have in a long time.

JUNE 5

Today I am twenty-two. I woke up this morning with absolutely no expectations, but Howard was waiting for me with a gift — a thin gold ring that he bought from a secondhand shop in Florence almost a year ago. He said he didn't know why he bought it; he just loved it.

The thing I love about it most is that it has history. The man who sold it said it belonged to an aunt of his who had fallen in love but was forced by her family to join a convent. Her lover had given her the ring and she'd worn it secretly her entire life. Howard said the shopkeeper made up a story to add some value to the piece, but it really is pretty and somehow fits perfectly. I was feeling exhausted, so instead of going out to dinner tonight like we'd planned, we stayed in and watched old movies. I barely even made it through the first one.

JUNE 6

Tonight Howard and I were sitting on the swing on the front porch, my feet in his lap, and he asked me a question: "If you could photograph anything in the world, what would it be?" Before I could even think about it I blurted out "hope." I know, cheesy, right? But I mean hope as in <u>stillness</u>, those moments when you just know that things are going to work out. It's the perfect description of my time here. I feel like I've hit the snooze button, and I'm taking a breath before I face whatever comes next. I know that my time is slowly ticking down here, but I don't want it to end.

JUNE 7

I want to record every minute of what happened today. Howard woke me up just before five a.m. and told me he wanted to show me something. We hiked back behind the cemetery, me half-asleep and wearing pajamas. It was still gray out, and it felt like we walked for hours. Then finally I saw where we were going. Ahead in the distance was a small round tower. It was old-looking and completely on its own, like something that was waiting to be discovered.

Once we got to it, Howard led me to the entrance. There was a small wooden door that had probably been put there to keep out trespassers, but had broken down with time and weather. He moved it out of our way, and then we both ducked under the doorway and followed a spiral staircase out to the top of the tower. We were just high enough to get a view of everything around us, and I could see the tops of the cemetery's trees and the road that leads to Florence. I asked him what we were doing there, and he told me to just wait. And so we did. We stood there without talking as the sun rose in the most amazing pinks and golds, and before long the whole countryside was awash in color. I felt this sudden ache — it had been cold and dark for so long, and then suddenly, slowly, it wasn't.

When it was full daylight I turned around. Howard was watching me, and it was like I was suddenly seeing him for the first time. I walked over to him and suddenly we were kissing like we'd kissed a million times before. Like it was the most obvious thing in the world. When he finally pulled back we didn't say a word. I just took his hand and we went home.

JUNE 8

I keep thinking about what it was like to be with X. When I had his attention it was like a spotlight was shining on me and everything in the world was right. But the second he looked away I was cold and alone. I tried to find the word for "fickle" in Italian, and the closest I came up with was "volubile." It means "turning, whirling, winding." I was attracted to that whirlwind feeling with X, but it also left me feeling uprooted. I thought I wanted caprice and fire, but it turns out that what I really want is someone who will wake me up early so I don't miss a sunrise. What I really want is Howard. And now I have him.

JUNE 10

Francesca came for a visit yesterday. Maybe I'm just not used to her anymore, but in the course of three weeks she'd somehow managed to become an exaggerated version of herself. Her stilettos were a half-inch taller, her clothes were even more fashionable, and she was smoking a record amount of cigarettes.

After dinner we sat around talking. I thought Howard and I were doing a great job of hiding this new thing between us, but as soon as he went to bed Francesca said, "So it happened." I tried to play dumb, but she said, "Please, Hadley. Don't patronize me. I don't know why you think you have to keep all your relationships secret. I could tell the second I walked in that something had happened between the two of you. Now tell me all the details. Subito!"

I told her about the past few weeks — how peaceful and healing they've been. And then I told her about the morning at the tower and how perfect everything has felt for the past few days. When I finished she sighed dramatically. "It's like a _favola_, Hadley. A fairy story. You've fallen in love for real. So now what will you do? Aren't you returning to America?" Of course I had no answers for her. I've submitted my portfolio to several schools and should hear back from most of them by the end of summer. Yesterday, on a whim, I asked Petrucione if he'd ever consider hiring me as an assistant teacher, but he silenced me with one look and then told me I was too talented to waste any more time.

That's when Francesca told me. At first all she said was, "He contacted me." I asked who, but by the way my heart was beating I knew who she meant. "He found me working on a set in Rome. His excuse was to congratulate me on my internship, but I knew the real reason. He wanted to find you." For a moment I couldn't think of a single thing to say. (He was trying to find _me_?) "He said that you'd changed your phone number and now that you're no longer enrolled at the institute, your school e-mail doesn't work." I'd never considered that I might be unreachable. I had about a million thoughts running through my mind, and Francesca was watching me carefully. "I didn't give him your information, but I took his. Hadley, I think it would be a mistake, but I didn't want to play God. If you want to contact him I have his new phone number. He said he's had a change of heart. That he has something he wants to tell you." Then she handed me a business card. His name was embossed on it in large letters and his new phone number and e-mail were spelled out like a trail of bread crumbs.

That night I could hardly sleep, but it wasn't because I was conflicted. It was because I was so sure. X could appear on a white stallion carrying a dozen roses and a perfectly crafted apology, and I still wouldn't want him. I want Howard.

———～———

"How's the journal?"

I looked up. Ren's expression was way more relaxed than it had been at the station, and my heart sprouted a tiny pair of wings. *Forgiven?* I tried to meet his eye, but he looked away again.

I dropped my gaze. "It's OK. And I was really wrong about something."

"What?"

"Howard wasn't just the rebound. She fell in love with him." I tilted the journal so he could see the page I'd been looking at. "What does this mean?"

After the entry about Francesca's visit there was an entire page scribbled with the words *"sono incinta"* over and over.

"*Sono incinta.* It means 'I'm pregnant.'"

"That's what I thought."

I looked sadly at the page. I know it pretty much meant self-annihilation, but I almost wished she weren't pregnant. Her fairy tale had just blown up.

Chapter 22

JUNE 11

<u>Sono incinta. Sono incinta. Sono incinta.</u> Would it feel different if those words were in English? I'M PREGNANT. There. I can barely think. This morning I puked up my breakfast like I have every day for the past week, and as I was flushing the toilet a horrible thought occurred to me. I tried to brush it off, but then ... I had to know. I've always been sort of irregular, but had I been more irregular than normal? I walked to the pharmacy but forgot my English-Italian dictionary and had to go through this horrible pantomime to tell them what I needed, and then I rushed home and took the test and — positive. I went back for two more. Positive. Positive.

They were all positive.

JUNE 13

For the past two days I've barely come out of my room.
Francesca left yesterday, and now every time Howard knocks
on my door I pretend to be asleep. I know I need to leave
here. Howard loves me. And I love him. But that doesn't
matter anymore, because I'm pregnant with someone else's
baby. I know I have to tell X, but the thought of it makes
me want to die. What will he say? According to Francesca
he's been looking for me, but I know for a fact that he
wasn't looking for this. And the timing is so unbelievable.
Is it a sign that Matteo and I were meant to be together?
But then what about this time with Howard? Three days
ago I wrote that he was the one for me. And now <u>this</u>.

I want to tell Howard so badly, but what do I say? I
have called my mother and hung up twice. I keep dialing
Matteo's phone number but only getting a few digits in.
I'm giving myself until tomorrow night and then I have to
decide something. I can't even think.

JUNE 14

I called Matteo. He's working in Venice and I'm going there
to meet him. I can't tell him over the phone.

JUNE 15

I'm on the train now. Howard insisted on giving me a ride

there, and even though I didn't tell him why I was going, I think he knew. Tears just kept running down my face, and the last thing he said was, "It's OK. Please be happy."

As soon as the train pulled away I started crying so hard that everyone around me stared. I've gone over this again and again in my mind, and everything points to Matteo. I'm having his child. I have to put Howard out of my mind. I have chosen Matteo. <u>Fate</u> has chosen Matteo. Our baby has chosen Matteo. He has to be the one.

JUNE 15 – LATER

Venice might be the worst place in the world for a pregnant woman. Of course it's beautiful. One hundred and seventeen islands connected by boats and water taxis and those striped-shirt gondoliers paddling tourists around for ridiculous fees. The Floating City. But it smells horrible, and the water lapping against everything makes me feel like I'm going to topple over at any second. As soon as the train arrived I dried my tears, then forced myself to eat a salty piece of foccacia bread. One hour until Matteo and I meet. One hour until he knows. I read that Venice is sinking into the ocean, an inch and a half every century. What if I sink with it?

JUNE 16

We met in Piazza San Marco. As soon as I'd gotten my bearings I left Venice's train station and went straight to the piazza. I was early, so I walked around looking at the Basilica of St Mark. The Basilica is so different from Florence's Duomo. It's Byzantine-style with lots of arches and a flashy mosaic on the exterior. Part of the piazza had flooded and there were tourists rolling up their pants and wading through the water.

Finally it was five p.m. I realized we hadn't said where to meet, so I just walked into the center of the piazza. Pigeons were everywhere, and I just kept seeing children. A little boy with dark hair and eyes ran past me shouting something, and my first thought was <u>How clever, he speaks Italian so well.</u> Will I have a child that speaks a language I hardly understand?

And then I saw Matteo. (Why call him X anymore?) He was walking toward me in a suit, his jacket in one hand and a bouquet of yellow roses in the other. I just watched him for a moment, feeling everything that this moment meant. Then, before I could say anything, he scooped me up in his arms and pressed his face into my hair. He just said over and over, "I've missed you, I've missed you," and feeling his arms warm and solid around me, I closed my eyes and exhaled for the first time since I found out I'm pregnant. He isn't perfect. But he's mine.

JUNE 17

I still haven't told him. I'm waiting for everything to feel natural between us again. He has been incredibly kind and gentle with me, and we've been spending most of our time walking through the streets of Venice. He is renting a small apartment with a view of a canal, and every half hour or so a gondolier passes below, usually singing to his passengers. Matteo told me he knew he'd made a mistake the second my train pulled away in Rome. He said he saw me everywhere — once he followed a woman who looked like me for half a block before realizing it couldn't have been me. He said he couldn't concentrate and that he'd started spending hours studying the photographs he'd taken when he was with me. He said I'd inspired some of his best work.

He invited me to stay in his apartment with him, but I booked a room in an inexpensive hotel. It's run by an older woman and has just three bedrooms that all share one bathroom. There are lace doilies covering everything and I feel like I'm staying at an elderly relative's house. I haven't taken a photograph in more than three days, which may be a record for me. My mind is just too full. Tomorrow I'll tell him about the baby. Tomorrow.

JUNE 18

I have to write this. It's ugly and brutal, but it happened and I can't leave it out.

I took Matteo to dinner at this gorgeous little restaurant near my hotel. It was candlelit and quiet and absolutely everything about the moment was perfect, except when it came time to tell him. I couldn't get the words out of my mouth. Once the bill came, I asked if he'd like to go back to my hotel with me.

My room was messy — my clothes and photography equipment were everywhere — but at least it was quiet and private, and when we stepped into the room I told him to have a seat. He sat down on my bed and then he pulled me so I was sitting next to him. He said he'd been thinking about something for a long time and he believed it was time for us to take the next step.

My heart started beating so fast. Was he proposing? Then I looked down at my hand and panicked. I was still wearing Howard's ring. Would I just have to take it off? Can you say yes to someone when you're wearing someone else's ring? But instead of pulling out a diamond, Matteo laid out what basically amounted to a business plan. He said he's tired of making almost no money working for schools, and he wants to start his own business, leading retreats for English-speaking photographers who want to spend time in Italy. He's already booked two tours and he said I'd make the perfect addition. I could help organize travel and accommodations, and once I have a little more experience I could teach photography as well. Then he put his arms around me and said he'd been an idiot to let me out of his sight. It was time for us to join our lives together.

I hadn't let him kiss me until then, and as soon as his lips were on mine the only thought I had was <u>Howard</u>. And that's when I knew things would never work out with Matteo. Pregnant or not, I love Howard. You can't be in another relationship when you feel that way. So I pulled away from Matteo and blurted out the two words I'd come to tell him.

The words hung heavy in the air. And then he jumped up like the bed had burned him. "What do you mean, <u>pregnant</u>? How did this happen? We've been broken up for two months." I explained that it must have happened just before he left and I hadn't known until earlier this week.

That's when he freaked out. He started yelling, calling me a liar and saying there was no way this baby was his. He said I'd gotten pregnant by someone else — probably Howard — and now I was just trying to pin it on him. He started grabbing all my stuff and throwing it around the room — my camera, pictures, clothes, everything. I tried to calm him down, but then he threw a glass bottle at the wall, and when he turned and looked at me, I was suddenly very afraid.

So I lied. I told him he was right, that the baby wasn't his, it was Howard's, and that I never wanted to see him again. I was telling him what I thought he wanted to hear, but it made him even angrier. He said he was going to ruin both of us and that Howard would regret ever coming

near me. Finally he shoved past me, then kicked the door
open and was gone.

———❦———

The ring. The denial. The lie.

I was finally getting a clear picture of my mother's life –
like up until now I'd been looking through a fogged-up
window and hadn't even known it. I'd had no *idea* she'd been
through so much heartache. Honestly, she was freakishly
cheerful. Like once our upstairs neighbor left the bathtub
running and when it flooded our apartment and ruined a
bunch of our stuff, my mom just pulled out a mop and started
talking about how awesome it was that we could clear out the
room and start fresh.

Had that bouncy, count-your-blessings attitude I'd grown
up with just been some kind of elaborate PR campaign? Had
she been afraid I'd find out what her pregnancy had forced
her to give up?

I closed the journal. I was pretty sure that if I tried
to keep going I'd have another massive breakdown, and
this time I didn't think even Ren could pull me out of it.
And besides, there was no point in reading any more. No
matter what my mom did next – flew by hot-air balloon
back to Florence, spelled out HADLEY LOVES HOWARD in
hundred-foot letters across Piazza del Duomo, sent him
a handful of love letters via Venice's plentiful pigeons – it
wasn't going to work out. Period. She was going to end up
living the rest of her life six thousand miles away with only
a slim gold ring to remind her of what she'd lost.

Oh, and me. Otherwise known as the world's most inconvenient souvenir.

I leaned back and closed my eyes, feeling the tiny back-and-forth movements of the train jostling on the track. I was approximately one hundred miles from a man who was about to get his world turned upside down and six inches from another who wanted nothing to do with me.

I literally wanted to be anywhere else.

When our train arrived in Florence it was after four o'clock. Ren had dozed off again, and his phone kept vibrating spastically on the seat next to him like some kind of giant bug. Finally I leaned over and took a look. Text message from Mimi. *Ouch.* Was he going to tell her about me kissing him? If so, I'd better brush up on my street-fighter moves. I was going to need them.

Ren opened his eyes. "Here?"

"Here. Your phone's been going off."

"Thanks."

He checked his messages, his hair hooding his eyes. As everyone around us gathered up their stuff, I picked up the journal and held it tightly in my hands. It had been one of the longest days of my life and I felt like I was wrapped up in a big, sad cocoon. I couldn't believe I had to add to it by going back to the cemetery and telling Howard what I knew.

The ride back to the cemetery was silent. Brutally silent. Everyone we passed seemed to be in the middle of a lively conversation, which made the blank space between Ren and me even more painful. I was pretty much a wreck. But I was angry, too. Yes, I'd messed up, but did that mean we couldn't even be friends anymore? And why did I have to meet Matteo and lose Ren all in one day? Don't most people get the luxury of spreading their life's drama over a couple of years?

When we finally pulled up to the cemetery a big bus of people was unloading in the parking lot, and they all stared at us like we were part of the attraction. Howard stepped out of the visitors' center and waved to us.

At the sight of him my insides froze and then shattered, but I managed to wave back. Even smile. What was he going to say?

"To the house?" Ren asked.

"Yeah."

He zipped up the road and a few seconds later pulled into the driveway, then turned off the scooter.

I climbed off the back and handed him my helmet. "Thanks for helping me, Ren. It wasn't great, but at least now I have some answers."

"Happy to." It was quiet, and we looked at each other for a moment. Then he looked down, starting up the scooter again. "I hope everything goes OK with Howard. It's going to be all right. He really cares about you."

His voice sounded like *good-bye* and I felt my throat tighten. "Maybe we could go running tomorrow?"

He didn't answer. Instead he walked the scooter around in a circle so he was facing the road and gave me a little nod. "*Ciao*, Lina."

And then he was gone.

Chapter 23

"SO EXPLAIN THIS TO ME AGAIN. HOWARD ISN'T YOUR father; he just thinks he is?"

"Yes. Or at least I *think* he thinks he's my father."

"You *think* he thinks he's your father?"

"Yes. Either that or he's lying. But I'm kind of leaning toward the former, because it's not like people are super-eager to take in random teenagers. Even if you did love their mother."

"But Howard isn't your father? It's that Matteo guy?"

"*Yes.*" I flopped back on my bed, holding my phone to my ear. We'd been going over this for like twenty minutes now. "Addie, I don't know how else to explain this to you."

"Just give me a second. It's not like it's complicated or anything."

"I know. Sorry." I covered my eyes. "And I still haven't told you the worst part."

"Worse than meeting your horrible jerk of a father?"

"Yes." I took a deep breath. "I kissed Ren."

"You kissed Ren? Your friend?"

"Yeah."

"OK... Well, what's so bad about that?"

"He didn't want to kiss me back."

"No way. Why?"

"He has a girlfriend, and we'd just met Matteo and I was having this big breakdown, which was like the most inconvenient moment to realize how I really felt about him. So then I like jumped on him and he kind of" – I cringed – "pushed me off him."

"He *pushed you off him*?"

"Yeah. And we were still in Rome, so then we had to take a train all the way back to Florence and he didn't talk to me like at all. So to sum things up, I'm all alone in Italy, I have to break the news to Howard that he isn't my father, and now I don't even have a friend."

"Oh, Lina. And to think, ten minutes ago I was jealous of you." She sighed. "What about what's-his-name? Underwear model?"

"Thomas?" *Crap. His text.* "He messaged me earlier and asked me out. Some big party for a girl who graduated from the school."

"Are you going?"

"Probably not. I mean, who knows what's going to happen once I tell Howard. For all I know he's going to kick me out."

"He's not going to kick you out. That's ridiculous."

"I know." I sighed. "But I doubt he's going to be very happy. I mean, how weird is all this? Honestly, I wish he were my father."

Words I never thought I'd utter.

Addie was quiet for a moment. "When are you going to tell him?"

"I don't know. He's still working, but he wants to go to a movie tonight. If I can work up my courage I'll tell him as soon as he gets home."

She exhaled. "OK, here's the plan. I'm going upstairs right now to ask my parents if you can move back in. No, I'm going up to *tell* them you need to move back in. And don't worry. They'll say yes."

I spent the next hour pacing around my room. I kept picking up the journal to examine the sliver of pages I still had left to read, but every time I tried to open it I ended up dropping it like I was playing hot potato. Once I read that last entry, it was over. I'd never hear anything new from her again. And I'd know just how badly she'd gotten her heart broken.

I kept going over to the window to watch for Howard, but he and the tour were moving across the grounds like garden slugs. Did they have to stop at *every* statue? And what was so interesting about that corner of the cemetery versus this corner? By the time they finished learning about WWII, WWIII would probably be done and over. Finally, when I thought I couldn't stand one more second of waiting, Howard led the group back to the visitors' parking lot and waited as they boarded the tour bus.

"You ready?" I whispered to myself.

Of course I wasn't.

Howard walked into the visitors' center, and then he and Sonia both came out and started walking toward the house.

Oh, no. I couldn't tell him with Sonia around. Was I going to have to sit on this all night? When they got to the driveway I took the stairs two at a time down to the living room and met them on the front porch.

"There you are," Howard said. "How's your day been?"

Horrifying. "It's been … OK."

He was wearing a light blue button-up with the sleeves rolled up and his nose was sunburned. Something I'd never experienced. You know, because I was *Italian.*

"I tried calling your phone earlier, but there was no answer. If we're going to make it to the movie, we'll have to go now."

"Right now?"

"Yes. Is Ren coming?"

"No. He … can't make it." How was I going to get out of this?

Sonia smiled. "They're playing a really old movie tonight, a classic with Audrey Hepburn. Have you heard of *Roman Holiday?*"

"No, I haven't." *And could everyone please just stop talking about Rome?*

Under normal circumstances I probably would have enjoyed *Roman Holiday.* It's a black-and-white movie about this European princess who is doing a world tour, but her schedule and handlers are superstrict, so one night when she's staying in Rome she sneaks out her bedroom window to go have some fun. The only problem is that she'd taken a sedative earlier in the night and so she passes out on a park bench and an American reporter rescues her. They end up exploring the city together and falling in love, except then they don't end up together, because she has too many other demands.

I know. Depressing.

I only half watched it because I couldn't stop looking at Howard. He had this big, booming laugh and he kept leaning over to tell me the names of places Audrey and her love interest were visiting. He even bought me a giant bag of candy, and even though I ate all of it I barely tasted it. It might have been the longest two hours of my life.

On the way back Sonia insisted I sit in the front. "So what did you think of the movie?"

"It was cute. Sad, though."

Howard glanced back at Sonia. "You still meeting up with Alberto tonight?"

"Argh. Yes."

"Why argh?"

"You know why. I swore off blind dates years ago."

"Don't think of it as a blind date. Think of it as going out for drinks with someone I really admire."

"Anyone but you and I'd say no." She sighed. "But then again, what's the worst that could happen? I've always said that a terrible date in Florence is better than a good date anywhere else."

Suddenly I realized I knew absolutely nothing about her. "Sonia, how did you end up in Florence?

"Came here on vacation the summer after grad school and fell in love. It didn't last, but it got me to plant some roots here."

I groaned inwardly. Maybe that was just part of the Italian experience. Come to Italy. Fall in love. Watch everything blow up in your face. You could probably read about it on travel websites.

Sonia met my eyes in the mirror. "You know, people come to Italy for all sorts of reasons, but when they stay, it's for the same two things."

"What?"

"Love and gelato."

"Amen," Howard said.

I looked out my window and put all my attention on keeping the tears from seeping out from under my eyelids. Just gelato wasn't going to cut it. I wanted the love part too.

When we got back to the cemetery Howard dropped Sonia off at her house, then circled back to ours. The headlights swept eerily across the headstones, and the combination of candy and nerves was making me absolutely sick to my stomach.

We were finally alone. It was time to tell him. I took a deep breath. I'd start talking in three ... two ... two ... two...

Howard broke the silence. "I wanted to tell you again how much it means to me to have you here. I know this hasn't been easy, but I really appreciate you giving it a try. Even if it's just for the summer. And I think you're great. I really do. I'm proud of you for jumping in and exploring Florence. You're an adventurer, just like your mom." Then he smiled at me, like I was the daughter he'd always hoped to have, and my remaining courage melted like an ice cube in the heat.

I couldn't tell him. Not tonight.

Maybe not ever.

When we got inside I made some lame excuse about another headache, then trudged up to my room and threw myself on my bed. I did a lot of throwing myself on the bed these days. But what was I going to do? I couldn't tell Howard, but I also couldn't *not* tell him.

Would it be so awful if I just stayed the rest of the summer and then went home without telling him? But then what about when Father's Day rolled around and he expected a card from me? Or what about when I got married and he thought he was the guy who was supposed to walk me down the aisle? What then?

My phone starting ringing and I jumped off my bed and crossed the room in two flying leaps. *Please be Ren. Please be Ren, please be—*

Thomas.

"Hello?"

"Hi, Lina. This is Thomas."

"Hey." I caught a glimpse of myself in the mirror. I looked like a puffer fish. Who'd suffered some kind of emotional breakdown.

"Did you get my text?"

"Yes. Sorry I didn't answer. Today's been kind of ... crazy."

"No problem. What do you think about the party? Do you want to come with me?"

His voice was so uncomplicatedly British. And he was talking about a *party*. Like it mattered. I ran my hand through my hair. "What is it exactly?"

"Eighteenth birthday party for one of the girls who just graduated. She lives in the coolest place – almost as big as Elena's. Everyone will be there."

"Everyone" as in Ren and Mimi? I shut my eyes. "Thanks

for asking me, but I don't think I'll be able to make it."

"Oh, come on. You *have* to celebrate with me. I passed my driver's test yesterday, and my dad said I could pick you up in his BMW. And you really don't want to miss this party. Her parents hired an indie band I've been listening to for more than a year."

I tucked the phone between my ear and shoulder and rubbed my eyes. After everything that had happened today, a party seemed laughably normal. Also, it seemed weird to go out with someone when I'd clearly fallen for someone else. But what do you do when your "someone else" wants nothing to do with you? At least Thomas was still *talking* to me.

"Let me think about it."

Thomas exhaled. "All right. You think about it. I'd pick you up at nine. And it's formal, so you'd need to dress up. I promise you'll have a good time."

"Formal. Got it. I'll call you tomorrow."

We hung up and I tossed my phone on the bed, then walked over to the window and looked out. It was a clear night and the moon winked at me like a giant eye. Like it had been watching this whole complicated story play out, and now it was having the last laugh.

Stupid moon. I put both hands on the window sash and practically threw myself on top of it, but the window wouldn't budge.

Fine.

Chapter 24

THE NEXT MORNING I WOKE JUST BEFORE DAWN. I'D passed out on my bed fully dressed, and there was a dish of spaghetti perched on the edge of my dresser, the tomato sauce pooled in oily clumps. Guess Howard had tried to bring me dinner.

Gray hazy light was filtering through my window, and I got up and walked quietly over to my suitcase, rummaging around for some clean running clothes. Then I picked up the journal and crept silently through the house, leaving through the back door.

I made my way toward the back gate. Not even the birds were up yet and dew covered everything like a big, gauzy spiderweb. My mom was right. The cemetery looked completely different at different times of day. Predawn cemetery was sort of muted-looking, like gray had been swirled in with the rest of the colors.

I went through the back gate, then broke into a run, passing where I'd met Ren for the first time. *Don't. Think. About. Ren.* It was my new mantra. Maybe I'd have it printed on a bumper sticker.

I shook the thought out of my head, then took in a deep breath, settling on a medium pace. The air was crisp and clean-smelling, like what laundry detergents are probably going for with their "mountain air" scents, and I was crazy relieved to be running. At least now it wasn't just my mind that was in overdrive.

One mile. Then two. I was following a narrow little footpath worn into the grass by someone who had made this route a habit, but I had no idea if their destination was the same as mine. For all I knew, I was headed in the complete wrong direction. Maybe it didn't even exist anymore, and then – BAM. The tower. Jutting out of the hill like a wild mushroom. I stopped running and stared at it for a minute. It was like stumbling across something magical, like a pot of gold, or a gingerbread house in the middle of Tuscany.

Don't think about gingerbread houses.

I started running again, feeling my heart quicken even more as I neared the tower's dark silhouette. It was a perfect cylinder, gray and ancient-looking and only about thirty feet tall. It looked like the kind of place where people had been falling in love for years.

I ran right up to the base, then put my hand on the wall, trailing it behind me as I circled around to the opening. The wooden door Howard had moved for my mom was long gone, leaving a bare arched doorway that was so short I had to duck to walk under it. Inside it was empty except for a couple of shaggy spiderwebs and a pile of leaves that had probably outlasted the tree they'd come from. A crumbly spiral staircase rose through the tower's center, letting a pale circle of light into the room.

I took a deep breath, then headed for the staircase. Hopefully all my answers were at the top.

I had to walk carefully – half the steps looked like they were just waiting for an excuse to collapse – and I had to do this acrobatic hurtle over the space where the final step had once been, but finally I stepped outside. The top of the tower was basically an open platform, its circumference lined by a three-foot ledge, and I made my way over to the edge. It was still pretty dark and gray out, but the view was stunning. Like postcard stunning. To my left was a vineyard with rows of grapevines stretching out in thin silvery ropes, and everywhere else was rich Tuscan countryside, the occasional house marooned like a ship in the middle of an ocean of hills.

I sighed. No wonder this had been the place my mom had finally noticed Howard. Even if she hadn't already fallen for his sense of humor and awesome taste in gelato, she probably would have taken one look at the view and gone completely out of her mind with love. It was the sort of place that could make a stampede of buffalos seem romantic.

I set the journal down on the ground, then slowly made my way around the platform, scanning every inch of it. I *really* wanted to find some sign of my mom, a stone scratched with H+H or maybe some lost journal pages she'd tucked under a rock or something, but all I found were two spiders that looked at me with about as much interest as a pair of British Royal Guards.

I gave up on my little scavenger hunt and walked back to the center of the platform, wrapping my arms around myself. I needed a question answered, and I got the feeling this was the best place to ask.

"Mom, why did you send me to Italy?" My voice threw off the quiet peacefulness of everything around me, but I shut my eyes tight to listen.

Nothing.

I tried again. "Why did you send me to be with Howard?"

Still nothing. Then the wind picked up and made a whipping noise through the grass and trees, and suddenly all the loneliness and emptiness I carried around with me swelled up so big it swallowed me whole. I pressed my palms to my eyes, pain ricocheting through my body. What if my mom and my grandma and the counselor were wrong? What if I hurt this badly for the rest of my life? What if every second of every day would be less about what I had than what I'd lost?

I sank to the floor, pain washing over me in big, jagged waves. She'd told me over and over how wonderful my life was going to be. How proud she was of me. How much she wished she could be there, not just for the big moments, but for the little ones. And then she'd said she'd find a way to stay close to me. But so far, she'd just been gone. Then gone some more. And all that gone stretched out in front of me like a horizon, endless and daunting and empty. I'd been running around Italy trying to solve the mystery of the journal, trying to understand why she'd done what she'd done, but really I'd just been looking for her. And I wasn't going to find her. Ever.

"I can't do this," I said aloud, pressing my face into my hands. "I can't be here without you."

And that's when I got slapped. Well, maybe not slapped – it

was more like a nudging – but suddenly I was getting to my feet because a word was pushing itself into my brain.

Look.

I shaded my eyes. The sun was rising over the hills, heating up the undersides of the clouds and setting them on fire in crazy shades of pink and gold. Everything around me was bright and beautiful and suddenly very clear.

I didn't get to stop missing her. Ever. It was the thing that my life had handed me, and no matter how heavy it was, I was never going to be able to set it down. But that didn't mean I wasn't going to be OK. Or even happy. I couldn't imagine it yet exactly, but maybe a day would come when the hole inside me wouldn't ache quite so badly and I could think about her, and remember, and it would be all right. That day felt light-years away, but right at this moment I was standing on a tower in the middle of Tuscany and the sunrise was so beautiful that it hurt.

And that was something.

I picked up the journal. It was time to finish.

JUNE 19

<u>Every new beginning comes from some other beginning's end.</u> I had that song lyric written on a piece of paper above my desk for almost a year, and only today does it actually mean anything to me. I've spent the entire afternoon wandering the streets and thinking, and a few things have become clear.

First, I have to leave Italy. Last September I met an American woman who's trapped in a terrible marriage because Italian law says that children stay with the father. I doubt Matteo will ever want anything to do with our baby, but I can't take that chance.

And second, I can't tell Howard how I feel about him. He thinks I've already chosen someone else, and he needs to keep thinking that. Otherwise he'll leave behind the life he's created for himself for a chance to start things with me. I want that so badly, but not enough to let him give up his dream of living and working in the middle of so much beauty. It's what he deserves.

So there it is. In loving Howard, I have to leave him. And to protect my child, I have to put as much distance between her and her father as possible. (Yes, I think it's a girl.)

If I could go back to one moment — just one — I would be back at the tower, a whole world of possibility ahead of me. And even though my heart hurts more than I ever thought it could, I wouldn't take back that sunrise or this baby for anything. This is a new chapter. My life. And I'm going to run at it with arms outstretched. Anything else would be a waste.

The End. The rest of the journal was blank. I slowly turned to the front cover and read that first sentence one more time.

I made the wrong choice.

Sonia had been wrong. My mom hadn't sent the journal to the cemetery for me – she'd sent it for Howard. She'd wanted him to know what had really happened and tell him that she'd loved him all along. And then, even though she couldn't go back and change their story, she'd done the next best thing.

She'd sent me.

Chapter 25

I PRACTICALLY FLEW BACK TO THE CEMETERY. I WAS incredibly nervous, but I felt light, too. No matter what Howard's reaction was, it was going to be OK. And he deserved to read her story. Right this second.

Daylight had totally transformed the cemetery, taking it from washed-out to vibrant, and I ran diagonally across the grounds, cutting through a batch of headstones and ignoring my blossoming side ache. I had to catch Howard before he started working.

He was sitting on the porch with a cup of coffee, and when he saw me he stood up in alarm. "You aren't being chased again, are you?"

I shook my head, then came to a stop, struggling to catch my breath.

"Oh, good." He sat back down. "Do you always sprint? I thought you were more into long-distance running."

I shook my head again, then took a deep breath. "Howard, I have to ask you something."

"What?"

"Do you know you're not my father?"

For a few long seconds my words hung in the space between us like a bunch of shimmering soap bubbles. Then he smiled.

"Define 'father.'"

My legs gave out and I stumbled toward the porch.

"Whoa, whoa. You OK?" He put his hand out to steady me.

"Just let me sit down." I fell to a seat on the porch step next to him. "And you know what I mean by 'father.' I mean the man who gave me half my DNA."

He stretched his legs out long in front of him. "Well, in that case, no. I'm not your father. But if you go with another definition, meaning 'a man who wants to be in your life and help raise you,' then yes. I am."

I groaned. "Howard, that's sweet and everything, but explain yourself. Because I have spent the last twenty-four hours completely confused and worried about hurting you, and you've known all along?"

"I'm sorry about that. I didn't know you had any idea." He looked at me for a moment, then sighed. "All right. You up for a story?"

"Yes."

He settled in, like he was about to tell a story he'd told a million times. "When I was twenty-five I met a woman who changed everything for me. She was bright and vibrant and whenever I was with her I felt like I could do anything."

"You mean my mom, right?"

"Let me finish. So I met this woman, and I fell completely head over heels in love with her. I'd never felt that way about anyone before – it was like I'd been looking for her all along and just hadn't realized it. I knew I had to do everything in my power to make her feel the same way, so I started by being her friend. I took an Italian class I didn't need just so I'd have some extra time with her—"

"The beginners' class?"

"Shh. Lina, listen. We took Italian together, I sat in on the rest of her classes, and I even worked my way into her circle of friends. But every time I tried to summon the courage to tell her how I felt, I turned into a blob of Jell-O."

"A blob of Jell-O?" I said incredulously.

"Yes. You know, the gelatin—"

"I know what Jell-O is!" Apparently "good guy" does not equal "good storyteller."

"What I mean by that is that I liked her so much it literally tongue-tied me. And then I found out I was too late. While I was bumbling around, carrying her books to class and pretending I liked to go out dancing, some other man had swooped in and carried her off."

"Matteo Rossi."

He flinched. "How do you know his name?"

"I'll tell you later."

He hesitated. "Anyway. I told myself that if this other guy was someone great, someone who really cared about her and made her happy, I would leave it alone. But I knew Matteo, and I knew what he was really like. Unfortunately, your mother was blinded by him for a long time, and even though we tried our hand at a relationship, she ended up choosing him. That's how you came to be – her relationship with Matteo. But when your mom got sick, I was the one she asked to step in. And so I did. Because I loved her." He nudged me. "And you're kind of growing on me too."

I groaned again. "OK, nice story. But you got some of it wrong, and why did you and my grandma tell me you're my father if it isn't true?"

"I can see now that that was wrong, and I'm sorry. I wasn't planning to at first. Your grandmother and I started communicating after Hadley passed, and a few weeks in I realized that your grandmother assumed I was your father. I knew it wasn't true, but I worried that if I told her the truth, she'd change her mind about sending you, and your mother had made me promise to bring you here. I also thought it might be better for you. I thought that if you believed I was your father it would make you more likely to come here and give me a chance."

"Except I was a total brat."

"No. Under the circumstances, you were actually pretty great."

"Liar."

He smiled. "I guess I just didn't know what else to do. Your grandfather was already struggling, and I didn't know what the situation was with Addie's family. I was worried you wouldn't have anywhere to go. So when your grandmother asked if she could tell you that I'm your father, I said yes." He shook his head. "I planned to tell you sooner rather than later, but after that night at the pizzeria, I thought I'd let you settle in first. But you don't seem to be much of the settling-in type. I should have known you'd see right through it."

"You're like twice as tall as me. And you have blond hair. We look nothing alike."

"True." He paused. "So now it's my turn. How long have you known?"

"About a day."

"How did you find out?"

I picked up the journal from the steps and handed it to him. "This."

"Your journal?"

"No, it's my mom's. It's the journal she kept when she was living here."

"This is *her* journal? I noticed it looked similar, but I thought it was just a coincidence." He turned it over in his hands.

"She wrote about everything that happened between her and Matteo. Only for most of it she just called him X, so at first I thought I was reading about you. But then you didn't know about the secret bakery."

"Wait a minute. The secret bakery? The place Ren asked me about?"

"Yeah. He was trying to surprise me by figuring out where it was."

"So Ren knows about all this too?"

"Yes. He actually helped me track down Matteo." I looked away. "We, ah, met him."

He levitated like half a foot. "You *met* him?"

I kept my gaze on the ground. "Uh-huh."

"Where?"

"Rome."

He was looking at me like I'd just told him I was actually half-ostrich. "When did you go to Rome?"

"Yesterday—"

"*Yesterday?*"

"Yeah, we took the express train. First Ren picked me up. Then we went to FAAF and I called Francesca—"

"Francesca Bernardi? How did you even know about her?"

"The journal. She told me what Matteo's last name was and we found him online and went to his art gallery and it was … well, a disaster."

His mouth was literally hanging open. "Please tell me you're joking."

I shook my head. "Sorry. I'm not."

He rubbed his hand across his chin. "OK. So the two of you tracked down Matteo. Then what? Did he know who you were?"

"He made up this story about my mom being crazy and faking her journal. It was ridiculous. I mean, we look exactly alike and he just kept telling me that he'd never had a relationship with her. We ended up just booking it out of there."

Howard blew the air out of his mouth. "Your mother would kill me. Here I thought you and Ren were just out eating gelato and going dancing, but you were tracking down your father in another city?"

"Yes. But I won't do that again," I said hastily. "It was kind of a one-time deal. Unless you're hiding something else from me…"

"Nothing. All my cards are out."

"OK, good."

"But where did you get the journal? Did you find it after your mom passed away?"

"No. Sonia gave it to me."

"*Sonia* Sonia? My Sonia?"

"Yeah. My mom sent it in the mail last September and when it got to the cemetery Sonia was worried it was going to upset you, so she held off for a couple of days. But then you told her about the plan for me to come stay here and she thought my mom had sent it for me. But it wasn't for me. It was for you."

Howard held the book up carefully, like it was a bird he didn't want to fly away.

"You should read it."

"Mind if I start right now?"

"Please do."

He slowly opened the cover, stopping at the sight of that first sentence. "Oh."

"Yeah. I'll leave you alone."

Chapter 26

TWO HOURS LATER HOWARD CAME TO MY BEDROOM door, journal in hand. "I finished."

"That was quick."

"Want to go sit on the porch again?"

"Sure."

I followed him downstairs and we settled ourselves on the porch swing. His eyes were kind of red.

"It was hard for me, reading all of that. I mean, she told me bits of it, but I didn't know the whole story. There were so many misunderstandings. Missed connections." He looked out over the cemetery. "She didn't get everything right. For one thing, I never dated Adrienne."

"You didn't?"

"No. Matteo did."

I looked at him blankly.

"Your mother wasn't the only student Matteo was messing around with."

"Ohhh." Another puzzle piece fell into place. "So is that why you told her the story of the bull and the baker? To tell her to look closer, because Matteo was two-timing her?"

He grimaced. "Yes, but I obviously wasn't very successful. She had no idea what I meant by that story."

"Yeah, that was pretty cryptic. Did you just make that story up?"

"No, it's real. I think it's pretty unlikely that it's true, but it's one of the legends that has been hanging around the city for centuries. I love stuff like that." He shook his head. "Anyway, I knew that your mom was involved with Matteo. She kept it a secret because she was worried he'd get in trouble with the school, but *he* kept it a secret because he was a dirtbag. I knew he'd had at least a few affairs with students, and from what I'd seen of him, I knew he was bad news. I had my suspicions, and then one day I walked in on Adrienne and Matteo in the darkroom. That night when your mom saw us outside the club, I had been confronting her about it. I wanted her to tell your mother."

"Why didn't you just tell her?"

He shook his head. "Everyone but Hadley knew that I was in love with her, and I knew it would just look like I was stirring things up. I was also pretty sure that Matteo would just deny it and then I would lose your mother's trust. Then once they broke up I couldn't see any reason to tell her. Also, I was kind of a coward. The breakup was my fault."

"Why?"

"Your mom was becoming withdrawn and started saying pretty critical things about herself and her work. So one week when Matteo went out of town for a conference, I called him up and told him that if he didn't stay away from her I'd tell the school."

"And that's when he broke up with her?"

"Yes. And then I went ahead and told the school anyway, and they ended up firing him. Hadley was so heartbroken it was like the color had been sucked out of her. I spent weeks wondering if I'd done the right thing." He pushed off, sending the swing gliding. "But then she seemed to get better. I convinced her to spend a summer here with me, and we were together for a while. But then I lost her again."

"Because of me."

He shook his head, gesturing to the cemetery. "She should have told me. I would have walked out on this in a heartbeat."

"That's exactly why she didn't tell you."

"I know." He sighed. "I just wish she'd let me make that decision. One day with Hadley was easily worth a lifetime in Italy."

"Tell me about it." I studied him for a moment. He loved her. Like *really* loved her. And he'd been missing her for even longer than I had. It made me want to throw my arms around him.

I looked away, blinking back tears. Hopefully my eyeballs would dry out one of these days. Otherwise I was going to be offered a job as spokesperson for Kleenex or something.

"Did you ever try to get her back?"

"No. In my mind she'd chosen Matteo. If I'd known the reason why, it would have been a different story. It wasn't until years later that I found out they weren't together and then only recently that I found out about you. I worried a lot about her, but every time I thought about reaching out, it was like something stopped me. Maybe my pride."

"Or just not wanting to get hurt again. She basically smashed your heart to bits."

He chuckled. "Smashed indeed. And of course, I was eventually able to move on. But having you here … well, I've kind of been reliving it."

We were quiet for a minute. The sun had risen full and hot, and my hair was practically sizzling.

He shook his head. "This isn't at all how I'd imagined we'd have this conversation, but I'm glad that things happened the way they did. And now we don't have to worry about Matteo. Your mom was really careful about keeping you away from him, especially once she was successful. She had always wanted to bring you to Italy but was too afraid to until now. I guess you being close to eighteen made her less afraid of Matteo."

"She probably never thought I'd be the one to go looking for him."

"Never. I think she underestimated you." He chuckled. "I think I did too. I can't believe you went to Rome."

"It was stupid."

"Well, that goes without saying. But it was also pretty brave."

"Ren came with me. He helped a lot." My expression fell. *Ren*.

"What?"

"Ren's not … talking to me anymore. I upset him."

Howard's forehead creased. "Did you get in an argument?"

"Something like that."

"I'm sure whatever happened, you two can work it out. He really cares about you. I can tell."

"Maybe." We sat there for a moment, swinging back and forth, when suddenly a thought occurred to me. "Howard, were you trying to tell me something when you told me that weird story about the woman who gave birth to the boar?"

He laughed. "The *porcellino*. I'd better stop doing that. It really doesn't seem to work."

"No."

"All right, yes. I was trying to tell you something. When we went to see the statue I realized it was the perfect symbol. Even though our circumstances are strange, and we're a bit of a mismatch, I really do want to be a part of your life. We may not be a regular kind of family, but if you'll have me, I'll be your family just the same."

I looked up at him and a thousand feelings swelled up inside me until I was as taut and full as a balloon. My mom had been totally right. No one would ever come close to replacing her, but if I had to choose someone, it would be Howard. She'd just been a few steps ahead of me.

"So what do you say, Carolina?"

I hesitated. I didn't want to rush into anything, but I did know that today it felt right. And that was going to have to be enough.

"OK." I nodded. "I'm in if you're in."

He gave me one of his lopsided smiles, then leaned back in the swing. "Good. Well, now that we have all that cleared up, what about this Ren business?"

Chapter 27

HOWARD INSISTED I COULDN'T GIVE UP. IF I WANTED
to see things through, I needed to be good and sure that there
hadn't been some kind of gross miscommunication between
Ren and me.

That's really how he said it. Gross miscommunication.

I shoved my remaining shreds of dignity into the back of
my closet, then called Ren's cell phone. Twice. Both my calls
went straight to voice mail and I did my best to block out the
image of him hitting REJECT.

Finally Howard helped me track down the Ferraras'
number, and I called their house.

"*Ciao*, Lina!" Odette trilled. She obviously hadn't been
filled in on the state of affairs.

"Hi, Odette. Is Ren home?"

"Yes, just a moment." She set the phone down. Then there
were some muffled noises. Finally she picked it up again.

"Lina?"

"Yeah?"

"Ren can't talk right now."

I grimaced. "Could you ask him a question for me?"

"What's that?"

"Is it OK if I come over? I need to talk to him."

There was a pause. "Ren? Why are you shakin—" Then she must have put her hand over the mouthpiece, because I couldn't understand anything else.

It was so unbelievably humiliating. My remaining shreds of dignity caught on fire.

When she came back on the line she sounded confused. "Sorry, Lina. He said he's too busy. He's getting ready to go to Valentina's party."

I perked up. "He's going for sure? It's for the girl who graduated last year, right?"

"Yes. I think it's to celebrate her eighteenth birthday."

At least I'd see him face-to-face. I took a deep breath. It was better than nothing. "Thanks, Odette."

"No problem."

I hung up the phone and sent a quick text to Thomas. Then I booked it all the way to the visitors' center. I needed a favor.

When I came bursting into the visitors' center, Howard and Sonia looked up in alarm. They were both going through a stack of papers and Howard was wearing these tiny old-man reading glasses that made him look like a nearsighted lumberjack. I giggled.

He put his hand on his chest. "Lina! One of these days you're going to give me a heart attack."

"Your glasses are so…"

"So what?" He drew himself up to his full height and I laughed again.

"Just … ignore me. Listen, I really need some help. I'm going to a party tonight and I really need to look amazing. I think it's my best shot at winning Ren back. I need to find The Dress."

He took his glasses off. "The one guaranteed to make anyone fall in love with you?"

"Yes! Exactly. Just like my mom had. Only hopefully I'll actually get to wear it and it will do its job."

"The Dress?" Sonia asked, looking back and forth between us. "I'm sorry, but I'm not following."

Howard turned to her. "Sonia, we'll have to close the cemetery early. Finding a new dress is probably pretty easy, but *The* Dress? It's going to take some time." He winked at me. "And by the way, I remember catching a glimpse of your mother in her version of The Dress. I think I walked into a wall."

Sonia shook her head. "I'm still a little unclear about what we're talking about here, but you know we can't close the cemetery. It's completely against regulations."

"Fine, we won't close it. We'll abandon it for a few hours while the three of us take an emergency shopping trip into Florence."

I bounced up and down. "Thank you! That would be really awesome!"

Sonia still didn't look convinced. "Howard, I'll just stay behind in case any visitors show up."

He shook his head. "No, we're going to need you. You know I'll be completely useless when it comes to shopping. My closet is where things go to die. We need a woman's opinion."

She shuddered. "Your taste is pretty bad. Remember

when I made you get rid of that horrible pair of corduroys? They were sprouting *hairs*."

I clasped my hands in front of my chest. "Please, Sonia. I don't even know where dress stores are, and I'm going to need all the help I can get. I have to look incredible tonight. Will you help me?"

She looked back and forth between Howard and me, then shook her head. "I think you've lost your minds. But all right. Pick me up at my house."

"Yes!" Howard and I high-fived. Then I waited outside while he closed up the visitors' center and we both jogged up the path to the house.

On the way into Florence, Howard and I filled Sonia in on our status as not related—sort of related.

She looked shocked. "You're telling me you're not actually father and daughter?"

"Not technically," I said.

"And, Howard, you've known all along?"

"Yes."

She shook her head, then started fanning herself with her wallet. "Only in Italy."

Howard looked at her. "And, Sonia, in the future please don't redirect any of my deliveries. Although in this case I think it worked out OK."

"Cross my heart. I'll never do anything like that again." She turned around so she was facing me. "What time does Ren pick you up?"

"At nine. But I'm not going with Ren. I'm going with Thomas."

"Oh. But I thought that you and Ren…" She trailed off.

"You thought me and Ren what?"

Howard glanced at Sonia, then met my eyes in the rearview mirror. "You know how in English we say that people wear their hearts on their sleeves? Well, in Italian, you say *'avere il cuore in mano.'* You hold your heart in your hand. Every time Ren looks at you I think of that saying. He's crazy about you."

"No, he isn't."

Sonia chimed in. "Of course he is. And you can't blame him. Look at you. The poor thing can't help himself."

"He has a girlfriend."

"He does?" Howard asked.

I nodded.

"Well, how do you feel about him?"

They both looked at me and I managed to stay quiet for about three seconds before blowing like a volcano.

"Fine. I'm in love with him. I'm completely in love with Ren. Besides Addie, he's the only person I've ever been around who makes me feel normal, and he's hilarious and weird and he has a gap between his front teeth that I love. But none of that matters because he has a girlfriend, and yesterday I must have had a momentary lapse in sanity, because I kissed him and it totally freaked him out. Also, his girlfriend looks straight out of a fashion magazine and whenever Ren sees *me* I'm either sweaty or crying. So now I'm dressing up and going to a party in hopes that I'll get his attention long enough for him to at least talk to me, so I can tell him how I really feel and try to at least salvage our friendship. So there. *That's* how I feel about Ren."

Howard and Sonia both looked stunned.

I slumped back in my seat. "That's why I need the perfect dress."

It was quiet for a moment, and then Sonia turned to Howard. "Is money an object?"

"No."

"Then turn left. I know where we need to go."

Howard drove us straight to a dress shop near the center of the city, and after we'd parked, all three of us got out and ran the three blocks from the parking center. When we burst into the shop, the woman behind the counter looked up in alarm.

"Cos'è successo?"

"Stiamo cercando il vestito più bello nel mondo." He turned to me. "She needs *The* Dress."

The woman studied us for a moment, then clapped her hands. "Adalina! Sara! *Venite qui.*"

Two women emerged from the back room, and after going through the same exchange with Howard, they pulled out their tape measures and started measuring my waist and butt and bust and … yeah. It was pretty embarrassing.

Finally they started grabbing dresses from all over the store, then hustled me over to a dressing room and stuffed me and the dresses inside. I wriggled out of my running clothes and pulled the first one over my head. It was cotton-candy pink and reminded me of the time I'd thrown up on a Ferris wheel. The second one was yellow and feathery and looked suspiciously like Big Bird's carcass. The third wasn't terrible, but the straps were so big they hovered a full inch above my shoulders, and the party was tonight – I couldn't just take it to a tailor for alterations. I looked at myself sternly in the mirror. *Don't panic.* But my hair panicked anyway. Or maybe that was just how it always looked.

"How's it going?" Sonia called from outside.

"Nothing yet."

"Try this one." She tossed another one over the door and I quickly changed into it. White and poofy. I looked exactly like a marshmallow. On her wedding day.

"Oh, no," I wailed. "None of these are right. What if I can't find it?"

"I brought you to this place for a reason. Let me see if the shopkeeper's oldest daughter is around. She's a dress genie. Be right back."

I stepped up to the mirror and looked at myself again. Not only did I not look forgivable, but I looked ridiculous. There was no way I was going to win Ren back looking like something I roasted at Girl Scout camp.

"Lina?" Sonia knocked on the door. Then the door opened and she and another woman stepped in.

The woman was in her late thirties and had her hair pulled up in a bun with a pencil stuck through it. She looked like she meant business. She gestured for me to spin around.

"No. *Tutto sbagliato.*"

"*D'accordo,*" Sonia said. "She says this one is all wrong."

"Will you ask her to find me one that's all right?"

"Don't worry. It's what she's good at. Let her work."

The woman stepped forward, cupping my chin in her hands. She turned my face back and forth, studying my features, then stepped back and motioned for me to do another spin. Finally she nodded and held up her hand. "*Ho il vestito perfetto.* Wait."

When she came back she was holding a pinkish-nude-colored dress with embellished lace all over the top and a short flowy skirt. I took it from her, holding it up in front of me.

"This one?" I asked.

"Yes. Thees one," she said firmly. She stepped out of the room, pulling the door shut behind her.

I took off the marshmallow dress and eased the new one over my head. The fabric was smooth and silky-feeling, and it slipped easily over my chest and hips, landing in the exact right spot.

I didn't even have to look in the mirror to know that it was the one.

By the time Thomas pulled up in his dad's car – a silver BMW convertible – I had managed to completely transform myself. Sonia had helped me style my hair so it fell in soft un-Medusa-ish curls, and had loaned me a pair of heels and diamond stud earrings. I'd put on makeup and perfume and had practiced my speech to Ren over and over. *Ren, I have something to tell you.* When I looked in the mirror I almost did a double take. I couldn't believe how Italian I looked.

"He's here!" Howard yelled from downstairs.

"Coming!" I took a deep breath to steady my nerves, then teetered down the stairs. Sonia's high heels were really gorgeous but *crazy* high. I miraculously made it to the bottom of the stairs without performing any sort of involuntary gymnastics, and when I looked up, Howard was giving me this misty look.

"You look beautiful. I don't care what Ren's girlfriend looks like. She doesn't stand a chance."

"That would be nice. But I'll be happy if he just talks to me again."

"I'm betting on the former."

There was a knock on the door and Howard crossed the room to open it. "Hello. Are you Thomas?"

"Yes. Nice to meet you."

I clattered over to the doorway.

"Woah! Lina, you look…" Thomas's jaw literally dropped. But then he noticed Howard looking at him like he was a deer during hunting season and he quickly cleared his throat. "Sorry. Nice dress. You look really pretty."

"You look nice too." Gray fitted suit. Hair styled messily. I could practically hear Addie spontaneously combusting.

"You ready to go?" he asked.

"Ready." I walked over and gave Howard a hug. "How long can I stay out?"

"As long as you want. Well, within reason." He winked at me. "It's going to work out."

"Thanks."

I followed Thomas out to his car and he opened the door for me. "You really do look gorgeous."

"Thanks."

"What did your dad mean by 'it's going to work out'?"

"Uh, I'm not sure." I glanced at my phone for about the millionth time. All afternoon I'd been hoping Ren would call. And all afternoon he'd kept *not calling*.

Thomas got in the front seat and put the keys in the ignition. "Nice car, right?"

"Really nice."

"My dad has a Lamborghini, too. He told me if I have a clean driving record for a year I can take it out sometime."

"Too bad it's not tonight."

"I know, right?" He backed carefully out of the driveway, then took off down the road. "Did you know you have to be eighteen to drive a car in Italy? I think I'm the only one at our school who even has a license."

"Ren will get one next year."

"But he's only a junior."

"He'll be eighteen in March."

"Oh." He pulled out onto the road and accelerated, turning up the music too loud to talk.

I'm sure riding through the Italian countryside in a luxury convertible with a young 007 should have been a magical experience, but it was lost on me. I was too busy mentally rehearsing what I was going to say to Ren. And trying to keep young 007's hands off me.

"Valentina's dad works with my dad, only he's even higher up. I've been to lots of parties at their house and they're always crazy. One year they did this big Japanese dinner and there were women lying on the serving tables. You had to eat your sushi off of them."

"Ew. Really?"

"Yeah, it was awesome." He slid his hand onto my bare knee – again – and I made a big show of rearranging my legs so he'd move his hand. Again. I looked at him and sighed. Any other girl would trade all the gelato in Florence for a chance to be sitting in my spot. But they weren't me. And they didn't know Ren.

When we finally pulled up to the party, I was shocked. Not because the house looked like Dracula's castle – of course it did – but because of how many people were there. Cars and cabs were all funneling into the driveway while throngs of ecstatic partygoers weaved their way toward the front door. It took us ten full minutes and three leg rearrangings just to wind our way up to the valet station.

When we got to the top Thomas threw his keys to the valet, then made a big show of helping me out of the car. A red carpet was draped on the big stone steps leading up to the entryway and tons of people were making their way inside. I'd been a little worried I'd be overdressed, but everyone looked like they were on their way to some kind of red-carpet premiere. This was definitely a The Dress occasion.

"This is way bigger than I thought it would be," I said, grabbing Thomas's arm before I could lose my balance on the stairs.

"Told you. It's going to be awesome."

"Do all of your friends live in houses like this?"

"Just the ones who throw parties."

The entryway had a long, curving staircase and an extravagant chandelier made of colored glass. A man holding a big stack of papers stopped us.

"Name, please." His accent was as thick as his biceps.

"Thomas Heath." Thomas turned and grinned at me. "And my date."

The man shuffled through his papers, marking Thomas's name. *"Benvenuti."*

"Do you mind if I check your list really quick?" I asked. "I'm wondering if my friend is here."

"No." He scowled at me, covering the list with his hand. "It is *privato*."

It wasn't like we were attending a party at the Pentagon or something. "I just need to look for one sec—"

"Come on." Thomas grabbed my hand and yanked me away from the list and farther into the house. Everyone was sardine-ing themselves into this big, overly frilly room with high ceilings and like five more chandeliers, and we had to push our way in, tripping over all the fancy dresses and guys sweating into their jackets. All the furniture was moved to the outer edges of the room, and a makeshift stage had been set up in one corner. So far there was just a bunch of instruments up there, but music was playing from speakers around the room at a level that could kill small birds. It was *so* crowded. How was I going to find Ren?

"Lina! Thomas!" Elena emerged from the crowd, grabbing my arm. She was wearing a short gray dress and her hair was pulled up in a high ponytail. "Wow. Lina, you look *bella*. This is the color for you."

"Thanks, Elena. Have you seen Ren?"

"Ren? No. I don't know if he's even coming. Mimi would probably kill him."

"Why?"

Thomas cracked up. "Guys, look. There's Selma." He pointed to a tall middle-aged woman who had climbed onto the stage and was fumbling around with cords. She was wearing a tiara and a hot-pink minidress that was about ten seconds from giving up on keeping her boobs covered.

"Ugh," Elena said, shaking her head. "That is Valentina's mom. She was a supermodel in the nineties, and she displays sexy pictures of herself around the house. I think I would rather die than see my mom's cleavage on a daily basis."

"Your mom's *bionic* cleavage," Thomas said. "We should try to get a good spot by the band. Valentina said they start playing at ten."

Elena shook her head. "I'm waiting for Marco."

"Marco, huh?"

Elena scowled at him. "*Dai.* I just told him I would. It doesn't mean anything."

"Uh-huh."

"Elena, if you see Ren, will you tell him I really need to talk to him?" I asked.

"Sure, no problem." She glanced at Thomas, then leaned in. "Wow. Thomas looks *incredibile.*" She pronounced it the Italian way. "Good choice. He is *troppo sexy.* I'm pretty sure every girl who's met him has tried for him. I guess you are the lucky one. It sucks that Ren broke up with Mimi for you, but I totally understand why you are here with Thomas."

Eight hundred exclamation marks went off in my head. "Ren broke up with Mimi? When? Today?"

She frowned. "I don't know. Maybe yesterday? Mimi said

she was glad, though. No offense, but Ren can be very strange. He always says whatever pops into his head."

"Yeah, but that's what's so great about him."

She slid her eyes at Thomas. "Yeah, I guess so. See you later. I'm going out front."

"Bye. Just tell Ren where I am if you see him, OK?"

"You OK?" Thomas asked when Elena had left.

"Yeah, sure." Maybe better than OK. Ren had broken up with Mimi for *me*? Then what was all that in Rome? The urgency of my Find Ren mission had pretty much hit the roof.

"Let's get a drink and go over by the stage," Thomas said.

"Sure."

The next couple of hours were incredibly slow. The band was Spanish, and after every couple of sets the drummer got carried away and threw his drumsticks into the crowd, where they had to be fished out again before they could start playing the next song.

Thomas kept disappearing for more and more drinks and Ren kept *not showing up*. Where was he? What if he *didn't* show up? Was this whole The Dress thing actually a curse? If so, I would have come in running clothes.

Finally I excused myself. "Thomas, I'm going to the bathroom. I'll be back in a while."

He gave me an unfocused thumbs-up and I pushed myself through the crowd, doing a quick scan of the party. As far as I could tell, Ren wasn't in the main room. And he wasn't on the front steps or in the entryway, either. Where was he? Finally I decided to actually use the bathroom, but there was a long line, and I kept my neck craned to watch for Ren.

When it was my turn I locked the door behind me, then looked in the mirror and sighed. My dress still looked great, but I was sweaty and I could tell my hair was plotting a mutiny. I pulled it back into a ponytail, then checked my phone again. Nothing. Where was he?

Thomas was waiting for me outside the door. "There you are. We have to hurry. Everyone's supposed to go outside. There's a big surprise."

I gave up on my shoes, taking them off and carrying them as we moved with the crowds toward the back doors. When we finally stepped outside I sucked in my breath. The yard was the size of a football field, and dozens of large white blankets checkered the ground, their edges lit with tea lights. It was nauseatingly romantic. Half the people out there were going to get carried away and start professing their undying love to each other.

"Thomas, you didn't see Ren while I was in the bathroom, did you?"

"No, no, no." He stopped at the bottom of the stairs, putting both hands on my shoulders. "Let's make a pact. No more talking about Ren. I just want to talk about you." He grinned. "And me. Now come on."

He pulled me forward, and I stumbled a little as we made our way across the grass.

"Where are we going?"

"I told you, it's a surprise."

We walked all the way to an empty blanket on the out-skirts of the yard and Thomas sat down, loosening his tie and taking off his jacket. His shirt and hair were rumpled and I wished for about the thousandth time that Addie were here to enjoy all this hotness. It was totally wasted on me.

"Now lie down," he said.

"What?"

"Lie down." He patted the blanket.

"Thomas…"

"Relax. I'm not going to do anything. Just lie down for a second. I promise I'll stay right here."

I looked at him for a moment, then lay down on the blanket, smoothing my dress around me. "Now what?"

"Close your eyes. I'll tell you when to open them."

I looked at him, then exhaled, half closing my eyes. Did he have to be this gorgeous? It was really complicating my life.

He started counting down slowly. "Twenty … nineteen … eighteen…" By the time he got to "one" I'd been lying there for half a century, and I opened my eyes to the sound of a collective cheer going up from the lawn.

All around us, white paper lanterns lit by candles were rising into the air. There were *hundreds* of them.

Thomas grinned at my stunned expression. "Valentina told me they were doing this. Cool, right?"

"So cool."

We watched quietly for a moment, the lanterns twirling up to the stars like graceful jellyfish. The night was beautiful and magical and *ugh* – I was so miserable I could cry. Here I was in *Italy* witnessing a scene out of a fairy tale, and all I could think about was Ren. Was I going to be like Howard? Heartbroken for life? Was I going to have to buy my own long board and start baking blueberry muffins in the dead of night?

"Told you you'd like it. They're doing fireworks later too." Thomas reclined on one elbow, lowering his face close to mine. A bunch of lanterns were reflected in his eyes and for a second I lost track of why I wasn't into him. And then I remembered.

"Thomas, I have to tell you something."

"Shh. You can tell me later." Before I could react, he rolled on top of me, pressing his lips against mine and my whole body into the ground. For a second it was like Christmas and my birthday and summer vacation all rolled into one, but then it was all so *wrong*. I wriggled out from under him and sat up.

"Thomas, I can't do this."

"Why?" He sat up too, a confused look on his face. This was probably his very first experience with rejection. Poor devil.

I shook my head. "You're great. And so good-looking. But I just can't."

"Because of Ren?"

"Yeah."

"Why'd you even come here with me if you're into Ren?"

"I'm sorry. It was really lame of me. And I should have told you earlier."

He stood up and grabbed his jacket, brushing grass off his pants. "Lucky for you, lover boy's right over there."

"What?" I whipped around. Ren was standing a few yards away, his back to me. I scrambled to my feet.

"See you around," Thomas said.

"Thomas, I really am sorry!" I called after him, but he was already on his way back to the house.

I took a deep breath, then scooped up my shoes and half ran over to Ren. He was wearing a navy blue suit and it looked like someone had held him down and given him a haircut.

I touched his back. "Ren?"

He turned around and I felt the shards of my broken heart crumble to dust. He looked so good. Like *so* good.

"Hey." Not even a hint of surprise.

"I was really hoping you'd be here. Could we talk?"

Suddenly Mimi materialized from a nearby group of girls. She was wearing a fitted black dress with cutout panels along the rib cage, and her eyes were outlined in dark liner. She looked like a tiger. I'd never seen anything more terrifying.

She linked her arm with Ren's. "Hello, Lina. How's Thomas?"

"He's OK," I said quietly.

"Ren, let's go back inside. I think the band's going to start again."

"Ren, can I talk to you for a minute?" I asked.

He was looking just past my right ear. "I'm kind of busy."

"Please? It will only be a minute. I just have to tell you something."

"He's busy," Mimi said, tightening her grip on his arm.

He looked down at her hand, then back up at me. "OK. One minute."

"Seriously, Ren?" Mimi growled.

"It will just be a second. I'll be right back."

She turned and flounced away. That girl knew how to flounce.

"What's up?" Ren asked quietly.

"Will you go for a walk with me?"

By the time we made it to the edge of the yard the lanterns were just tiny little specks in the sky, and I was a hundred percent sure that Ren hadn't gotten over what happened in Rome. He just kept trudging after me like a well-dressed robot, and I felt myself sinking lower and lower. Was this even going to work?

The yard was terraced and we walked down some steps, passing a couple making out against a tree and a group of guys riding around on croquet mallets like they were jockeys. Totally something we'd laugh about. That is, if we were talking.

Finally we came to a white stone bench and Ren sat down. I sat down next to him.

"Amazing party," I said.

He just shrugged.

OK. He wasn't going to make this easy on me.

"I guess I'll just get right into it." My voice was wobbly. "I've never met anyone like you. You're smart and funny, and really easy to be around, and you're basically the one person I've met since my mom died who I don't feel like I have to act fake around. And I'm really, *really* sorry about what happened in Rome. Kissing you wasn't fair because you have a girlfriend ... or *had* a girlfriend..." I looked at him, hoping he'd clarify, but he didn't say anything.

"Anyway. I didn't know right until that moment how

I felt about you, but I should have just told you instead of basically jumping on you. Anyway, what I'm trying to say is, I really like you. A lot. But if you don't feel the same way about me, it's OK. Because you're really important to me, and I hope we can still be friends."

Suddenly a second round of cheering started up on the lawns and there was a hissing noise followed by the *pop* of a red firework exploding across the sky.

It would have been the perfect moment for Ren to gather me in his arms and profess his undying love.

Only he didn't.

I shifted uncomfortably. A few more fireworks went off, but Ren didn't even look up.

"It would be really awesome if you'd say something."

He shook his head. "I don't know what you want me to say. Why didn't you tell me sooner? And back in Rome, why'd you say that you'd never thought of me as more than a friend?"

Crap. I shouldn't have said that.

"I guess I was trying to save face. You obviously didn't want to kiss me, and I was so embarrassed. I was just trying to fix the situation."

He looked up. "Well, you're wrong. I really did want to kiss you, but I stopped because I was worried you didn't mean it. Meeting Matteo was pretty crazy, and I didn't want things to happen just because you were in the middle of some kind of emotional roller coaster. And then afterward, you told me you *didn't* mean it."

"But I did. That's what I'm—"

He cut me off. "I liked Mimi for a long time. Like two

years. I thought about her all the time and then when things finally started happening between us I thought I was the luckiest guy ever. But then I met you and suddenly I was avoiding her calls and trying to think of ways to get you to hang out with me. So the night we went to Space I called her and broke up with her. I didn't know if things were going to work out between you and me, but I really wanted the chance."

He shook his head. "Then we went to Rome. And then all that stuff happened. And now tonight..." He stood up. "Why do you think you can be all over Thomas and then come tell me you like me?"

A whole different kind of fireworks exploded behind my eyes. "Why do you think *you* can be all over Mimi and then tell me you liked me all along? You're the one who's had a girlfriend all this time."

"You're right. *Had* a girlfriend. Who I broke up with. And I'm not the one who was just rolling around on the ground with someone else. What am I? Your backup plan?"

I jumped to my feet. "If you'd actually been watching, you would have noticed that I pushed Thomas off me and told him I like you, but forget it. I don't even care anymore."

"Me neither. I'm going back to the party. And you'd better get back to your date." He turned and walked away.

"*Stronzo!*" I yelled.

A heart-shaped firework exploded over his head.

Chapter 28

IT TOOK HOWARD ALMOST AN HOUR TO FIND Valentina's house. For one thing, I didn't know who Valentina was, and for another, I couldn't find anyone who knew the address. Selma and her bionic cleavage were nowhere to be found, and I couldn't find Elena or Marco or anyone else I recognized. Finally I got the bouncer to tell me where I was, but he didn't speak much English and kept guarding his clipboard from me like he thought I was trying to trick him into giving me access. Finally I just forced my phone on him and he gave directions to Howard.

By the time Howard's car pulled up to the driveway all the anger had drained out of me and I was about as perky as a wet noodle. I felt crumpled. No, *bedraggled*, and when I got in the car Howard didn't even ask how it had gone. He could tell by my face.

When we got to the house I threw my dress on the floor, then put on a T-shirt and a pair of pajamas pants and went downstairs. I was on the verge of tears, but I couldn't handle the thought of crying alone in my room. Again. I'd reached my threshold of pathetic.

"We have gelato and we have tea," Howard said when I walked into the kitchen. "Which sounds best?"

"Gelato."

"Excellent choice. Why don't you go sit in the living room? I'll bring you a bowl."

"Thanks." I went and sat cross-legged on the couch, resting my head back against the wall. I'd spent all night looking for Ren and then he'd seen me in the exact moment that Thomas had made his move. What were the chances? Was fate just against us? And had I really called him a *stronzo*? I didn't even know what that meant.

Howard walked in with two bowls. "I got you two kinds, *fragola e coco*. Strawberry and coconut. I'm sorry we don't have *stracciatella*. I can tell it's a *stracciatella* night."

"It's OK." I took the bowl from him, balancing it on my knee.

"Rough night?"

"I don't think things are going to work out with Ren." My eyes teared up. "Not even friend-wise."

"Your talk didn't go well?"

"No. We actually got into this awesome screaming match and I called him a bad word in Italian. Or at least I think it was a bad word."

"What was it?"

"*Stronzo.*"

He sat down on the chair across from me, nodding gravely. "We can recover from *stronzo*. And remember, it isn't over until it's over. For years I thought things were completely finished with your mother, but we actually started talking again before her diagnosis."

"You did?"

"Yes. She sent me an e-mail and we corresponded for almost a year. It was like we picked up right where we left off. We didn't talk about any of the heavy stuff, just kind of fun banter back and forth."

"Did you ever see each other?"

"No. She probably knew that if I ever saw her again I'd carry her off. No questions asked."

"Like the Sabines." I tried to take a bite of gelato, but it just sort of slid off my tongue, and I let my spoon clatter back into the bowl. "You two basically have the saddest story I've ever heard."

"I wouldn't say that. There was a lot of good."

I sighed. "So how do I get over Ren?"

"I'm the worst person to ask. I fell in love and stayed that way. But if you ask me, it's worth it. 'A life without love is like a year without summer.'"

"Deep. But I'm about ready for summer to be over."

He smiled. "Give it some time. It will be all right."

Howard and I stayed up really late. When I checked my phone I had a three-word text from Addie (THEY SAID YES!!) and Howard and I spent more than an hour discussing the pros and cons of staying or leaving Florence. He even pulled out a lined notebook and made two columns with REASONS TO STAY and REASONS TO GO at the top. I didn't add Ren to the list because I couldn't decide which side he belonged on. Brokenhearted and see him every day?

Or brokenhearted and never see him again? Either one sounded incredibly miserable.

Finally, I went up to bed where I spent the night tossing and turning. Turns out there's a reason they call it *falling* in love, because when it happens – really happens – that's exactly how it feels. There's no doing or trying, you just let go and hope that someone's going to be there to catch you. Otherwise, you're going to end up with some pretty hefty bruises. Trust me, I would know.

I must have dozed off eventually, because around four a.m. I woke in a five-alarm panic. Had something just *hit* me? I scrambled to my feet, my heart racing. My window was as wide-open as ever, and a dusting of stars glittered at me from the cemetery's treetops. Everything was as calm and still as a lake. Not a single ripple.

"Just dreaming," I said, my voice sounding supercalm and in charge. It was literally the only part of me not freaking out over the fact that I may or may not have just been woken up by something cold and hard hitting me in the leg.

Not that that made any sense.

I shook my head, pulling back the covers to get back in bed like a rational person, and then I yelped and jumped like half a foot, because there were coins everywhere. Like, *everywhere*.

They were scattered across my bed and rug and a few of them had even made it onto The Dress, which was still lying in the world's saddest heap on the floor. I fumbled for my lamp, then bent down to take a look, being careful not to touch any of them. They were mostly copper-colored one- or two-cent coins, but some of them were twenty or fifty cents. There was even a two-euro coin.

My bedroom was raining money.

"What is going on?" I said aloud.

Just then another coin arced through my open window, hitting me square in the face and causing me to do this dramatic tuck-and-cover move that I'd learned in elementary school earthquake drills. But by the time I hit the floor I wasn't freaked out anymore. I knew what was going on.

Someone was throwing money at me through my window. Which meant that either a government official was here to let me know that I'd won the Italian Powerball or Ren was trying to wake me up. Either way, my night had just gotten a whole lot better.

I jumped up and ran over to the window.

Ren was standing about six feet from the house, his arm cocked back to hurl another coin.

"Look out!" I dropped to the floor again.

"Sorry."

I slowly raised myself back up. Ren's jacket and tie were sprawled out on the grass, and he was holding a white paper bag in his nonthrowing hand. I was so happy to see him it made me want to punch his lights out.

I know. Mixed signals.

"Hi," he said.

"Hi."

We just stared at each other. Part of me wanted to chuck The Dress at him and the other part wanted me to let down my Medusa hair so he could use it climb up to my room.

I guess it all depended on why he was here.

Ren seemed like he was having an internal debate as well. He shuffled around for a second. "Would you mind coming down here?"

I held out for exactly nine-tenths of a second, then threw one leg over the windowsill and slowly lowered myself out. Some of the bricks were uneven, and I used them as footholds to slowly climb down the house.

"Be careful," Ren whispered, holding his arms out to catch me.

I had to jump the last few feet, and I smashed right into Ren, who did this awkward crumpling thing that left us tangled up on the ground. We both sprang to our feet, and Ren took a step back, looking at me with an expression I couldn't read.

"You could have used the stairs," he said.

"Stairs are for *stronzos*."

He cracked a smile. "You left the party."

"Yeah."

Suddenly a light turned on in Howard's room.

"Howard!" Ren whispered. He looked like he'd just spotted a yeti in the wild. He was never going to get over that first conversation.

"Come on." I grabbed his hand and we ran for the back fence, trying – and failing – to not trip over every single curb we came across. Hopefully we'd never have to resort to a life of crime, because I was pretty sure we'd be the worst fugitives in the world.

"There's no way he didn't hear us," Ren panted when we reached the back wall.

"I think he went back to sleep. Look. His bedroom light is off again."

Minor lie. Most likely Howard had figured out what was going on and decided to let my middle-of-the-night escapade slide. He really was kind of the best. I turned to look at Ren, but I was so nervous that my eyes kept sliding off his face. He seemed to be having the same problem.

"So what did you want to talk to me about?"

He kicked at the grass. "I, uh, didn't tell you earlier, but you really looked amazing tonight. It was your version of The Dress, wasn't it?"

"Yeah." I looked down too. "I don't think it worked, though."

"No, it did. Trust me. So back there … at the party." He breathed out. "I was pretty upset when I saw you with Thomas."

I nodded, doing my best to ignore the flicker of hope in my chest. *And…*

"I really need to apologize. I was pretty upset back in Rome when you said you'd never, ever, ever, *ever* considered me as more than a friend—"

"I only said 'ever' twice," I protested.

"Fine. Never, *ever, ever.* It was like a slap in the face. And then when it comes to Thomas, I'm a total idiot. He's like a British pop star. How do you compete with that?"

I groaned. "British pop star?"

"Yeah. With a fake accent. He actually grew up near Boston, and when he gets really drunk he forgets about the whole British thing and sounds like one of those guys you see yelling at Red Sox games with letters painted on their beer bellies."

"That's horrible." I took a deep breath. "And I'm really sorry that I told you I'd never, ever, ever—"

"Ever," Ren added.

"... ever consider you as more than a friend. It wasn't true." I cleared my throat. "Ever. Also, you're not a *stronzo*."

Ren grew a tiny, hopeful smile on his face that immediately transplanted itself onto my face too. "Where'd you learn that word, anyway?"

"Mimi."

He shook his head. "So, did you mean it back there? When you said you aren't with Thomas?"

I nodded. "Are you really not with Mimi?"

"No. I am one hundred percent available."

"Huh," I said, my smile ramping up like ten more degrees.

We looked at each other for another long minute, and I'm pretty sure all four thousand headstones leaned in to hear what was going to happen next. So ... were we just going to stand around *looking* at each other? What about all that crazy Italian passion we supposedly had?

He took a tiny step forward. "Did you finish the journal?"

"Yes."

"And?"

I exhaled. "I think they were perfect for each other. Things just got in the way. And Howard knew all along that he wasn't my father. He just really wanted to be in my life."

"Smart, scary Howard." He held out the white paper bag he'd been carrying all this time.

"What's this?"

"An official apology. After I left the party I went into Florence and started driving around asking people where I could find a secret bakery. Finally some women walking home from a party told me where to go. For future reference, it's on Via del Canto Rivolto. And it's awesome."

I opened the bag and warm, buttery heaven wafted up at me. A flaky, crescent-shaped pastry was wrapped in white tissue paper. "What is it?"

"*Cornetta con Nutella.* I bought two of them, but I ate the other one on the way. And then I used my leftover change to wake you up."

I reached reverently into the bag, then took a big bite of the *cornetta.* It was warm and melty and tasted like every perfect thing that could ever happen to you. Italian summers. First loves. Chocolate. I took another big bite.

"Ren?"

"Yeah?"

"Next time, please don't eat my other one."

He laughed. "I wasn't sure if you were going to talk to me at all, but I knew food was probably my best bet. Next time I leave you standing alone in the dark like a total jerk, I'll buy you a dozen."

"A dozen at least." I took a deep breath. Now that I had Nutella coursing through my veins I felt invincible. "And just so you know, I meant what I said at Valentina's. You're the one I like. Maybe love."

"Maybe love, huh? Well, that's good news. Because I maybe love you too."

We grinned at each other and then a warm, spicy feeling dripped straight though my core, and I could tell Ren was feeling the same thing, because suddenly we were standing so close I could see every single one of his eyelashes. *Kiss me, kiss me, kiss me.*

He squinted. "I think you have Nutella on your face."

I groaned. "Ren, would you just kiss me alre—"

But I didn't finish because he dived on me and we kissed. Like really, really kissed. And it turns out I'd been waiting absolutely my entire life to be kissed by Lorenzo Ferrara in an American cemetery in the middle of Italy. You're just going to have to trust me on that one.

Finally we broke apart. We'd somehow ended up on the grass and we both rolled on our backs and lay there looking up at the stars with these big Christmas-morning smiles that should have been cheesy but really were just awesome.

"Can we please count that as our first official kiss?"

"First of many," he said. "But if it's OK with you, I'm not going to forget that one in Rome, either. Before I so rudely interrupted it, that kiss was pretty much the best thing that had ever happened to me."

"Me too," I said.

He rolled to his side, propping himself up on one elbow. "So … there's been something I've been wanting to ask you."

"What?"

He pushed his hair out of his eyes. "Have you ever thought about what it would be like to stay here in Italy? Permanently? Now that you have a boyfriend and all that?"

Boyfriend. The stars winked ecstatically.

I propped myself up too. "I was actually kind of working on that earlier. Addie texted and told me that I could live with her family next year, and Howard and I spent a long time talking about it."

"And?"

I took a deep breath. "And I'm staying, Lorenzo."

He gasped. "Did you just roll your *R*? I swear you just rolled your *R*. Say it again."

I smiled. "Lo-ren-zo. I'm half Italian, right? I should be able to roll my *R*. And come on. I tell you I'm staying in Florence and you get excited that I can say your name?"

"Never been so excited in my life."

We grinned at each other. Then I leaned over and kissed him again. Because that was totally something we did now.

"So you're telling me that not only do you like, maybe *love* me, but you're staying here indefinitely?"

"That's what I said."

"This is officially *la notte più bella della mia vita*."

"I'm sure I would totally agree if I had any idea what that meant."

"You'll be speaking Italian in no time." He interlaced his fingers with mine. "So now that we won't be chasing your mom's ex-boyfriends around, what are we going to do?"

I shrugged. "Fall in love?"

"Way ahead of you." He extended his index finger, lining it up against mine to make a little steeple. "Hey, I just thought of something."

"What?"

"When we're together, we make one whole Italian."

I smiled, looking down at our fingers and feeling my heart grow so fast and big I had to shut my eyes to keep it from bursting out.

He leaned in to me. "Hey, what's the matter? Are you crying?"

I shook my head, slowly opening my eyes and smiling at him again. "No, it's nothing."

But it wasn't nothing. I didn't want to ruin the moment by explaining it to him, but suddenly it was like I had a zoomed-out view of this moment and I never, ever (ever) wanted it to end. I had Nutella on my face and my first real love sprawled out next to me and any minute the stars were going to sink back into the sky in preparation for a new day, and for the first time in a long time, I couldn't wait for what that day would bring.

And that was something.

Acknowledgments

Before *Love & Gelato* I had only a vague understanding of how many people it takes to make a book happen. Turns out it takes lots. Scads. Heaps. Oodles. So here's my best attempt at narrowing that number down.

My first thank you has to go to my parents, and especially my mom, Keri DiSera Evans, for giving me Italy. Those two years expanded my world exponentially and were pure magic. Thank you for never settling for the status quo. You're my hero.

Thank you to my inspirational dad, Richard Paul Evans, who not only led me to the cliff of Authorship, but shoved me over the edge. I can only dream about writing as many books or impacting as many lives as you have. Thank you for not letting me give up. (Thank you, thank you, thank you.) I am doing my best to repay you in hilarious grandchildren.

A special thank you to my son, Samuel Lawrence Welch. I got the news that *Love & Gelato* was going to be a real live book just minutes after you blew out the candle on your first birthday cake, and I still can't believe I get to live out both my dreams at once. Thank you for making sure I took time out to play cars and read silly books. And you're right – pencils should be used for drawing choo-choos, not writing endings. Those can wait. (Also, grown up Sam: Did you need a sign that you can accomplish your biggest, scariest dream? This is your sign. Go for it, Sammy Bean.)

Thank you to my lifelong friend/family member/fairy godmother, Laurie Liss. I've been so lucky to have you in my life and feel even luckier to have you as my agent. I simply couldn't love you more than I do. Thank you for believing in me.

Thank you, thank you to everyone at Simon Pulse, and in particular my brilliant editors Fiona Simpson and Nicole Ellul. This story could not have happened without you. Thank you for being enthusiastic about Lina and Ren, telling me what was and wasn't working (in the kindest way possible), and for helping me to find my voice. I honestly don't know how to thank you for helping me write a book I love. So just thank you.

Thank you to my friends at the American International School of Florence – in particular Ioiana Luncheon, the real live girl who grew up in the Florence American Cemetery. I've obviously thought a lot about you and your runs through the cemetery over the years. Thank you for your help with translating and getting all the facts straight. You were awesome. (Also, an apology to the current groundskeeper at the Florence American Cemetery. I was just the tiniest bit overexcited about my visit and really didn't mean to set off the alarms or ruin your family dinner. I pretty much want to die every time I think about it.)

Also, a heartfelt thank you to the fourteen-year-old boy who asked me on a date while I sat working on my novel in the Millcreek Library. I was having a tough writing day and you totally turned it around. Also, I forgive you for yelling, "She's *OOOLD*!" to your friends. I'm sure you didn't mean that.

And best for last, thank you to my husband, David Thomas Welch. You are immensely talented, kind, and strong, and I have relied on you so much. Thank you for believing I could do this even when I didn't. Thank you for all the extra carrying you did to allow me to fulfill my dream. Thank you for listening to every crazy direction this story could have gone and for allowing Lina and Ren to hang out in our home like they were real people. (They are, aren't they?) But most of all, thank you for choosing me. This December will mark thirteen years since I sat in your car and worked up the courage to say, "Um, hey. Do you maybe want to hang out for a little bit longer?" I'm so glad you said yes.